TRACKS IN THE SNOW

a novel by

SANDRA H. ESCH

A LAMP POST BOOK

TRACKS IN THE SNOW
BY SANDRA H. ESCH

ISBN 10: 1-60039-191-5
ISBN 13: 978-1-60039-191-0
ebook ISBN: 978-1-60039-717-2

www.lamppostpubs.com

TRACKS IN THE SNOW

BY

SANDRA H. ESCH

ACKNOWLEDGEMENTS

Writing Tracks in the Snow, my first novel, has been anything but a solitary endeavor. It has morphed into our novel and a surprisingly fascinating adventure.

My heartfelt thanks to my Acquisitions Editor, Ashley Ludwig, and Lamp Post Inc. for seeing potential in this work, offering me a contract, and guiding me through the ropes. Many thanks also to Elizabeth West for her brilliance in editing with a light hand.

Thanks to Natalie Jensen Baker for her sacrificial caring and expertise, and to my writers critique group (Martha Gorris, Diana Wallis Taylor, Jean Mader, Mary Kay Moody, Maria Sainz, Cheryl Ford, Sharon Geyer, and others traveling through our group) for keeping my writing on track.

A special thank you to Doug Sterner from the Home of Heroes for his permission to craft and include a paraphrased accounting of the true and heroic story of the Four Chaplains. Thanks to Don Byington, Larry Hank, Bob Shafer, and Rick Sheldon for their smiles and nods as to the historical accuracy of the World War II details presented.

Thanks to my dear friends Bonnie Aase-Roach, Cindy Belshan, Ellen Sheldon, Fran Jenkins, Lois Kuehnast, Lori Lobnitz, Lorraine Hooks, Nadine Washburn, Pam Coley, Patti Tzannos, and Roselyn Collver, among others, for their valuable input and encouragement as well.

Last but definitely not least, my profound thanks to my dear husband Fred; my sisters, Ardena Okland and Lois Williams; and my niece, Sheila Okland, for their amazing support. I couldn't be more blessed.

CHAPTER ONE

We are now in this war. We are all in it—all the way.
Every single man, woman, and child is a partner
in the most tremendous undertaking of our American history.

—*Franklin Delano Roosevelt*

EARLY FEBRUARY 1942—AMBER LEAF, MINNESOTA

T*his* is London? Jo Bremley looked at the radio as if she could actually see the words flowing from its speaker. Edward R. Murrow had it all wrong. What about the Blitz? Air raid sirens wailing night after night. Hailstorms of bombs pounding the city. Tens of thousands killed. Over a million homes damaged or destroyed. *That* wasn't London. *That* was hell.

While a menacing darkness consumed Europe and the Pacific, quite the opposite cloaked Jo's sleepy Minnesota town. But that, too, was changing. Now, the war had wrestled its way into America, igniting a blaze in the bellies of men all across the country, her husband Case, included. Pulling a full length of yarn, she unleashed her nerves on her knitting. But not without an occasional glance at Case, who listened intently and paced, wearing a trail through a good stretch of linoleum.

"Come," she said, patting the sofa. "Sit down."

He shook his head. Then, for the duration of the broadcast, the clicking of knitting needles and creaking of the floor beneath Case's footsteps fell mute against Ed Murrow's reporting of a drama so intense it flowed like a work of fiery fiction.

After the broadcast Case turned off the radio but continued to pace, war worry dimming the spark in his eyes. "Where's this all headed, Jo?"

She didn't want to think about the war or worry about it. She just wanted it to go away. "Would you mind turning up the heat in the oil burner, Case?"

"Sure thing."

"In answer to your question? I don't know where this is all headed, and I'm not sure I want to know. That gathering storm everyone used to talk about has swelled into a tempest. Just talking about it gives me the chills."

A good half hour and three sharp raps on the door later, Trygve Howland whisked into their small asphalt-shingled home. Smelling of leather and fresh soap, his hawkish eyes darted about with a sense of urgency, taking in everything. Everything, that is, except Jo.

No surprise there.

She folded her arms over her apron and watched his stealthy gaze shift from Case toward the front porch, shooting him a can-we-have-a-private-chat-out-there look.

Case snatched a jacket from the closet and mumbled, "We'll be out on the porch," but his gaze failed to meet Jo's.

She returned to their daughter's sweater, weaving her needles loosely, slowly at first—knit one, purl two, knit one, purl two—her attention all the while locked on the thin front door. Not wanting to eavesdrop, she couldn't help overhearing the hushed words drifting through the gap beneath it.

Case and Tryg made the war sound idyllic. They discussed Marauders and Wildcats, howitzers and Tommy guns, and shells measured to the millimeter as though admiring lovely ladies instead of hard, cold weapons designed to destroy. They talked about the thrill of free falling from planes as if paratroopers, without a care in the world, actually fell through the heavens and onto plush meadows on clear summer days.

Her knitting lay forgotten on her lap as she tortured herself with the dark side they chose to ignore—pilots spiraling down in flame-engulfed planes with acrid smoke smarting their eyes and choking their lungs; paratroopers dropping from starless skies, dodging bullets, yanking desperately on ripcords; and brave young men with no arms or legs and partial faces coming back from the war, if they came home at all.

With Tryg just having passed the bar and Case still studying for his CPA, though, she wouldn't have to worry about them, she told herself. At least not yet.

Hearing a muffled cough from the back room, Jo went to check on Brue. "Do you need anything, sweetie?" she asked as she entered their daughter's room.

"I'm okay, Mom."

Touching Brue's forehead, Jo grinned. "Are you ever! Your fever finally broke. Looks like you're well on the mend." After smoothing Brue's bedding, Jo gave her a quick hug. "Get some more rest, all right?"

Jo stopped at the door and looked back at Brue. How she favored Case. Thick blond hair. Eyes the color of midnight with sweeping lashes. Same strong yet gentle presence. Jo smiled warmly then blew her a kiss and quietly closed the door.

When she returned to the living room and picked up her knitting, she could still hear the men talking.

"How's it possible for so many people to be that deceived?" Case asked. "What are the Germans thinking? I can't understand for the life of me how things got this far out of hand."

"I don't understand it either," Tryg said. "What I do understand is that it's high time we showed them what we've really got."

That's the problem with the two of you. You compete. You're courageous to a fault. Take risks at the edge. When everyone else backs off, you rush in and take things a step farther. You just can't stop yourselves.

Tryg's voice softened, but not enough that she couldn't hear. "I'm signing up."

Jo dropped a stitch.

"When?" Case asked.

"Tomorrow. I want to get in the Airborne."

After a prolonged pause, she heard Tryg say, "You look like you might want to come along."

"I do."

The air squeezed out of Jo's lungs.

"What's holding you back?"

"You don't have a wife and little girl," Case replied.

Jo scoured the small living room, taking in the pungent-smelling oil burner, soot-streaked walls, scanty furnishings, the yellowing sheers bookended with aging drapes, and the worn gray linoleum. Searching for something, *anything,* to keep Case home.

Her fingers moved mechanically back and forth over her needles, then suddenly stopped when Tryg said, "I know. But we just can't sit back and let the Krauts take over the world."

We?

"What time you going?" Case asked.

"Thought about ten."

"I'm coming along."

"Good. When will you tell Jo?"

"Tonight, maybe. After you leave," Case said, his tone sounding uncertain. "I've got to."

Jo shifted on the sofa then worried her way through a few more stitches before catching herself. Having been down this deadly road before, she needed to get behind Case or intervene.

For a short while, the drone from the oil burner brought relief as it muted the men's exchange. But the longer they talked, the louder their voices became. Excitement had a way of doing that.

"I'm worried about Jo," Case said.

"Don't be. She may not be happy about your signing up, but she'll get over it. Just give her time."

Tryg couldn't be serious. What kind of wife with a hint of sense ...

"You make it sound so easy," Case said. "When I bring it up, she gives me her back. Walks away. Won't talk about it."

"She'll have to now. The way I see it, if Ed Murrow had the moxie to report from the rooftops during the Blitz and now he's got the mettle to tag along on bombing raids, we've got the grit to jump from an airplane or two. We pass our physicals, we're on our way to Fort Benning."

"Please. No." Jo's whisper, a prayer.

CHAPTER TWO

J o dropped her knitting. Her feet hit the linoleum, slapped across the living room, and marched through the front door. A silver moon beaming through the windows illuminated the porch like early dawn, like late dusk. Stopping in front of Case, she adjusted her stance to avoid casting a shadow. She needed to see his face.

Tryg, who was balancing his spindle chair on its two back legs, looked up expressionless while maintaining his posture.

Not Case. He took one look at her and his eyes widened.

"Kind of cold out here, isn't it?" she asked.

"It's not too bad."

"Mind if I join you, then?"

"Not at all. Please do." Case's apprehensive look indicated he would rather avoid this conversation at all costs. He gave Tryg a sidelong glance. "In case you overheard, Tryg and I are talking about joining the Airborne."

Jo turned to her husband's best friend. "This was your idea, wasn't it?"

Before Tryg could respond, Case said a bit too quickly, "I'll be in just as soon as he leaves, sweetie. Maybe it would be better if we talked about it then."

Tryg, she saw, could not leave well enough alone. He leaned back, stretched his arms, and finger-brushed his thick sable hair, then interlocked his hands behind his head. "The Airborne could use a couple of good men."

Jo choked at his pride-filled statement. "Really?"

He punted it back. "Really."

"What about Elizabeth? Does she know?"

"Yes, ma'am."

"And?"

"She's just fine with it."

His haughty tone nettled Jo's already frayed nerves. "What about her job at Naeve Hospital?"

"She quit. The Army needs nurses."

"You'll be postponing your wedding until after the war, then."

He pulled off his wire-rimmed glasses, held them up to the dim light filtering into the room, and casually examined them. "We'll have to."

His nonchalance hit Jo like a flying fist. "Look," she said, her voice intense, "this isn't an invitation to a fraternity. This is war, for heaven's sakes. This may be a game to you, but it sure isn't to me. Why did you have to talk Case into signing up, too?"

Tryg leaned forward. The full weight of his chair cracked against the hardwood floor, his eyes tapering into narrow slits. "It didn't take a whole lot of doing."

Case reached for Jo's hand. "Come on, you two."

She pulled back and tried to speak, but her words got stuck. Lacking worldly experience, Case and Tryg clearly had no comprehension of what it meant to give all for God and country. But Jo did. That wasn't Tryg's fault, but pressuring her husband without thinking things through sure was. "Have you given any thought to Case's having a child?"

"You mean a *wife* and a child," he corrected. "This war is a lot bigger than the two of you. Have *you* given any thought to *that*?"

That smarted.

"Tryg, don't," Case said softly, his voice firm yet thoughtful.

Jo needed to back down. Tryg did have a point—a cold and judgmental point, but a point nonetheless. These past months, talk about the dark winds of war had been nothing more than that—talk, too far removed to feel threatened, but not anymore. She slipped her hands into her apron pockets and leaned in. "I've given it a lot of thought."

Turning and looking at Case, her fear was confirmed. War fever. It blazed in his eyes. To her dismay, they were consumed by it, both of them.

"That door is awfully thin," Jo said, nodding in its direction. "I couldn't help overhearing nearly every word you said. It's apparent you haven't given a lot of thought to the danger before running full-speed ahead."

The muscles in Tryg's jaw tightened. "That's what you think?"

"Yes, it is."

"Really?" Tryg barreled on, amusement now playing in his voice. "I find it hard to believe you'd actually say that. We want in on the fight just like every other Tom, Dick, and Harry."

A maddening grin creased Case's cheeks. "He's right, Jo. You don't go marching into these things deliberately trying to scare yourself. We're going to be fine."

"How can you possibly know that?"

Tryg cut in, answering for Case. "Get out of his way, Jo."

She winced at the sound of his stern and impatient tone.

"We'll talk about this privately just as soon as Tryg leaves." Case looked at her affectionately, his voice sincere. "That's a promise."

Jo gave him a passive nod then headed back into the living room. Gathering her needles and yarn, she settled onto the sofa to sort through her troubled thoughts, but before she could throw herself back into her project to help quiet her angst, she heard Tryg ask, "What's the matter with that dame, anyway?"

"She's terrified. Can't stand the thought of me getting into a plane."

"She's got to get over it."

"It's not her fault, Tryg."

"Yeah? Why not?"

"She watched her dad go down in flames."

"She what? You got to be kidding me. What happened?"

"National Air Race. Engine caught fire. She couldn't have been any more than four or five at the time."

Tryg let out a breathy groan. "No wonder she was such a pistol."

"She doesn't have much in the way of fallback, either. No parents. No brothers. No sisters. None. Only a cousin in Minneapolis, another one in New York, and a few distant relatives up in Fort William."

"I should have known something was going on. She's never been combative before. I've got to make this right."

"I'll talk to her. She's a sport. She'll be fine."

As Jo listened to the words spilling from their lips, she could feel the thin walls of her heart constrict. She had seen how her father's sudden death drained the life out of her mother and needed to protect Brue from experiencing that same plight.

Case and Tryg's voices became quiet for a long moment, silently shifting gears, and then started in again. As Jo listened, the colder and bleaker the dark February night seemed to grow. She swallowed hard, fighting back the tears hanging heavy in her eyes, but it took no time at all for her to lose the battle. She mopped the moisture from her cheeks, refusing to let Case catch sight of a tear-stained face when he finally walked through the door.

Five minutes later, Tryg called out, "See you in the morning." The screen door slammed followed by the sound of boots pounding down the stoop.

Jo drew in a deep breath. *Here it comes.*

CHAPTER THREE

The living room door groaned open, and Case stepped in from the shadows of the chilly front porch. He stopped just inside their small living room.

"I really am sorry, sweetie."

Sensing Case's heart had already landed on foreign soil, Jo nodded with resignation. She folded Brue's sweater onto her lap before looking away.

"I should have told you Tryg was coming over," Case admitted, "but I knew it would upset you."

"How could it not? This is happening way too fast."

"I know."

Jo grimaced. "Why on earth would you discuss something this important with Tryg before you'd discuss it with me?"

"I didn't. Lately we've had a number of conversations about it, remember? Unfortunately, they've all been one-sided."

Reluctantly recalling how frequently Case had broached the subject, a pang of guilt tore through her.

Case leaned against the faded floral-papered wall. Pressing his hands deeply into the pockets of his trousers, he scanned the living room.

"How's Brue? Any improvement?"

"Fever lifted a little while ago. I'm sure she'll be fine by morning."

Case stood quietly as the clock noisily ticked away the seconds, no doubt choosing his words carefully. "Look, college is behind us now, and Tryg and I want to serve our country just like everyone else. We figure the Airborne could use a couple of fine paratroopers."

"Are you absolutely sure you want to do this?"

"I'm positive, and having your support would mean the world to me. I know I'm asking an awful lot of you."

Jo turned briefly, her lungs crying for a natural flow of breath. "But what about your interview with Haskins & Sells? Our possible move to New York?"

"Nothing's changed. We can still do that after the war is over."

"But you've never jumped from a plane in your life."

"No one ever does until they get the proper training." Case flashed a rascally grin. "Tryg and I have jumping in our blood."

Jo pressed her fingers to her temples. Her tears dried. Her thoughts froze. The war represented the world's unfinished business. How long would it last? How many more lives would be lost? Which side would win? But her tight grip on Case and her growing conflict with Tryg represented her unfinished business, unfinished business she wanted to get past but had no idea how.

She tucked Brue's sweater into her knitting bag wishing for a moment she could tuck her feelings in there, too. "I hate having a chokehold on you. I know I'm being selfish. I really don't want to be this way. You are doing the right thing. It's just that Brue—"

"You aren't being selfish. Anyone who's experienced as much loss as you have would understand that. You don't have a cushion."

Jo shuddered at the unwelcome reminder and the awful feeling of vulnerability sweeping over her. "Our friends are the family of our choosing, right?"

He gave an unhurried and questioning nod.

"I'll do some relationship building, Case. I *will* thicken my cushion."

"That's my girl."

"You might want to hold back your praise."

"Why?"

"Because we haven't discussed Tryg yet. He's your best friend." She still cringed at the memory of his meddlesome performance at their wedding, and here she thought she had put that nightmare behind her. "Unfortunately, he isn't mine. Not by a long shot."

Case held up his hands. "You're on your own with that one."

"Thanks a lot," she said with a chuckle, but then turned serious. "He had the audacity to make light of your family responsibilities. Again."

"You know he does that. He can't stop himself."

Jo's cheeks flamed. "Can't you see what he's doing? It's not surprising he's the one who talked you into this."

"He didn't talk me into anything. Look, I know your relationship—"

Jo stood and closed in on Case. "No. This isn't about my relationship with Tryg. This is about you risking your life, going off to a heinous war where you could easily be killed."

"But—"

Jo shook her head, a knot strangling her voice. "And who am I kidding? It is about Tryg. We've been in competition for your attention ever since our first date. He is the one pressuring you."

"I need to do this, sweetheart, and not because of him."

Jo folded her arms, holding herself. Aching to hear anything but strength in his response, she asked, "Why, if not because of him?"

"Because it's the right thing to do. We have to view the war from a higher hill. Hitler is on the march and he's got to be stopped. Now the Japs have bombed Pearl Harbor." Case pulled his shoulders back, lifted his chin, and expanded his chest. "Look, I refuse to let anyone else do my fighting for me. I need to carry my own weight."

"But why?"

"I want to fight, Jo—for our country, for you and me, and for our little girl. Brue deserves to have a safe world to grow up in. And I want us to grow old together in that same decent world."

Jo's shoulders fell limp. "You're right. Hitler does need to be stopped." What an insane reality that one megalomaniac had the power to destroy so many lives. She knew the Americans would never bow down to Hitler or to the Axis powers. They couldn't. Her own fear aside, she needed to get behind Case, take pride in his courage and sense of duty.

But she couldn't. Not yet. Better to live with lifelong guilt than lifelong widowhood, not that she possessed the power to hold him back.

"If you have the grit to face battle, you need to do that," she offered, her voice losing strength. "But it's going to take a while before I can give you my wholehearted support."

Case embraced her rigid frame. She relaxed as he held her in his arms. "I know," he murmured softly.

Her head on his shoulder, she mulled over his well-beyond worrisome confidence and sense of duty.

But her trepidation was short lived.

On Wednesday afternoon, Jo stopped drying a plate in midair when Case slouched through the back door, his face drawn, his eyes cast downward.

"What's the matter?"

"I fell one nod shy of passing my physical, but not Tryg. He was a shoo-in."

Jo placed the plate and towel on the table and eased her way toward him. "Why did you fall one nod shy?"

"High blood pressure."

"What? How bad is it? Are you okay?"

"I'm fine. It's only high enough to knock me out of the running."

Jo reached up and lightly touched his cheek. "I'm sure you feel awful, but I can't tell you how relieved I am. Can you imagine how torturous it would have been worrying about you? Never knowing what was happening? Fearing little Brue and I might lose you?"

Case slid his hands around her waist and drew her into his arms, but Jo pulled back.

"Now that you aren't going, I can tell you that if we lost you—"

Case quickly placed a finger on her lips. "Don't say that."

He studied her long and hard as if his eyes could draw her into his heart, but then he shook his head and looked away. "Look, this isn't over. I'm going to check out the other branches of service. I still need to get in on the action. Until then, I'll have to settle for living vicariously through Tryg."

Within a matter of days, the war so far away closed in on Jo as they gathered at the train station to bid Tryg farewell.

"Watch for my letters, Case," he said.

Even thousands of miles couldn't separate best friends. The thought alone of seeing Tryg's letters falling through the mail drop suffocated her.

"I'll thread the first names of our schoolmates throughout them to get past the censors. Like a world map, their nationalities should dot a trail across the countries I pass through."

"All aboard!" the conductor announced.

Tryg gave the conductor a quick and excited glance then said, "I'll refer to some of our childhood shenanigans, too, so you'll get a good idea of what sorts of things we'll be butting up against. Sure wish you were coming with me, buddy."

Jo's muscles cemented at Tryg's touch as he leaned forward and gave Case, then her, and then little Brue a quick hug good-bye.

He picked up his gear, hopped on board, then quickly turned back and called out a hearty, "So long!"

The whistle blew, the steam hissed, and the iron crunched and shrieked. Relieved that Case remained at her side, Jo watched the heavy train lumber down the tracks, having no idea that the bond polarizing her and Trygve Howland would one day change the course of their lives forever.

CHAPTER FOUR

OCTOBER 13, 1943

Shafts of light speared through the windows of the sun porch for the better part of the morning, mirroring brightly off the far wall and hardwood floor. Still the chill remained. In mid-October, Jo's breath already took form in a puff of mist.

She bent down by the mail drop and snatched up two letters that had fallen to the floor. The familiar penmanship on the top envelope gave her a shiver. Precise ink strokes—not too hard, not too soft. Precise letters—not too large, not too small. Precise slashes across the *t*'s—not too long, not too short.

She forgot about the cold and simply stared at the envelope. The letter was from Tryg.

She dropped it to her side and patted it against her hip, thinking.

Tryg's letters reminded Case that he had been left behind, but he lived for them just the same. Jo thought about the many times she'd watched Case decipher his messages with the curiosity of an amateur about to crack a secret code. What a shame he had to wait until Tryg's return to learn if he'd decoded them correctly.

Honestly, what am I doing still standing out on the porch?

Walking back into the living room, she pulled out the bottom letter from an old friend up in Fort William. Maybe she and Case could read their letters together when he got home. Good idea. She slipped them both into her wide apron pocket and resumed her daily chores. But it took no time at all for a niggling thought to prod her, a thought that refused to be ignored.

Tryg.

There had been a longer span of time between his last two letters. Why? Case had voiced concern about it lately, worried that something might have happened to him. Tryg had to be okay, though, or he couldn't have written.

At half past two the crunch of tires on gravel, the purr of the engine, and the grating of their '37 Packard's handbrake drew her to the kitchen window. She peered out into the crisp autumn afternoon. Case was stepping off the running board. Her heart still pitter-pattered at the sight of his Ivy League good looks. She smiled at the sound of his boots trudging up the hollow stairs. First the steady footsteps, followed by the mischievous glance from around the back door, and then the warm and welcome embrace.

"Did you have a good day?" he whispered as he wrapped her in his arms.

Her day? Jo sighed then slowly broke free.

"What's the matter?" he asked. "Why the less than happy look?"

"You got another letter from your friend."

Case's eyebrows shot straight up. "You mean he finally wrote?"

Jo pulled the letter from her pocket. "Yes, he did. I got a letter from Jane today, too."

"Really? What did she have to say?"

"I don't know yet. Thought we could read our letters at the same time."

Case headed straight for the living room and dropped into the easy chair. At his invitation, Jo lowered onto his lap. She sliced open Jane's envelope only to have a newspaper clipping spiral to the floor.

Case swept it up and handed it to her, not lifting his eyes from Tryg's letter.

Jo read the clipping not once, but twice, and then moaned.

"What's the matter?"

She stretched her arm around Case's shoulder and rested her cheek against his forehead. "Remember Brady Malone?"

"Your old neighbor from up in Fort William? Sure I do. Why?"

"He lost two of his grown kids."

"Not on the battlefield?"

"I'm afraid so."

Case pulled back, deep lines creasing his forehead. "Two?"

She nodded, moisture forming in her eyes.

"He had three kids, right?"

"Right."

"And now he only has one?"

Jo's heart constricted. "And now he only has one."

With a slow and thoughtful shake of his head, Case lightly stroked Jo's back. "That poor, poor man. How do you ever live with something like that?"

"I don't know. It's really getting to me. This war won't stop escalating. I keep wondering who's going to be next."

"Me, too," Case said. "It's growing more personal all the time."

"And painful."

As Jo unfolded her accompanying letter, Case returned to his. A few more pages into it, he looked up at her and said in an unusually tight voice, "There's something else you might want to know."

"What is it? More bad news?"

Case drew his letter closer. "No wonder we haven't heard from Tryg." He then slapped the open letter on his thigh and stared off as he ironed it mindlessly with the flat of his hand. "He's on his way home."

"So soon? Why?" Overwhelmed by a sudden sense of foreboding, she said, "He wasn't wounded, was he?"

"I'm afraid so."

"What? No!" Squeezing her eyes closed, Jo touched her cheek again to Case's forehead. These things happened to strangers, not to people they knew well. "How bad was it? Does he say? Is he all right?"

"Doesn't sound good. Says he can get around pretty well now, but he'll be on crutches for a while."

Jo pulled back. "What happened?"

Case lifted the letter again and leafed back a page. "Let me read it to you. Let's see. Here it is ...

"'I just returned stateside and will be heading home soon. Got shot down in Sicily in early July—the tenth, to be exact. We were executing an attack behind enemy lines. You may have heard about it. Operation Husky? Just past midnight, we flew in over the Mediterranean to the Gulf of Gela. Parachuted into strong winds. Got blown off course and on our way down we got riddled with shrapnel. I got separated from my buddies. Next thing I knew, my chute shredded like a rotting sheet. The limbs of a well-placed mulberry tree cushioned my fall, but also made me easy prey. I got snared high up on a compromised limb. Couldn't get down.'"

Case thought for a moment. "Unbelievable, isn't it?"

"Very," she said softly as shame subdued her. She regretted her resentment that morning when she'd plucked Tryg's letter from the porch floor. To think he'd risked his life for his country and how easily he could have been killed.

Case continued reading.

"'My buddies were on the alert. I'll bet it took them no more than a couple of minutes to find me. When I heard the crunch of the underbrush, at first I thought the Italians had rooted me out or, worse, the Krauts. I thought for sure my tender days on earth were coming to a swift and sorry end. I froze, scared stiff the violent thumping of my heart would expose my location.'"

Jo's lungs emptied of air as she visualized Tryg's terror. "How frightening."

"Sure is. Wait until you hear this." Case returned to the letter. "'Suddenly, some twigs snapped on the ground below and one of the guys looked up. "This is no time to be picking berries," he whispered. "What are you doing hanging around in a tree when we have a war to win?" When I saw they were from the 82nd I wanted to shout, but under the circumstances I didn't. With the Krauts closing in, they sliced me loose from the chute, grabbed my arms on either side, and hauled me off so fast the soles of my boots barely touched the ground. We practically smelled the Krauts' sweat, they were that close. Fortunately, it took no time at all for us to lose those devils.

"'After slamming into that tree, my hip gave me a little trouble, but not enough to slow me down. We heard gunfire in the distance, maybe two or three miles away. Thought it might be from a concrete pillbox we spotted during the drop. We sliced a few power lines before closing in on it.

"'Remember how you used to wear me out with your obsessive football passes out there on the field in Academy Park? Precision throws, you called them.'"

Case glanced at Jo, a grin pulling at his lips. "Remember that?"

"Yes, I remember," she said regretfully, recalling the many times she'd sat on the sidelines and watched—on the outside looking in.

"'Turns out you did me a favor. When it came down to "it's either them or us" with time running out, my instincts kicked in. I had just tossed a live grenade when I took a couple of good slugs in my leg, but my toss? Precise. We cleaned out that pillbox with one hit. The good and the bad of it was that it was my first drop behind enemy lines, but I'm sorry to say it was also my last. My million-dollar wounds sure took care of that.'"

"I can't imagine anyone wanting more of that kind of action," Jo said.

"I can. I'm proud of him. He's all man through and through, and a courageous one at that."

Jo nodded skeptically. What a shame he wasn't all gentleman, too. "You think he's on his way home for good now? Or do you think he'll head back to the Airborne after his wounds heal?"

"He won't be going back." Case looked up at Jo with worry-filled eyes. "You can bet he's been reclassified already."

"As?"

"Unfit for further combat duty."

"Do you think he'll be able to accept that? I mean, I can't imagine Tryg letting anyone label him as unfit for anything without putting up a good fight."

"He won't have much choice." Case studied Jo for a long moment. "At least Tryg should be able to set up his law practice now," he said with his words, but his tone revealed something altogether different.

"What's wrong?"

"He wants me to pick him up in Minneapolis on the eighth of November."

CHAPTER FIVE

ase folded Tryg's letter, placed it back in the envelope, and rhythmically tapped it against his thigh. He stared toward the far wall, looking bothered.

Jo was bothered, too. She didn't mind seeing Tryg again and knew he would need Case's support. But ... "Couldn't someone else pick him up?"

"I'm his best friend. I can't turn him down. He would've done the same for me."

"But he's going to take over our lives again. You'll be giving him a good foothold if you go."

"Now, Jo."

"Look, I feel awful about it, especially with him getting wounded the way he did. And I appreciate his heroism. That's incredible, really. But I need time to sort this out. It's happening way too fast."

Case propped his elbow on the arm of the easy chair and anxiously massaged his cheeks and chin. "We don't have time."

"But what about the train? Couldn't he take the train?"

"He could, I suppose, but he'll get home sooner if I pick him up. Besides, I'm sure he'll have had his fill of riding the rails by then."

Jo got up and padded toward the window, the linoleum floor

groaning beneath the soles of her shoes. Not about to give up, she folded her arms, leaned against the window frame, and gazed absently up the short gravel road. "What about gas? You don't have enough rationing stamps for a round trip."

"I'll be fine. I'll do some bartering. There are plenty of people around who wouldn't mind sharing. After all, he is a war hero now."

"But what about the tires?"

"You certainly are covering all the bases, aren't you?" Case asked, a smile breaking through his voice.

"I'm trying."

"The tires still have plenty of tread, and a quick trip to the Cities isn't going to hurt them any. The rubber should last quite a while yet."

Giving Case a sidelong glance, Jo deliberately changed the subject. "Case?"

"Hmm?"

"Tell me more about the war. Why are the Allies invading Sicily?"

"Why do you think?"

"They want to topple Mussolini's government to get Italy out of the war. But why invade Sicily? Why not head directly into Italy?"

"You've got to get past your hard feelings about Tryg."

Jo hesitated, glancing once more through the window, her fingertips resting lightly on the sill. "I can't. They have a mind of their own. They come and go at will. Anyway, I'd like a response to my question, please."

"Yes, ma'am," Case replied, sounding uncharacteristically worn down. "I'm sure they're trying to get a good foothold so they can open the shipping lanes in the Mediterranean. If we invade Sicily, I doubt that island can be used as an Axis base anymore. So, can we get back to Tryg?"

Jo strolled back, settled onto Case's lap, and fingered a button on his denim work shirt. Saying nothing, she looked into his eyes, studying them.

"Too bad the timing of that job in New York comes when it does," he said, gently smoothing her forearm. "Your conflicted feelings aside, I wouldn't mind spending some quality time with him. I'm sure he could use a good friend about now."

Jo frowned. She didn't begrudge Case's spending time with Tryg. She begrudged Tryg.

Case shook his head. "When are you going to give him a chance? I mean really give him a chance?"

"Never."

"Now, Jo."

Weary from all of her attempts at letting go of the past, forgiving, and starting all over again, she said, "I keep trying, Case. Honest, I do. But a wall keeps shooting up. I'm still trying to figure out a way to tear it down. I have to admit, though, that I do feel a little silly sulking now that I know he's been wounded."

Case looked into her eyes, lightly touching her chin. "One of these days the bad feelings will disappear. Until then, just know that I love you and you love me, and other than God and our little girl, nothing else really matters. I believe in you."

"I know," she said softly.

Since Case could undoubtedly use some time to figure out other, more suitable ways to get his best friend home, Jo got up and opened the living room door.

"What are you doing?" Case asked.

"I'm looking for Brue. She should have been home from school by now."

"But about the trip to Minneapolis—"

Jo looked out across the sun porch toward Harrington Park only to find Brue bounding up the steps. Jo swept her daughter up into her arms, gave her a big hug, and sent her on to her father. Jo then made her way into the kitchen, comforted by the sound of warm laughter as Case twirled Brue through the air. Having bought more time to think through the Tryg Howland quandary comforted her, too.

CHAPTER SIX

T he grandfather clock struck six. Jo placed a basket of fresh homemade bread on the table then lifted a steaming pot of beef stew from the stove and called her husband and daughter for supper. They gathered around their wooden table and bowed their heads. While Brue said grace, Jo whispered a prayer of her own. *God, help me with Tryg. Please.*

She ladled the stew into their bowls and passed the breadbasket. As she and Case buttered slices of warm bread, Jo noticed Brue resting her head on one hand. Long strands of blond hair hid her eyes as she mindlessly stirred her stew.

Jo raised a brow toward Case, who redirected his attention.

"What's going on in that pretty little head of yours?" he asked, his deep voice resonating concern.

Brue stopped stirring. "I'm cooking my thoughts."

"Is that right? Are you cooking up new thoughts, or are you stewing in old thoughts?"

"I don't know," she said innocently. "Which one's better?"

"Well, I'd say cooking up new thoughts is probably better, wouldn't you? Did anything out of the ordinary happen at school today?"

Brue broodingly patted a chunk of beef with the back of her spoon. "I guess maybe it sorta did."

"Maybe it sorta did, huh? What happened? Do you want to tell your mother and me about it?"

Brue slumped in her chair. "Miss Porter got mad at me. She scolded me in front of the whole, entire class."

Concerned, Jo leaned forward, but before she could speak, Case asked, "Why? What did you do?"

"I had a messy desk."

Jo took note of the amused grin Case held in check. Her heart swelled with gratitude to have him at home. She reflected for a moment on the horror and physical pain Tryg experienced and Brady Malone's loss of his two grown children, shuddering to think how easily Case could have numbered among the casualties as well. That thought alone made her want to weep.

"I see," Case said. "And how'd she find out about that?"

"I spilled my milk, and when she looked inside to help me clean it up, she said first graders should know how to keep a tidier desk."

Raising an amused brow at Jo, Case shifted his attention back to Brue. "Hmm. And what did you learn from that?"

"That she has a real bad temper?"

"Anything else?"

"That I need to keep my desk clean? Are you going to punish me, Dad?"

Case smiled sympathetically. "Sounds to me as if you've had enough punishment already."

Uncertainty clouded Brue's gaze. "I have?"

"Definitely. Being scolded in front of your whole, entire class couldn't have felt very good." Case cupped his hand lightly beneath Brue's chin. "I don't think this is the end of the world, and I doubt it will ever happen again."

After supper, Case opened his Bible. "It's time for our nightly reading. This passage is from the second chapter of the book of James."

Jo heard far more than words rolling from his lips. Through the deep tenor of his voice, she heard the sound of true reverence and witnessed his faith. He provided their family with a rock-solid foundation, but a foundation that could easily turn brittle and crumble if Jo didn't pay attention.

After the reading, he recited the Lord's Prayer then led the family into the living room where they listened to the nightly news on their Motorola and learned that Italy had done an about-face, siding with the Allies by declaring war on Germany. Jo glanced at the troublesome letter lying on the end table near the radio—and Trygve Howland was coming home.

After the broadcast, Case whisked Brue up in his arms. "Time for bed, young lady."

He carried her off to her bedroom, Jo following close at his heels. They kneeled at Brue's bedside as she said her nightly prayer, then they tucked her in and took turns kissing her lightly on the forehead. Case switched off the light. "Sweet dreams," he said, closing the door behind them.

When they returned to the living room, Case seized Jo's hands, and pulled her close. "Look, I've given this more thought. I do want to go to Minneapolis to pick up Tryg, but I won't if you don't want me to."

Weary of battling her conflicting feelings, she shook her head. "I hate this war so much."

"You're in good company. Even God hates it, but that's not going to stop evil from spreading, now, is it? Or all of those innocent lives from being snuffed out?"

"I know."

Case searched her eyes. "What are you thinking?"

"Oh, nothing much. Just that when I watched you interacting with

Brue tonight, I couldn't shake off my conflicting feelings of relief and guilt."

"How's that?"

"Relief that you're safe at home where we don't need to worry about you, and guilt that our family is still together when so many others have been torn apart." She looked away as the weight of her words squeezed her heart. "All those courageous dads who've answered the call."

"I know. And to think they keep rejecting me because of high blood pressure."

Jo took a step back. "I haven't answered your question about going to Minneapolis."

"I noticed that."

"You're free to do whatever you want. You know that. Besides, you'd give me the same freedom. I know you would."

There. Jo did it. She said the right words, the words Case wanted to hear. But for some inexplicable reason a resounding *no* battered her insides.

CHAPTER SEVEN

NOVEMBER 8, 1943

Something about the blizzard didn't feel right—the suddenness maybe, coming on too hard and fast. Jo drew back the tired curtain and with the warmth of her hand melted a wide swathe of frost.

Case was out there.

For hours now, snow had descended on southern Minnesota like flour out of a sifter. The squat clapboard houses hugging the narrow gravel road were all but buried beneath a thick blanket of white. Although beautiful, the glow from the windows and wisps of smoke from the chimneys of the neighboring homes felt cold and lonely without him.

"What time did Dad leave?" Brue stayed silent for a moment and then said, "Mom?"

Jo glanced back at her. "Hmm?"

"What time did Dad leave?"

"Oh, pretty early. This morning around three, I guess." Jo touched her forehead lightly to the window. Remembering. The door yawning open. Case disappearing into the black of night. The unmistakable look of apprehension in his weary eyes. "He took a thermos of coffee with him," she said softly. "Should've kept him well awake for the drive."

Jo understood what troubled him. She, too, had witnessed the fire in Tryg's eyes the day he boarded the train, the day he went off to save the world. What would Case find in those eyes now? What lurked deep in the heart of a man forced out of a good fight by a perilous twist of fate?

She stared off into the unrelenting storm. The narrow roads would be treacherous with ice and drifting snow.

"If your dad and Tryg can get through, the drive from the Cities could take a while."

And then she would learn far more than she wanted to know about the cruel realities of war, about what awaited Case at the train station, how incapacitated or agitated Tryg had become, how deep and visible his scars.

Jo broke away from the window. "Ready to finish?"

"Ready."

Brue stood in the middle of the living room with a tufted pincushion balanced perfectly in the palm of her small hand. Her hair tumbled over the collar of her rummage-sale dress, which needed to be hemmed at least an inch, if not two. She looked adorable, but the expression on her fair features was another matter, not because of the dress, but because of the cross-country move it represented.

Jo had taken no more than a couple of steps when the telephone rang. *Finally.*

An explosion of static crackled in her ear. She shoved the handset out at arm's length and listened intently, trying to make sense of the fractured words spurting through the wires.

"Case, is that you? What? Axe? I can't hear you," she shouted. "What? Farmhouse?"

She paced as she threaded the phone wire through her thin and jittery fingers.

Brue nudged up against her, wide-eyed.

"When will you be home?" Jo asked, pulling her daughter close.

He said something about calling again later, and then the line went dead. Jo cradled the handset, confused by the short conversation.

"Dad's okay?"

"I'm sure he is, sweetie." Jo slowly shook her head as she said thoughtfully, "I can't believe how much he sounded like Tryg."

Brue gave Jo a questioning look before resuming her stance.

But was Case okay? The call made no sense. An axe? A farmhouse?

Lowering her slender form to her knees, Jo resumed pinning the hem, as mindful of her daughter as she was of her daughter's dress. Brue was standing too quiet and still for a six-year-old. Lately, the life in her vibrant eyes dimmed with any mention of New York. Case's getting the job at Haskins & Sells certainly clinched the move. But with him wanting to see Tryg through his time of need and with Brue's added reluctance, Case could easily change his mind about leaving.

Jo slipped a bent pin into Brue's hem, not realizing for a moment she'd pricked her finger. She ignored it, dwelling instead on Case and how hard he'd studied for stellar grades. Anything to attract the attention of a prestigious accounting firm. If he had been worried, he'd never said a word. She often fell asleep to the sound of the teapot whistling, a sure sign he'd be poring over his books until late into the night. The glow from the kitchen light seeping under the bedroom door had become commonplace. It bothered her to watch him work so hard, but now that he'd secured a good position, off to New York they'd go.

And the first thing on their to-do-list?

Buy new clothes—new socks, shirts, suits, and shoes. No more mounting bills for his education. Jo would finally get away from their small home with its weather-beaten siding and bare-bones furnishings. They would have a nice home, a complete change of scenery, and a wonderful new life. And Tryg? He would be reduced to a faded memory.

Slowly and methodically, Jo worked the hem of Brue's dress, nudging her a quarter of a turn at a time, all the while thinking of Case. The moaning wind, ticking grandfather clock, and sputtering flames in the oil burner couldn't compete with her angst about his safety. If it hadn't been for Tryg, Case wouldn't be out in this storm.

Neither could the sounds compete with her daughter's frustrating silence. Now, what was Brue's sudden change of heart about? Jo needed to find a way to draw her out of her reluctance. No matter how large or small, conflicts without words were not acceptable, not in the Bremley household.

"I wonder who'll be coming to our going-away party on Saturday night," Jo said as she pulled another pin from her pincushion and nudged it through the hem of Brue's dress. "It should be lots of fun. Evelyn is the real goods when it comes to playing hostess."

Brue stared straight ahead, looking troubled.

"I can't tell who's more talkative these days, young lady, you or your doll, Shirley Ann," Jo said, her frustration in full restraint.

Brue shrugged.

Jo inserted the last pin, unbuttoned Brue's dress from behind, and helped her slip out of it. Then as she threaded a needle, an anxious feeling churned in her stomach, the sort of feeling she found difficult to quell. Her eyes carved a path from the window to the telephone and back again.

Brue broke her silence. "Are you okay, Mom?"

"I'm fine."

"You don't look fine."

"You don't look fine, either. Do you want to talk about it?"

Brue sighed and tilted her head. "Why do we have to move?"

"We don't. We can stay right here. But we'd only be staying in Amber Leaf because that's what you want to do. Would you feel good about yourself if we did that?"

Brue's nose wrinkled. She bolted up onto the sofa, clutched her doll, and wedged her chin firmly on top of Shirley Ann's long flaxen ringlets. She hesitated before finally shaking her head.

"That's what I thought. When your dad first mentioned New York, you couldn't wait to go. What changed your mind?"

Brue fussed with the lace on her doll's dress and frowned. "Poke said all the boys at the school for the gifted are pudgy and wear glasses so thick their eyes look funny."

Poke. So that was it. "Really?"

"Yup, and he said all the girls wear their hair parted down the middle and they have long perfect braids. And when the teachers aren't around, the boys grab them by their braids and pull them backward around the classroom."

Jo turned away for a moment to conceal her smirk. "And you believed him?"

"I didn't at first. But then he said I wouldn't find any friends there, either. He said they're already taken, and no one will want to play with me."

Brue took one look at her mother and her eyebrows shot up. "Why are you laughing?"

"I'm not laughing—yet." Jo set the dress aside and reached for Brue's hands. "You know who'll miss you the most, don't you?"

Brue shook her head.

"Poke. And do you have any idea who you'll be missing the most?"

"Who?" she asked, her eyes wide with anticipation.

"Poke. I think you'll miss him a lot. He certainly doesn't lack for personality."

Brue's dimples deepened, her lips tightening into a straight line.

A quick gust of wind plunged deep into the oil burner, setting off a flurry of sparks that popped and fizzled like Jo's jumpy nerves. She watched the flames dance around before settling down, and then she returned to her sewing.

"What other sorts of nonsense has Poke been feeding you?"

"He said that the teachers in New York are all mean to the kids. They smack them on the backs of their hands with rulers when they don't behave."

"Some might, I guess. Remember, some are pretty strict here, too. But all of them?"

"I know. When I told him he was wrong, he said I was being a naive little kid."

Jo shook her head. "I'm afraid your father and I may have made a terribly big mistake."

"How come?"

"I'm not sure you're ready for the gifted classes yet."

"Huh?" Brue said, disbelief evident in her tone.

"I thought you were too smart to be taken in by Poke's nonsense."

"Do you really think we'll like New York, then?"

"I don't know. You tell me. Do you think we'll like eating at Tavern on the Green? Taking the ferry to the Statue of Liberty? And we can ride the elevator to the top of the Empire State Building." Jo shivered at the dizzying thought of looking far down at the city but quickly shook it off. "Don't forget, there are lots of nice restaurants, too. And Macy's. And Gimbels."

Brue squeezed her doll closer. "What's Macy's and Gimbels?"

"They're department stores."

Brue let out an unhappy sigh.

"How about riding in a horse and carriage through Central Park and ice skating at Rockefeller Center at Christmastime?"

"We can do that?"

"We can do that." A grin tugged at Jo's cheeks. "Come to think of it, you might want to tell Poke his family is welcome to come to New York for a visit any time. That's probably what it'll take for him to find a few kind things to say about it."

Brue giggled.

Good. She was on board now.

The grandfather clock chimed twelve, drawing Jo's attention once again toward the window. The broken message continued to gnaw at her. An axe and a farmhouse. An axe. Wait a minute. Was he trying to say accident? No, he couldn't have.

She flipped on the radio for a weather update but immediately regretted it. The record-breaking storm had already deposited as much as a foot of snow with more on the way. Road closures brought movement to a halt across the entire state.

"Do you think Dad might have been in an accident?"

Jo let out a ragged sigh. Nothing got past that child. "What? Where'd you ever get an idea like that? They called us, didn't they?"

Worry wrinkles lined Brue's forehead. "Yes, but when you heard the word 'axe', maybe they were trying to tell us they were in an accident."

"Well, even if they were, it couldn't have been too bad or they wouldn't have been able to call, now would they? They must be waiting out the storm at a farmhouse somewhere. Don't worry. We'll find out soon enough. I'm sure your dad is just fine."

A gust of wind whipped back the outer screen of the rear door, banging it hard against the house. Jo jumped at the sound then hurried to the back porch. As she pulled the door closed, an icy draft gave her a fleeting chill, as did a loud muffled knock resonating from the front porch. How strange. Who could possibly be coming for a visit in the middle of a blizzard?

"I'll get it," Brue cried, her footsteps pitter-pattering toward the door.

"Is Mrs. Bremley in?" a deep voice asked.

Jo drew the sleeves of her burgundy cardigan up toward her elbows and headed for the front porch. Another quick gust of wind slapped the screen door back, hurling large white flakes into the enclosed porch.

"I'm Jo Bremley. Can I—?"

Out on the steps, a lone policeman stood like a cement statue, his face crestfallen. "Ma'am, I'm Officer Dunhope."

"Yes?"

"I'm afraid I have some bad news," he said, his tone ominous.

Jo's heart thumped violently against the walls of her ribcage while an uncontrollable trembling played havoc with her knees.

The officer removed his hat, walking thick and nervous fingers around its rim. "Your husband has been in an accident. They rushed him to Hennepin County General up in Minneapolis earlier this morning."

"Hospital?"

He gave her a faint nod.

Her breathing became shallow and labored.

"I've been asked to tell you that the doctors did all they could."

Jo's head spun, blackness stealing her vision as she collapsed onto the cold porch floor.

CHAPTER EIGHT

ONE YEAR LATER ...

Jo gazed at the calendar hanging in the laundry room of the O.M. Harrington House, at the turn-of-the-century picture of lovely ladies in flowing silk dresses meandering about a town square. They wore elegant ostrich plume and floral hats and held delicate parasols in impeccably gloved hands.

Smiling at the image, she promised herself she would build her job into a career. Yes, that's what she would do. One day she and Brue would clothe themselves in elegance and they, too, would enjoy a fine life. She would learn how to live again, not merely exist. Then an aloof Trygve Howland would see that she would not have been a hindrance to her husband's success after all. And by then she would have nothing to prove and would no longer care what that man thought or felt.

Her eyes lowered to the day and month. The ninth of November. Looking back a day, she reached out and ran the tips of her fingers lightly over the number.

How long does the grieving process last?

She had promised herself three hundred and sixty-five days. Not one day more.

That was three hundred and sixty-six days ago.

She straightened her shoulders and returned to work, gathering a heavy load of soiled linen. Backing out of the laundry room, she glided down the rear steps, hoisted her wicker basket onto Brue's little red wagon, and started for home.

"Hellooo, Mrs. Bremley."

Startled, Jo looked up, the clatter of the wagon coming to a halt.

Calvin Doherty, who manned the boarding house's registration desk, stood on the front porch with his arms folded, the full weight of his shoulders resting against a white column. He looked taller than his height of five foot ten. Sophisticated. Soft-spoken. Middle-aged, with thinning dark hair flecked with gray at the temples. But his fine looks were tinged again with sadness as they often were, a sadness that did not disappear even when he smiled.

"Afternoon," she replied.

"Thought I'd take in the fall colors for a few minutes." He straightened and his gaze found its way toward Harrington Park while his shoes made a slow trek down the steps. "Certainly is spectacular out here today."

Jo looked out across the park, too. What would it hurt to join Mr. Doherty for a minute or two? The air smelled of autumn with hints of smoke from distant fireplaces. Dry leaves scraped across the sidewalk in the light, crisp autumn breeze. The last time Jo had paid attention to the view, thinning maple and oak leaves of red, yellow, and gold had painted the trees with broad strokes. Now a brilliant blue sky peeked through barren branches. "You're right. It is beautiful. I'm afraid I've been focusing on my work too hard. This view nearly slipped past me."

He lowered his gaze to the wagon and kept it there. "You certainly look well."

Was it Jo's imagination, or had a sudden fascination spurred away his sadness?

That same fascination seared her cheeks with unwelcome heat.

Towing Brue's little red wagon only embarrassed her when people were around. Unfortunately, that was most of the time.

She inched to the front of the wagon to divert Mr. Doherty's attention.

"So tell me, how's Brue enjoying school these days?" he asked. "She's in the second grade, isn't she?"

"No, she jumped from first to third."

"That's swell," he said with a puckish grin that appeared unrelated to Brue. "She's smart and mature well beyond her years. You must be very proud of her."

Jo took note of the glint in his eye. "Are you wanting a ride in my daughter's little red wagon, Mr. Doherty?"

"It's tempting, but I'm afraid the fit might be a bit prohibitive."

She chuckled at his lighthearted comeback.

After a few pleasantries, she said a quick good-bye then hurried across the park with the wheels of the wagon thudding against the cracked and broken sidewalk. At least the weight of the linen muted the clatter.

She nudged the wagon close to her front porch and looked back across the park. She had nothing but gratitude for her income from the O.M. Harrington. She needed it for the massive debt that piled up after Case's death. Her washing machine, and only means of support, was harder to coax into working these days than a headstrong mule. The house was in dire need of repair. And one too many of Brue's clothes had received one too many washings.

But the Allies were making progress in Europe. She and Brue had each other and their health. A farmer that Case had worked for gifted her with an old car, which she used as little as possible, but at least she had something to drive. And with financial restraint and the help of a victory garden, she kept food on the table.

The jangle of a bicycle bell distracted Jo from her reverie. She heaved her basket onto the porch and peered up the gravel road. A thin young man wearing a Western Union cap and uniform pedaled toward her at full speed. He looked lost and out of place, and he may well have been. The nearest soldier's family was several blocks away. With the exception of the O.M. Harrington House, this wasn't the sort of neighborhood that received telegrams.

He hopped from his bike and wedged his kickstand. Jo assumed he stopped to ask for directions, but he glanced at the number on the doorframe. "Are you Mrs. Jo Bremley?"

"Yes."

"Telegram, ma'am. Please sign here."

After quickly scrawling her signature, Jo stood dazed as she watched the young man pedal away. A moment later, she hurried into the house. The hinges creaked and the door slammed closed behind her. Just inside the porch, Jo ripped open the telegram, read it, and then slapped it against her side. Once again her world was crashing in on her. She made her way listlessly across the living room and collapsed on the sofa. Her entire inheritance from her grandfather's estate—gone.

Before she had time to process what she'd read, the telephone rang. She got up and answered it on the first double ring with the telegram still in hand.

"Mrs. Bremley?" said a stern and commanding voice.

"Yes?"

"Mrs. Bremley, I'm Marjorie Ennis Bickford calling from the five-and-dime."

"The dime store?" No one received telephone calls from the dime store.

"Yes, ma'am. It's about your daughter."

Jo dropped the telegram on the end table and leaned back against the side of the sofa, gripping its arm for support. "What about my daughter?"

"I assure you, she's absolutely fine," Miss Bickford said, her tone a bit too reassuring, "but you might want to bring her a change of clothing.

There's a sizable tear in her dress from an incident immediately outside our store."

"What sort of incident?"

"With Big Ole. I'll tell you all about it when you get here."

"Big Ole? Wh—"

"Yes."

Jo could not get a word in.

"Again, I assure you, your daughter is just fine and in good spirits. Oh, and there's another issue I'd like to discuss with you as well."

Jo's lungs collapsed. "What?"

"We'll be expecting to see you soon, then."

Click.

"I'm on my way," Jo mumbled into the dead receiver.

CHAPTER NINE

Jo snatched a dress from Brue's closet and bounded out the door without bothering to lock it. She gave the '31 Chevy a quick and apprehensive glance before hopping in. Not only had she not had a chance to fix the clutch, the car had been sitting idle in the driveway far too long. It sputtered, belched, whined, and fell silent.

Come on. You can do it!

She pumped the pedal and twisted the key again. As the engine kicked in and the car roared up the gravel road, she held the steering wheel with a vice-like grip while shifting her worrying from her car to the incident Brue had allegedly escaped from unharmed. If that incident somehow further threatened Jo's fragile financial situation, she could be in real trouble.

Stones crunched beneath her balding tires. The instant the car crossed over River Lane and onto the blacktop, the crunching ceased and the tires whirred. The road smoothed out, but not her thoughts. They ran faster than the car. Thoughts about Big Ole—ever since he'd set foot in town earlier in the summer, his name seemed to surface more and more frequently, but not in a complimentary way. Thoughts about Brue—her torn dress; wondering how she could possibly be fine after having had an incident with the hulking old man.

After the short drive to town, Jo pulled into a parallel parking space immediately in front of the dime store and aligned her car perfectly to the curb on her first attempt. Feeling good about her efforts, she gathered her purse and Brue's change of clothes.

But when Jo got out and closed the car door behind her, something felt amiss.

She looked up and down Broadway. Other than an inordinate number of people milling about the sidewalks, it looked the same as it had last autumn. She wasn't sure exactly what she was looking for. Same poplar trees sprouting tall out of the wooden planter boxes along the same concrete sidewalks. Same streetlights. Same First National Bank on the northeast corner and Freeborn County National Bank on the southeast corner. The same corner drugstore across the street to the south with the same café next door. Swinging in the breeze above the door immediately to the west of the café, however, a sign caught her eye and siphoned her breath. A sign she hadn't seen before.

In bold letters, it read T.W. "Tryg" Howland, III, Attorney-at-Law.

CHAPTER TEN

C alvin Doherty gave the laundry room a long and appreciative look and then grinned as proudly as if he'd done the work himself. That Jo Bremley could not be more organized or efficient. The stacks of linen lining the shelves could easily pass boot-camp inspection, and the hamper had already been emptied. But as he turned to leave, he hesitated. He knew she needed her job, but did she need it that badly?

Calvin returned to his post. Not more than five minutes later, the roar of a low-flying plane vibrated the boarding house, shifting his attention to more personal issues. He white-knuckled the registration desk as if the plane spat bullets and only the desk could shield him.

Spitfire, the old house dog, ran whimpering into Calvin's room behind the registration desk, and Calvin took off after him. "Here, boy," he said, peering under the bed. With paws shielding his ears, the cocker spaniel refused to respond. "Come on, boy. Don't be afraid."

After several unsuccessful tries, Calvin gave up and returned to his desk only to hear another deafening roar. *That Charlie.* Being an ace pilot did not make him lord of the sky. With the sky so huge, if he needed to show off, why couldn't he find another place to do it?

Suddenly, the door swung back and Calvin watched a rush of

long-term guests, along with the maids, cooks, and handyman, tramp out into the brisk autumn afternoon, all no doubt wanting in on the excitement.

Not Calvin.

The door swung open again, but this time Jonathan, a resident of the boarding house, poked his head in. "Hey, Calvin," he said, his voice tight with concern.

Calvin glanced up from his desk and peered warily over his bifocals. Jonathan's steel-gray eyes had lost their luster.

With an unlit pipe cemented between his teeth, Jonathan shook his head. "You might want to think about coming out to join us."

"Why?" Calvin asked although he didn't care to know. "What's going on?"

"Doc."

"He's having problems again, is he?"

Jonathan politely widened the door for a few more guests drifting through then said, "He could use an encouraging word or two."

Calvin did not feel as politely inclined.

Jonathan stepped inside the great room, closing the door behind him. He removed his pipe from his thin lips and held it close to his chest. "He's acting kind of strange."

"You know as well as anyone that I don't counsel any more. I'm afraid you'd better find someone else."

Jonathan padded toward the registration desk. "I don't think so."

"You don't, huh?"

"No, I don't. You care too much to say no, and you know it."

Calvin leaned back in his chair and rubbed his hands against its arms. "I left the chaplaincy when I left the service. You know that."

"Sure. And like a starving vulture pecking at a warm carcass, the cries for help aren't going to stop coming no matter how hard you try to avoid them."

Calvin looked away.

"That's what you get for being so good at what you do," Jonathan said.

"I need a reprieve."

"Forget it. You're not getting one."

"What about you? It's not like you don't know what you're doing. I've heard rumors."

"What kind of rumors?"

"Word's out you played the stock market better than Babe Ruth hit home runs. So what's your problem? Why can't you handle Doc's little quirks?"

"Cuz he ain't money."

The instant Calvin blew out an exasperated breath, Jonathan revealed a gotcha grin. "You're the only one I can think of who has the savvy to draw him out."

Right.

Doc needed Calvin, though. "I'll be there in a minute."

Calvin watched the door close behind Jonathan then reluctantly tossed his pen aside and stepped out into the cool, mid-afternoon sun. He wove a path to the far gate, stopped for a moment, and stood rigidly against it. He did not want to be here. That he wasn't happy about it didn't matter. He had a job to do and a fair amount of that job included serving the guests of the boarding house.

Suddenly, the Cessna Model T-50 roared again, tearing up the sky. It dipped its wings left, then right, before dive-bombing.

Calvin dug his shoes into the brown tufts of grass, forcing his attention away from the chattering bystanders, banging door, and flow of footfalls behind him. Having been a chaplain during two world wars, he'd experienced enough stimulation to last several lifetimes. Didn't care for any more. He glanced up at the plane. "Way to go, Charlie," he muttered and then slowly muscled his way toward Doc and Jonathan's small piece of turf.

For the most part, O.M. Harrington's residents appeared relaxed in its tranquil setting, but not Doc. Tall, lean, and recently retired, an obvious nervousness had forced him to give up his medical practice; the same nervousness that compelled him to jingle the coins in his pants pockets, and incessantly at that. He stood disengaged, as though far off in another world. Calvin knew what troubled him before coming outside, but wondered if Doc could be lured to the other side of it.

"Doc. Jonathan. I see you gentlemen found a not-too-bad view."

Jonathan nodded. "Sure did. There's nothing in the way here to block Charlie's flight pattern."

Doc kept his eyes riveted on the Cessna, his silence thundering louder than the plane.

"That Charlie is a real ace, Doc," Calvin said with an upward glance. "You must be very proud of him."

Jonathan caught Calvin's eye. "You aren't going to get anything out of Doc here. According to him, Charlie's no ace."

"Is that a fact?"

"Yup. Doc insists he's nothing more than a thrill seeker. Says he gets a rush out of pushing small planes to their limit and the faster, the better. Calls it tomfoolery and says he wants Charlie to get it out of his blood. Isn't that right, Doc?"

Still lost in his private world, Doc continued to ignore them.

The light plane circled then made another pass, zooming lower and closer to the ground this time. Through the cockpit window, they could see Charlie's standard military whiffle cut and the glint of his teeth. A man of few words and tremendous confidence, he excelled at making sport.

As the Cessna's propeller threatened to snip the treetops like a razor shearing hair, Doc let loose a few harsh words, all the while keeping his attention fastened on the plane.

Calvin reflected for a moment on Doc's assessment of his son. He then considered his own life, the complete antithesis of Charlie's. That troubled him. While home on furlough, Charlie stayed with Doc at the

O.M. Harrington, seizing every opportunity to hone his skill as a pilot. To him, the real thrills lay ahead as soon as he could finish training and get overseas.

Calvin's days on the battlefield were behind him, however, along with his sense of fulfillment. Like Charlie, who was born to fly, Calvin was born to preach. But unlike Charlie, who couldn't wait to get overseas, Calvin not only would not return to the battlefield, he vowed not to return to the pulpit, either. Ever.

A sharp elbow jabbed Calvin's side.

"Look at the way he's dipping those wings," Jonathan boasted. "Now, that's skill. Have you ever seen anything like it?"

"No, I sure haven't. Looks like something out of an old war movie."

"You can say that again. I swear that kid could pilot a torpedo, given half a chance."

"Him pilot a torpedo?" Doc said, finally engaging in their conversation. "He'd have a tough time piloting a rowboat, and if he doesn't pay closer attention, that plane's gonna plow down that entire row of trees and explode into flames. That kid's reckless beyond belief."

Jonathan shook his head. "Doc, you've got to get behind him. He's your son."

"No boy of mine is getting killed overseas because of some harebrained notion to show off," Doc spat, and then he turned toward Calvin, pointing a hard thumb Jonathan's way. "Can you believe this guy?"

I can, actually. Calvin had seen firsthand the courage of young fighters on the battlefield, but never before had he witnessed such fear in the heart of a protective father on the home front. Doc was scared out of his wits, but the grim die was cast. Calvin needed to encourage him, even if his son's chances for survival were bleak.

"He has nerves of steel," Jonathan shot back. "He's got the sort of stuff legends are made of."

"Sorry, Doc," Calvin said, "but Jonathan's right. I've seen enough fighter pilots in action to know you don't need to worry about that boy."

The don't-need-to-worry part was anything but the truth, but neither did Calvin envy enemy pilots who one day soon would make the mistake of crowding into Charlie's slice of sky. Why exacerbate Doc's worst fears? "He's got what it takes in spades."

"You think so, do you?"

"I know so. Take a look at him, Doc. Take a long, hard look. I've seen my share of ace pilots, but I've never seen a boy handle a plane like your son. A kid with that kind of mettle won't falter in the heat of battle. Our country could use a lot more like him."

The tight lines creasing Doc's face faded. "I sure hope you're right."

The howl of the small plane ebbed. It broke right and circled once again, climbing high into the clear sky before making a final raucous, low-sweeping pass. Then the hum of the engine grew faint as the Cessna dwindled to a needlepoint far off in the distance.

For now, Calvin's job was done. "If you'll excuse me, gentlemen, I'd better get back to my post." He strode to the porch and held the door for the guests as they filed back into the boarding house. Fortunately, more often than not, he'd found a semblance of happiness here.

Calvin watched a few of the guests disappear into the library. Others went into the great room for high tea; some wandered back outside toward Harrington Park for a leisurely game of shuffleboard or croquet or to feed the birds from one of the park's wooden benches. Someone always lingered around, someone for Calvin to have a conversation with, someone to help him keep his mind off himself.

"Hey, Calvin," Jonathan said as he passed by, "when Big Ole gets back, would you mind telling him Doc and I will be waiting for him in the coffee room?"

Calvin restrained a grin. "Yes, I would."

"I'm sure Big Ole will be more than pleased to hear that. And you were planning to hold onto your job for how long?"

Calvin's laughter filled the room. "Speaking of Big Ole, you might want to keep your head down. I think the cook's been lacing his eggs with a little too much Tabasco the past few days. He looked cranky again when he headed off for town this morning."

Big Ole. Jonathan. Doc. No one could fill the void in Calvin's social calendar better than they could. All widowers, they had never remarried. Now, they frittered away their afternoons playing cribbage in front of the bay window. What would Calvin do without them? Come to think of it, what would they do without him?

"Hey, Calvin," Jonathan said, giving Calvin a sudden jolt. "That young woman. Attractive little lady. Long, wavy hair the color of dark chocolate. The one with that little blond girl."

"Yes?"

"What's her name? The one who does the laundry?"

"Jo Bremley?"

"That's it. When's she coming to pick up the next load? I've got a few things in my room that are crying for starch and soap."

"Later this afternoon. She said she'd stop by around five. You can count on her to be prompt."

"Good." Jonathan hesitated. "You know, I see her coming out of that small house out there on the north side of the park every now and then, but I never have seen her husband. He's overseas, I take it."

"No. I'm afraid not."

Jonathan's face sobered. "What's her story, then? Not that it's any of my business, you understand."

"Bad accident. About a year ago." Calvin paused. "Took his life."

"No! What a shame. She sure is young to be a widow. Looks like a schoolgirl yet."

"It's a real tragedy. They don't come any finer than her."

"Too bad we can't keep her on indefinitely." Jonathan wrinkled his nose and scratched at his upper torso with a loose hand.

Calvin's forehead twitched. "What?"

Jonathan apparently misunderstood the reasoning behind the

question. "Remember that last one—Mrs. Starch Happy? What was her name? Mrs. Gates, wasn't it?"

"That's right. But—"

"I swear that woman managed to keep me in rashes head-to-toe four seasons out of the year."

"About Mrs. Bremley," Calvin said. "Until Mrs. Gates got in a family way, Mrs. Bremley filled in as backup, but I don't think Mrs. Gates will be coming back any time soon. If all goes well, I'm hoping we can give Mrs. Bremley a contract come the first of the year. She certainly seems interested enough. So, what's this 'too bad we can't keep her on indefinitely' business all about? Do you know something I don't?"

"Charlie mentioned the other day that Big Ole wanted the boarding house to switch over to some big laundry outfit uptown. You didn't know, then?"

"No, I sure didn't."

Jonathan's gaze met Calvin's and they studied one another soberly.

"Maybe I misunderstood," Jonathan said. "I'll go gather a few things and, while I'm at it, double check my information."

Calvin drummed his fingers on his desk. "I'd appreciate that."

This news didn't sit right with Calvin. Mrs. Bremley needed the laundry job and certainly worked hard enough to deserve it. He wiggled uncomfortably in his chair, identifying all too well with the young widow's loss and wishing he didn't. He'd had his own love torn away in his youth, too. When he saw Jo, she triggered disturbing memories and feelings he couldn't seem to get past, feelings about abandoned love and faith gone bad. Calvin had made the most of his faith while on the battlefield to meet the requirements of his job. Like they say, there are no atheists in foxholes. Although he walked away from the ministry and his past when he stepped back on American soil, he remained conflicted, vacillating between shunning people and wanting to help them, depending on his mood. The ministry had felt right to him once, but not any more. No, his ministering days were definitely over.

Helping Jo Bremley keep her job, though, wasn't that a different matter? Since arriving at the O.M. Harrington less than a year ago, Calvin
had successfully ignored her grief. Maybe he should do an about-face.
Have a chat with Charlie. Get more information. Maybe approach Big
Ole on her behalf. Who knew? If the rumor was true, he might help
salvage her job.

Jonathan emerged from down the wide hallway, approaching at a
fast clip. "It may already be a done deal. Big Ole didn't know that the
owner of the laundry outfit lost his son overseas. When Charlie mentioned it, Big Ole made up his mind to use the man's services right there
on the spot."

Calvin shook his head. "Thanks for the heads-up." He picked up his
pad and pen and got back to work. A moment later he stopped abruptly
and tossed his pen back onto his desk. He had work to do, all right. The
kind of work he excelled at, but only when he wanted to.

Helping.

CHAPTER ELEVEN

Tryg? Jo lingered by her car, absorbed by the sight of his shingle and numbed by the sight of his name. He definitely had an air about him. Always had. In the past he had introduced himself as Trygve. Only his closest friends called him Tryg. What a surprise to see that he'd gone informal now. Maybe posing as a regular guy drew business.

How she dreaded the thought of seeing him again. He had robbed her of her future. Confiscated her peace. Only she possessed the power to get that back, but she wasn't ready. Not yet.

The door beneath the Attorney-at-Law sign suddenly swung open, and a dark-haired gentleman with wire-rimmed glasses stepped out onto the busy sidewalk, glancing at his watch as he hurried down the street.

Tryg.

Well dressed in a charcoal suit and fedora, he stood nearly six feet tall, only an inch or two shorter than Case had been. From all outward appearances, he had only one imperfection—a limp from his war wounds. No, on second thought, the limp wasn't an imperfection. Even that he wore like a badge of honor. *As well he should,* she conceded.

He cut through the crowd at a fast clip, seemingly unaware of his audience across the street. After the many long hours Jo had spent in his presence during his numerous chats with Case, what was in the chestnut eyes behind those wire-rimmed glasses still remained a mystery. Even now she couldn't read him as he hurried down the busy sidewalk, breaking free from the crowd.

"Mrs. Bremley? Mrs. Bremley, is that you?"

Jo jumped at the intrusion of the authoritative, high-pitched voice. She turned and shifted her gaze into the eyes of a wrinkled and determined face immediately outside the five-and-dime. "Yes?"

The slightly-built woman placed a hand over her heart. "Oh my, I didn't mean to frighten you. You look as though you've just seen a ghost."

Jo glanced across the street to where she'd last seen Tryg. "In some respects, I feel as though I might have."

A wary expression cut across the stranger's intense face. "I'm Marjorie," she said, extending a stiff hand, "Marjorie Ennis Bickford. Come with me, please."

Jo pulled back. "What was this incident with Big Ole all about?"

As though she hadn't heard Jo, Miss Bickford ushered her by the elbow toward the far outside corner of the store. "Your daughter is waiting. But before I take you to her, there's something I'm sure you'll want to see."

Jo stopped hard. "What happened?"

"I'll tell you all about it in just a minute," Miss Bickford insisted and then once again guided Jo along. "You have a very lovely little girl, by the way."

Jo smiled weakly. Marjorie Ennis Bickford was as officious in person as she had been on the telephone. But the strength in her voice would have seemed more appropriate coming from someone much larger. While pressing her thin fingers like sharp talons into Jo's arm, Miss Bickford nudged her toward the wide corner window of the five-and-dime.

What could be so important in a store window?

Miss Bickford raised her chin. "So, you're the poor, young Widow Bremley. I've heard all about you."

Jo didn't feel particularly comfortable being referred to as the poor, young anything. "You have?"

"I certainly have. Not having much in the way of family to speak of. Then losing your young husband in that horrible accident the way you did. My, my! That's way too much for any one person to endure."

Jo's cheeks warmed. Curious that the woman could switch so effortlessly from sensitive to insensitive in her fast-clipped voice, Jo thought it best not to respond.

Miss Bickford's mouth formed an instant and precise O. "I'm so sorry. Where are my manners? What a dreadful thing to say."

"Don't give it another thought," Jo said, dismissing the woman's sharp edges with a casual shake of her head. "We're doing just fine."

Miss Bickford maneuvered Jo close to the glass and lowered her voice. She pointed toward a small black box holding a Cinderella watch and glass slipper sparkling beneath the lights of the display case. "That's the other issue I wanted to tell you about. I thought you'd appreciate knowing your daughter stops by frequently to admire that watch. I've never seen a child so taken with something." Then, lifting her nose and with a heavy dose of pride, she added, "I used to be a school teacher, you know."

"So that's it."

"Pardon me?"

"No wonder she's been getting home from school late. *Cinderella* is her favorite story. My husband read it to her so many times I swear the two of them had it memorized."

"Oh my. That's why the watch means so much to her, then." The woman took quick, shallow breaths and kept right on talking. "You know, it nearly brought me to tears when I saw her this afternoon. If only you could have seen your little girl, too. She leaned against the window here with those tiny, little hands of hers cupped to the glass and rubbed the tops of her bulky shoes against her socks, first one and then the other. You'd have thought a good buffing could have turned them into something feminine and beautiful."

Compassion flowed into the chambers of Jo's heart. "I can only imagine."

"Now that you've seen this, do come along. We can go in through the back door."

Jo reached out, lightly touched the window, and lingered for a moment. No wonder her little girl was smitten. The Cinderella watch and glass slipper were enchanting. With Christmas just around the corner, they would make an ideal gift. Jo needed to make that happen, but would it be possible? She turned and glanced back at Miss Bickford, who stood waiting. "Thank you for telling me about the watch."

"Think nothing of it. If she were my child, I would have wanted to know, too." Marjorie Ennis Bickford slipped her thumbs into the pockets of her pea-green smock, made a comment about how easily Franklin Roosevelt had just won the presidential election, took a nervous glance up the street, and kept right on talking.

But as the woman's words poured emptily into the air, Jo had thoughts only for Brue.

Suddenly, Miss Bickford hesitated and her countenance warmed. "Again, I really am sorry. I don't mean to be so rude. I can be at times, you know. I guess I'm still a little nerved up about the run-in between your daughter and Big Ole."

Jo's heart thumped. "Run-in? I thought you said Brue was okay."

"Heavens, yes. She's just fine."

Miss Bickford guided Jo into the narrow alley where they sidestepped wooden crates and stacks of old newspapers butted up against its rough brick walls. She stopped short just outside the back door and spilled the details of the incident with relish. "Big Ole looked startled when your little girl backed into him. But when he raised his cane in anger the way he did, it was no wonder her dress got torn. I thought sure that old man was going to wallop her but good."

Jo's breath seized in her lungs. "But he didn't."

"No. Fortunately, he didn't."

Jo quickly took the lead through the back door and into a small room at the rear of the store where she found Brue standing with her back against the wall, her dress bunched at her waist. Jo knelt down, wrapped Brue tightly in her arms, and then pulled back to reassure her with a warm smile and soft, kind words. "Are you okay?"

Brue nodded.

"Good. Now let me take a quick look at your dress."

As she shook the dress loose from Brue's hands and carefully unfolded the wide tear along the dress's waistline, Jo stifled an alarmed gasp then glanced up at Miss Bickford. "You wouldn't happen to have any idea where that old man went to, would you?"

"I certainly do. He marched right across the street and into The Copper Kettle."

"I see." Jo held tight to her anger. "Brue, Miss Bickford tells me you had quite an incident with Big Ole."

Brue nodded apprehensively.

"I'm sorry that happened, pumpkin." Jo handed her a clean dress. "Why don't you change into that and wait here for me for a couple of minutes while I run across the street?"

"Where are you going, Mom?"

"I'm afraid I need to see a man about a dress. I'll be right back."

Miss Bickford gave Jo an approving nod. "I'll be more than happy to wait with her until you get back."

CHAPTER TWELVE

Resting her hand on the door handle of The Copper Kettle, Jo hesitated before walking in. It wouldn't take much for an uncomfortable conversation to get out of hand. She needed to weigh her words carefully.

When she finally stepped inside, all eyes were on her. Maybe she did open the door a bit too briskly.

Although the café was crowded, it took no time at all for Jo to find who she was looking for. People of Big Ole's stature could never get lost in a crowd; they were the crowd. To top it off, his less-than-pleasant demeanor made him stand out like white flecks of dandruff on a velvety-black collar. He was seated at a table with the chief of police, deeply engrossed in conversation.

Jo wove through the crowd, stopping short at their table. "Excuse me, sir. I'm sorry to interrupt, but I wonder if I could have a word with you in private, please. Would you mind joining me outside for a quick moment? It's important."

"Yes, I would mind," Big Ole said, shooting an incredulous glance toward the chief. "I would mind very much."

Chief Stout rose from his chair. "I'd better be on my way so the two of you can have a word."

"Nonsense. You stay right there," Big Ole insisted

"Chief Stout, did you happen to see the incident this man had with my daughter this afternoon?"

The chief lifted his hands, palms facing out, as if shielding himself from their encounter. "Sorry, but I'm afraid this conversation is between the two of you."

"I see," Jo said, but she did not move.

Big Ole's cheeks reddened, his eyes narrowing. "So, that was your daughter who nearly knocked me on my keister in front of the dime store."

"No," Jo said, struggling to keep her voice low, respectful, and controlled. "That was my daughter you nearly struck with your cane. That was my daughter whose dress you tore to smithereens."

"Obviously, you haven't taken the time to get the full story from her, Mrs. ...?"

"Bremley."

"Mrs. Bremley."

"Didn't need to. I saw her dress, and I think it might be for the best if you kept your distance from her in the future." Jo straightened her shoulders and frowned at the insufferable man. "*Sir!*"

Big Ole rose in his chair just far enough to peer down at her.

Disturbed by the manipulative move, Jo stood taller, meeting his gaze at his level.

"I'm sorry you feel that way," he said. "But while we're at it, you might instruct your daughter to keep her distance from me as well. *Madam!*"

Jo left The Copper Kettle a little less sure of herself. Big Ole's words rang true. She hadn't gotten the full story from Brue, but she certainly saw her dress. The tear said volumes.

Miss Bickford's eyes widened when Jo returned. "Did everything go okay?"

"You might say Big Ole and I reached an agreement."

"It's about time someone stood up to that man," Miss Bickford replied, but then she cleared her throat and glared at Brue's shoe.

Following the line of her gaze, a burst of heat scorched Jo's cheeks. Not only had the tear in Brue's dress been large enough to shove her head through, the sole of Brue's shoe had completely ripped loose.

"Nice meeting you, Mrs. Bremley," Miss Bickford said with a patronizing expression, as though she accomplished what she had set out to do.

Jo watched the door close and then knelt to take a good look at Brue's shoe. "How long has your sole been torn?"

"Not long."

"We'd better stop by the shoe repair shop and get it sewn."

Jo couldn't miss the sadness overtaking Brue's face. It hurt to look at her. "You hoped we'd buy new shoes, didn't you?"

Brue stared at nothing, saying nothing.

"We will." Jo got up and reached for her brown paper bag. "That's a promise, but we can't do it now. I'm down to thirty-five cents. We'll get this shoe fixed, and then I'll buy you a nice new pair just as soon as we can afford it, okay? It may take a while, but you have my permission to start looking."

"But—"

"I'm serious, Brue. Just as soon as we can."

Brue broke a grin.

Jo stuffed Brue's torn dress into the bag and said, "I couldn't believe my ears when Miss Bickford told me she was afraid Big Ole was going to wallop you with his cane."

Brue looked up at Jo, her countenance the picture of innocence. "He wasn't going to wallop me, Mom."

As they approached the candy counter on their way through the store, Jo hesitated. Candy. At the moment Brue could definitely use some. The counter stood on a wooden platform an aisle long with a catwalk cut through its center for a lone attendant. They strolled past the glass-covered bins. So many kinds of candies to choose from—taffy, maple sugar candy, licorice, lemon drops, peppermints, gum drops.

Jo pulled a nickel out of her wallet and pressed it into Brue's hand, then smiled as Brue hurried toward the counter. She stood on her tip-toes tapping her coin against the thick glass until a clerk peered over the top, no doubt standing on her tiptoes as well. The bins were on the high side—not practical, but quaint. When the clerk handed Brue a paper bag containing a nickel's worth of maple sugar candy, Brue grinned broadly with both hands reaching.

Jo smiled, appreciating that so little could buy so much.

As they neared the front of the store, the door opened, the bell above it jangled, and the door clacked shut. "Sweetie, wait a minute," Jo said, nostalgia flooding her senses.

She gazed up at the bell, inhaled the aroma of hot buttered popcorn, gaped at the bright lights and dazzling jewelry, and listened to the famil-iar tinkle of flatware at the food counter at the far end of the store. After a year of mourning, she felt as though she'd just stepped out of a cave and into the bright sunlight, and it felt good.

She spotted Miss Bickford standing near the display window and went to offer a quick good-bye. As she approached, a loud commotion from somewhere out on the street caught her attention.

"What's going on out there?" Jo asked.

Miss Bickford turned toward her and blinked. "War Bond Rally. The marching band is parading from Amber Leaf High to the band shell to add a little fanfare, I guess."

"Oh? No wonder I saw so many people roaming around in the street when I came."

"Chief Stout wants the town to do more to help finance the war effort."

Jo glanced out the window. "Oh, no. Look where I parked my car. Right in the midst of all the excitement."

Miss Bickford looked sympathetic and calmer than when Jo first arrived.

"We're on our way to get Brue's shoe sewn." Jo touched the older woman's arm. "I want to thank you for everything. Especially for looking out for Brue."

After saying a polite good-bye, Jo glanced back at Marjorie Ennis Bickford and decided the woman was rather pleasant after all.

Once outside, Jo seized Brue's hand and threaded through the crowd spilling across the sidewalk. Then they headed on toward the shoe repair shop a block and a half to the south on East Main.

A man slight in stature sat on a three-legged footstool buffing a shoe when Jo and Brue entered. The strong scents of leather and shoe polish filled his small, dark workshop.

"How much to sew my daughter's shoe?"

"Let's take a look." The shoemaker set his work aside and crouched down to help Brue slip off her shoe. He then held it up and, twisting it from side to side, he said, "I think a nickel should do the trick."

Noticing how inexpensive the price, his hesitation, and his apparent compassion, Jo asked, "Are you sure that's enough? I don't want to short you."

"I'm sure, and if you want to wait, I'd be happy to sew it right away."

A nickel for the candy. A nickel for the shoe. And what had Case called a quarter? Two bits? Two bits was all she had left.

CHAPTER THIRTEEN

That's quite the tear you have there. You know," the shoemaker said, "I think if I were a young lass about your age, I might have helped this tear get a lot worse by dragging my shoe along the sidewalk." He winked at Brue, a smile wrinkling the corners of his eyes. "But then I'm not a young lass, and I'm not about your age, either."

Brue's cheeks suddenly grew warm. He couldn't have seen her. How could he possibly know what she'd done?

When he slipped her bulky shoe onto his stitching machine, she looked down at the matching shoe on her other foot. They were the ugliest shoes she'd ever seen. But at least she didn't have to wear them much longer.

Dangling her feet from the tall chair, she looked up and around at the walls of the small shop. Rows of crumpled work shoes lined its shelves, each one looking like it had a story to tell.

Hanging above the shoemaker's toolbox was a picture of a scared kitten that was peeking out from behind the tongue of a scruffy work shoe. A golden retriever was howling at its side. The dog looked pitiful and sad.

"Brue?" Her mother reached for Brue's knee, touching it lightly. "I'm sorry I ever bought those shoes for you."

"You are?"

Her mother nodded. "I thought they'd last a long time. That's the only reason I got them."

How does Mom know what I'm thinking? She's just like the shoe repairman.

"I can't believe I didn't notice the tear before," her mother continued. "Why didn't you say something?"

Brue peered at her feet, slowly swinging them back and forth. "I dunno. When Poke saw the ripped sole, he looked real happy about it."

"Sounds like Poke."

Brue couldn't tell her mother she'd been happy about it, too, and excited to see it break loose. She knew the sooner the tear got big enough, the sooner she'd get a new pair. But it made her feel guilty at the same time because her mother couldn't afford to buy her new shoes.

"Brue," her mother said, "while we're waiting, why don't you tell me more about what happened today."

Brue glanced across the small room again, wishing she could crawl into that picture high up on the wall and hide behind that little kitten. Going uptown without asking permission? Ripping her shoe apart on purpose? Getting into trouble with Big Ole? She looked down and fingered a button on her woolen sweater. And now her mother was beginning to ask questions.

"I need to think this Big Ole problem through," her mother said. "Something isn't sitting right with me. You said you didn't think he would have hit you, that your dress got caught when he raised his cane."

"He always raises his cane, Mom."

"You're right. I have seen him do that. But I'm worried because he lives at the O.M. Harrington House, and your story and Miss Bickford's version don't quite match up. Why did Miss Bickford feel she needed to yell?"

Brue tapped her heel against the leg of her chair.

"Brue," her mother said softly, but with determination.

"I think she thought he was gonna trip over me."

"*Trip* over you?"

"Yup."

"Oh, dear. But ..."

Brue could see question marks bouncing around in her mother's eyes. Maybe if she didn't look at her mother this talk would be easier.

"Did anything else happen that I should know about?" her mother asked.

Brue admitted she'd run into Big Ole twice.

"You what?"

"I ran into him twice. The first time was when I turned the corner on Newton. He was way up the street in front of me. He looked like a grown-up Humpty Dumpty."

Brue was relieved to see her mother break a hint of a smile. The shoemaker glanced over and also smiled, but didn't say anything. He just stayed busy with his work.

"I had a hard time getting around him because he took up the whole sidewalk. When I said, 'Excuse me, sir,' he grunted." Brue's stomach tightened at the memory. Big Ole's eyebrows had raised at least an inch, if not two. Maybe looking at him hadn't been such a good idea.

"Nothing really happened, then? He just grunted?"

"Uh-huh."

"I guess that's okay. Sometimes people just have bad days."

Brue didn't like Big Ole's bad days.

"What about the second time you ran into him?"

Brue sighed and wished she didn't have to say anything, but her mom expected her to be honest. "I was looking through the window at the dime store."

"I need you to talk louder. The sewing machine is so noisy." Brue's mom leaned forward, straining to hear. "What were you doing in front of the dime store window?"

"Are you mad at me?"

"I'm not sure yet."

Brue hesitated, not really wanting her mother to know. "I wanted to look at Cinderella's glass slipper. That's all."

Her mother gave her a funny look but didn't say anything more about it.

Brue remembered how excited she'd gotten when she reached the corner of Broadway and East William. She could still see the sun's bright reflection on the window. On the other side in a small black box, a Cinderella watch and glass slipper had been on display for weeks. The glass slipper looked exactly like the one in *Cinderella*—the book her dad had read to her over and over and over again.

She hadn't been able to keep from touching the window. She liked the Cinderella watch, but it was the glass slipper that took her breath away. It carried her off to a beautiful world where people didn't die, where there wasn't any war, and where people could afford to buy beautiful things. But she could never have the watch and glass slipper. Her mother had been working awful hard ever since her dad went to heaven. She was tired most of the time. Brue saw hurt in her eyes when the bills came in and knew it wouldn't be right to ask for them. Her mother told her many times that being poor on the outside didn't mean you couldn't be rich on the inside. Brue knew exactly what she meant. The glass slipper made her feel rich just looking at it, and nobody in the whole wide world could keep her from dreaming.

Brue twisted and pulled at the corner of her sweater as she went on, telling her mother about hearing someone coming, but not knowing who it was, and how she'd moved closer to the window to get out of the way. "I just heard the sound of a stick hitting the sidewalk and footsteps getting closer."

The loud clunking of the cobbler's sewing machine distracted Brue for a fleeting moment, but it stitched through the leather pretty well. Brue found it hard to look at her brown shoe. It still looked ugly.

Thinking about the glass slipper made her shoe look even uglier, if that was possible.

Brue then told about seeing that really nice clerk on the other side of the dime store window. "She waved her duster at me, and I could see her humming."

"I guess I can see her doing that, too," Brue's mom said.

"She got closer to the window like she wanted to see something. That's when I turned around and saw that it was Mr. Big Ole that was coming. He plowed past two gray-haired ladies with big shopping bags. He didn't even bother to look at them. He just kept coming and forced them off the sidewalk. He was looking down and getting closer all the time."

"What did you do then?"

"I was too scared to move, so I pretended like I didn't see him. Then I heard Miss Bickford shouting through the glass. When I jumped back, I bumped right into Mr. Big Ole's stick. It caught my dress and that's when it ripped."

Brue's mother shook her head. "Wait a minute. Let me take a better look." She nudged the dress out of the paper bag and pulled at the fabric until she found the tear. She then smoothed it with her fingers and looked at it up close.

Brue didn't remember seeing Big Ole's cane touch the ground, but she did remember him swaying back and forth so far she was afraid he was going to fall. Without thinking, she'd grabbed his sleeve and pulled on it with both hands. The next thing she knew, he swatted her off his arm. He shoved his cane high up into the air and shouted at her.

The shoemaker removed Brue's shoe from his stitching machine and buffed it. He looked like a nice man, nothing like Big Ole. When Brue looked back, her mother was staring off like she wasn't sure about something.

"What's the matter, Mom?"

"This tear. I've washed your dress so many times, I'm afraid it wouldn't take a whole lot to give it a good-sized rip. I wonder if it would have torn at all if it had been newer." Her mother let out a deep breath. "Go on. I want to hear the rest of this."

"I didn't know what to do. I heard Miss Bickford come running around the corner. Her face was white, and it looked a lot more wrinkled in the sunshine. She headed straight for me, but she was watching Mr. Big Ole the whole time. He leaned on his walking stick with both of his hands and he looked real mad. Miss Bickford asked me to come into the store with her so we could call you. On our way, she marched right up to him and asked why he didn't pay better attention to where he was going. They yelled a bunch of mean words at each other. I wanted to run, but I couldn't because I was stuck in the middle of them. Mr. Big Ole gave Miss Bickford a real nasty look, then he hit his cane on the sidewalk and left."

Brue thought about Miss Bickford standing there, watching Big Ole stomp across the street and go into The Copper Kettle. As she did, Brue had looked down at the ground, worrying about what her mother would think when she found out what happened.

Brue should have known.

Feeling safe and secure, she rested her head on her mother's shoulder and draped her hand over her mother's thin arm, wondering for a moment why she wasn't angry.

Brue then glanced back at her newly sewn shoe. It didn't look anything at all like Cinderella's glass slipper.

The shoe repairman's work had been quick and good, but the look of the sole hadn't improved. Not in the slightest.

Jo helped Brue slip her small foot back into her shoe, thanked the man sincerely as she paid him the nickel for his work, and together she and Brue walked out the door. Jo wanted to say something, but words escaped her. The shoe still looked pathetic.

As for Brue, she didn't have to say anything. Her eyes said it all.

73

CHAPTER FOURTEEN

November. Jo loved this time of year—pilgrims, turkeys, stuffing and gravy, Indian corn, and pumpkin pie. But this November held a special significance. The year was 1944. An election year. And as far as she could see, campaign posters were still prominently displayed in storefront windows two days after the election. Roosevelt had been in office longer than any other president, yet few were surprised when he won a record fourth term. Even staunch Republicans had known Dewey stood little chance of defeating him, not in the midst of a world war.

War bond posters flanked the campaign posters, while Irving Berlin's theme song, "Any Bonds Today?" blared in the distance. Not only had Irving Berlin volunteered to help with the war effort, Norman Rockwell had painted a special bond series for *The Saturday Evening Post* and Hollywood film stars either signed up to serve or performed in rallies all across the country, among them the late Carole Lombard, Bette Davis, Greer Garson, and Rita Hayworth. Anything to help win the dreadful war against the powerful Germans and invading Japanese. The township of Amber Leaf, not about to be left out, was launching a Victory Bond Rally of its own.

Jo and Brue hastily retraced their steps up Broadway. Jo needed to get home. The overflowing baskets of soiled linen lining the walls of her basement would not clean themselves. She fumbled with her car keys. Just as they turned the corner onto East William, the dwindling sound of snare drums from the high school's marching band played havoc with her conscience. What was more important? Laundry? Or patriotism? They had to stay.

Stopping by the car long enough to drop off Brue's torn dress, Jo glanced at the law office across the street. Judging by the way Tryg had hurried away earlier, she doubted he would be at the rally. That thought alone brought her a significant measure of relief. She steered Brue gently by the shoulder. They continued walking north on Broadway, crossed Fountain Street, and descended the hill toward the snowy-white band shell crowning the shoreline of Fountain Lake. Old Glory stood prominently on the right of the stage, flapping proudly in the light gusts of wind. The crisp, dry autumn air smelling of a hint of smoke from a distant fire added a pleasant touch to the event.

As Jo found empty seats on the folding chairs near the back, she took note of the tempered activity about her—hushed voices seeking privacy in an anything but private setting; the striking absence of young men; held-back emotions; eyes revealing no passion or fear, only the uncertainty that comes with the anticipation of war news.

A gray-haired lady held a cigarette and coughed to the point of breathlessness before inhaling another choking drag. A young mother chased a screeching toddler with food-encrusted cheeks. A weathered old man in a shabby jacket stood hunched over an empty chair, scraping absently at his teeth with a toothpick while staring blankly at the whispering waves lapping lazily against the shore. What were they thinking? What were they feeling? How many husbands, sons, fathers, grandsons, brothers, and cousins represented here were sacrificing their lives in the name of freedom?

After the band noisily tuned their instruments, the conductor tapped his stick against his music stand and leaned into the microphone.

"Ladies and gentlemen, please stand and join in as we sing our national anthem."

The instant he waved his baton a rush of patriotism flowed through the musical instruments, touching off a groundswell of national pride. Broken emotions tore loose. Loss. Fear. Hope. Pride. Jo heard it all in the trembling voices surrounding them. As she clung tight to Brue, who buried her head in Jo's side, small hairs quivered down Jo's arms and legs as she, too, choked out the words.

The music stopped. The crowd, placing their hands over their hearts, recited the Pledge of Allegiance. After they were seated, the chief of police approached the microphone, not that he needed one.

"Last month I went out to sell war bonds the hard way," he said, "knocking on every door until my knuckles ached. You can imagine my surprise when one of those doors swung open, and I found myself looking into the sprightly eyes of a stooped and wrinkled, white-haired lady. Her dentures made a lot of noise as she talked. I think the clicking might have embarrassed her because she kept lifting her bony fingers to her lips to quiet them. Her house could have used a new coat of paint. Desperately, I might add. But her windows were spotless and her home spic-and-span."

Jo watched, fascinated, as the chief's gaze shifted from face to face as though he were having an intimate conversation individually with every person present.

"Under the circumstances," he said, "I didn't feel right asking her to participate in our worthy cause here. She must have sensed my reluctance, because she said, 'Sonny, what brings you to my door? The war effort?'

"I just nodded. With the water in her teapot still hot, she invited me in for a cup of tea. She mentioned something about my looking tired and probably needing a break."

"It's our boys overseas who could use a good break, not you," an overbearing voice shouted from the rear of the crowd. "Why don't you go back to where you came from?"

Stunned, Jo looked back. By the looks on everyone's faces, the chief's included, the voice must have been unfamiliar to them, but Jo was sure she recognized it.

The chief didn't respond and the brash voice cried out again, "Hey, I'm talking to you!"

When the chief glanced in the direction of the heckler, Jo followed the path of his gaze to Brady Malone. Having moved to Amber Leaf several months back, Brady wasn't well known. At least not yet. To the crowd and to the chief, it probably appeared as though he thought his opinions carried more weight than anyone else's, but Jo knew nothing could have been further from the truth.

From the front row, a well-dressed man got up, and with a purposeful limp, he slowly worked his way in Brady's direction like a sad old dog hobbling toward its defeated and broken master.

Jo wiped her perspiring hands on her skirt. It was Tryg.

Keeping a curious eye on Tryg's movement, the chief went on as though there had been no intrusion. "She asked how the bonds were selling. Told me she invests half of her pension every month in victory bonds. As she spoke, I couldn't help but notice a picture of two young soldiers sitting on a table at the far side of the room."

Jo glanced back at Brady, concerned. He looked noticeably agitated, his jaw clenched tight. She feared he might erupt again.

She also kept a reluctant eye on Tryg who moved in closer now. The overflow crowd standing at the far side parted, clearing a path for him. Seeing the sober and compassionate look on Tryg's face, Jo sensed that he might be feeling Brady's pain, that he might be feeling his own pain.

But what about her pain?

So, this is what deep-seated resentment feels like. But isn't this hate?

If ladies don't hate, what do they do when they feel justifiably overwhelmed with dark feelings? She couldn't let Tryg off the hook; that wouldn't be fair to Case. She couldn't bury it; that would only make it fester. But she couldn't bear to watch him play hero, either. It wasn't right for him to try to win the respect of this crowd or of any other crowd, for that matter.

She returned her attention to the chief's talk. *Focus, Jo!*

"She saw me glance at it," he went on, "and said, 'those are my grand-sons. I'm so proud of them. They're both off in the Pacific somewhere. The way I have it figured, if they can volunteer to put their lives on the line, the least I can do is volunteer to put my money on the line.'"

"Why?" Brady shouted again.

Tryg stopped short.

"Put her money on the line for what?"

Tryg stood motionless staring at the ground with one ear appearing tilted toward the commotion, another on Chief Stout as if listening intently for an unspoken directive from him before proceeding forward.

Brady's face burned crimson. He blinked at Tryg for a distracted moment before going on. "You didn't answer me. The question is *why?* We're getting our kids killed overseas and for what? Let the other countries fight their own battles."

"Oh yeah? What about Pearl Harbor, you dimwit?" someone yelled, setting off a muddled chorus of agreement. Heads turning. Questioning gazes darting every which way.

"Sir, if you even think of rudely interrupting me one more time," Chief Stout warned, "I've got a nice little eight-by-twelve-foot room where I'd be more than happy to give you plenty of time to rethink your position, and you can give the iron bars a nice little spit shine while you're at it."

Brue looked up. "Mom?"

Jo pulled her close. "It'll be okay, sweetie. Don't worry. Everything will be just fine."

Brady grimaced then took an empty swat at the air and stomped off with Tryg trailing along behind him, his hand reaching out.

Chief Stout finished his talk without any further interruptions. The crowd quickly dispersed. A number of townspeople lined up to purchase war bonds, a few would undoubtedly go on home, while the rest made their way back down Broadway, many heading through the open doors of The Copper Kettle.

Passing alongside the five-and-dime as they returned to their car, Jo noticed smudges on the store window, no doubt from Brue. She quickly buffed the prints away with her handkerchief. Then her eyes found their way to the Cinderella watch and her polishing slowed.

She turned and led Brue toward their car.

Feeling some resistance, Jo asked, "What are you—"

"Mom, look at that pretty car."

Brue broke loose and headed straight for the shiny new Packard parked immediately behind Jo's '31 Chevy.

"It looks like the one Dad wanted to buy us some day, remember?"

"Yes, I certainly do."

Concerned about her car's bad clutch, Jo balked at the bulging crowd across the street in the restaurant. Her car could be a challenge to drive under normal conditions, but even more so pulling out of a parallel-parking spot. Maybe she worried needlessly. After all, the clutch hadn't caused any problems on her way to town.

"Come, Brue," she said. "Let's go home."

Jo fired up the engine and shifted into reverse. Rolling down the window, she slid her arm into the correct position to signal—straight out.

So far, so good.

Next, she released the clutch, but it slipped as she stepped on the gas pedal. The car bucked, and she heard the sickening crunch of metal on metal and glass on glass.

CHAPTER FIFTEEN

Charlie rapped his knuckles against the registration desk as he bounded in the direction of the coffee room. "Afternoon!"

Calvin glanced up. "Time for a quick afternoon pick-me-up, I see."

"You bet."

Charlie!

Calvin hoisted to his feet and nudged his pants up a notch. "Mind if I join you? I could use a break here."

"Happy to have ya." Charlie led the way then poured two coffees, handing Calvin a cup. "Here you go. You take it black?"

"Black and bitter."

They settled in at a small table near the window. Charlie sprawled comfortably back on his spindle chair and looked around. "Say, where is everyone this afternoon?"

"I have no idea. It is a little on the quiet side, isn't it?" Calvin swept a stray cookie crumb under his napkin, set down his cup a bit too hard, then quickly wiped away a dribble of coffee that had sloshed on the table. "So what are you up to for the rest of the day?"

"Thought maybe I'd take another spin in the Cessna for about an hour or so. Might as well take advantage of the decent weather while I can."

"That's quite the little machine you've got there."

"It's not too bad, I guess."

"What do you mean, not too bad? I still hear people talking about it. You're quite the pilot, too. You'll do well overseas, son. You've definitely got the gift."

Charlie's face brightened. "Thanks."

"Speaking of overseas, any idea when you're heading out yet?"

"Day after tomorrow."

"The military doesn't mess around, does it?"

"No, sir, it sure doesn't. We got a war to fight, and I'm itching to get out of here. Boys over there could use a little help."

Calvin saw the unfettered eagerness in Charlie's eyes, the same eagerness he himself had felt before experiencing the sobering realities of war. Strange how the mind worked. In the throes of battle, Calvin had taken danger in stride. But now where none existed, the memory alone of the raw and distant cries from the battlefield made easy prey of his mind.

He still tossed and turned at night, cursing the times he'd been a sham as a chaplain, sharing head knowledge rather than heart knowledge with the mortally wounded. During their final moments, as the light faded from their eyes, those soldiers deserved better. Under less than ideal circumstances, what else could Calvin have done? Quit the Army when he returned stateside immediately following World War I? He'd considered it. But how could anyone have known that "the war to end all wars" wouldn't?

Calvin had held his own with lighter duty during the high times of the twenties and the hard-hitting Great Depression of the thirties. Then the new war heated up in Europe. He'd kept an eye on it with foreboding. But when it spread faster than a forest fire gone wild, it was too late to get out. He felt duty-bound to continue serving. Fortunately, he was home now. Home where he no longer needed to pretend to be something he wasn't.

"Hey, are you okay?" Charlie asked.

Calvin winced. Looking into the eyes of the young flier, he could still see countless soldiers scattered, wounded and lifeless, across the battlefield. "Guess I got a little too lost in my old world memories for a minute there."

Charlie gave him a confused smile that told him just how deep inside of himself Calvin had drifted. "You know, you never did tell me. What exactly were your duties back then?"

"The usual." As though repeating a monologue, Calvin added, "Blessings for the Jews, last rites for the Catholics, prayers for the Protestants, tourniquets, bandages, splints, medicine, and more words of encouragement and feeble hope than I or anyone else, for that matter, had the capacity to give."

"I envy your past."

Calvin scratched his chin, his smile reluctant. "Has someone been slipping something numbing into your drinking water?"

"No. Not at all. It's just that a good number of those days had to have been jam-packed with stimulation."

"They were. But it wasn't the kind of stimulation ..."

"Go on."

"I've got to tell you that every time I heard the cry, 'Chaplain!' I felt like the most vital human being alive. Stress sure took its toll, though. But every grateful look and every soldier still alive because of my efforts ..." Shaking his head while choking down a thick sensation forming in his throat, Calvin cast his gaze toward the small chandelier dangling from the ceiling. "No one can walk away from something like that without feeling some sense of satisfaction, a real sense of purpose."

"That's not all that easy to come by these days."

Charlie had that right. Calvin had been somebody back then— Captain Calvin H. Doherty, Chaplain, 88th Infantry Division, European

Theatre. Although his struggling faith taunted him relentlessly, at least he'd felt useful.

Now, Mr. Calvin H. Doherty, Clerk, O.M. Harrington House. A welcome break? Sure. But what about purpose?

Calvin rested his elbows on the table and clasped his hands together, his thumbs stroking one another. "You're right. Purpose is anything but easy to come by. But I'm afraid that's about the only thing I miss about active duty."

"I guess I can understand that." Straddling an elbow over the back of his chair, a downcast look sprouted from Charlie's worried eyes. "Keep an eye on Pop for me, would you? He's always been a little on the nervous side, but it seems to be getting worse the older he gets."

"Be happy to. Don't worry about it."

"Hey, Chaplain—"

"I'm not a chaplain anymore," Calvin said, his words spilling out in a rush.

"Right," Charlie acknowledged with a nod. "But I'm curious. When you were, did you ever get involved in any of those crawling out rescue jobs?"

"A few from time to time."

"You got guts."

Calvin pushed back in his chair. "Compassion, not guts. The guys who've got guts are the ones going out there ahead of the lines taking hits. Somebody's got to ferret the ditches looking for them."

"Like I said, you got guts."

Calvin shifted uncomfortably. Enough of this war talk. "Say, Charlie, I've been meaning to ask you. I heard a rumor that Big Ole wants this place to use some new laundry outfit uptown."

"What does that have to do with crawling out rescue jobs?" Charlie asked, looking puzzled.

"Doesn't. You wouldn't happen to know anything about it, would you?"

Charlie quickly gulped down a swallow of cooling coffee then said, "Sure do. Big Ole and I talked about it a couple of days ago. I know the guy who runs the place. Name of Ernie Pritchard."

"Don't believe I know him."

"His son was a good buddy of mine." Charlie hesitated, his hazel eyes emanating grief. "Got buried in Italy."

Calvin's heart sank, but what about Jo Bremley's husband? He also got buried. "That's a real shame."

"Ernie's a good man."

"I'm sure he is."

Uncertain as to how to proceed, Calvin peered through the window and ventured, "The young Bremley widow. She sure does a bang-up job with the laundry. You haven't had any problems with her work, have you?"

"Not me. I don't doubt she's pretty good at it." Charlie lifted his chin, his eyes revealing understanding. "You're worried about the widow getting aced out of her job here. Is that it?"

"Guess you might say that."

"Can't say as I blame you," Charlie said. "I doubt Big Ole's decision had anything to do with her, though."

"That's a relief, but why would you say that?"

"It was more of a whim. When he found out about Ernie's son, I think he wanted to help out. Ernie needs the work. With the war taking a toll on his business, he needs it bad. I know him. I think his outfit would do a swell job for the boarding house."

"But—"

"Look, I wouldn't mind revisiting this with Big Ole, but I'm not sure that would be such a great idea. You might want to give Ernie's place a try first. Maybe he won't make the grade." Charlie swirled what was left of his coffee and eyed Calvin for a moment before taking a sip. "Don't take it so seriously. Business is just business. You know that."

"I know, but with all due respect, I can't help but feel for the young widow. She's got a load on her hands, especially raising that little girl alone."

Charlie set his cup down, his gaze penetrating Calvin's. "Be careful about taking that on as your problem."

"Why do you say that?"

"Ernie's struggling, too. So much so that he's offered to give Big Ole twenty-four-hour turnaround service on his personal laundry."

Calvin gulped. "Twenty-four hours?"

"That's right. Big Ole's ears sure perked up when he heard that one, I'll tell ya."

"I can imagine. But about Mrs. Bremley ..."

Charlie stiffened. "That's Big Ole's decision." He then glanced distractedly around the coffee room and his voice softened. "Besides, I wouldn't worry about that dame. She's got chutzpah. She'll do just fine."

"Sure wish I could feel as confident as you." Calvin gathered his cup and slowly pushed up from the table. Things looked bleak. "Thanks for the coffee," he said and then headed back to the registration desk where he could worry with little-to-no pressure for conversation.

CHAPTER SIXTEEN

J o sat in her car in a daze before shifting her attention across the street toward The Copper Kettle. Wall lanterns flanked its double door front entry. "Happy Thanksgiving" was scrawled in colorful orange and brown script stretching across the entire length of its picture windows. And through the colorful penmanship on the other side of those windows, Big Ole sat front and center, looking back at her.

She shrugged off the sight and turned to Brue. "Maybe it would be best if you waited in the car."

"Why, Mom?"

"Because I don't want you to get hurt stepping on any chunks of glass or bumping into anything sharp. But you can roll your window down and look out if you want."

Jo breathed in a lung full of air then slid out of her Chevy, took that agonizing walk toward her back bumper, and crouched down for a good look. Broken headlamp. Dented rim. Thoroughly scratched paint. Slivers of glass from the Packard's headlamp and her Chevy's taillight scattered on the street like pieces spilled out of a kaleidoscope.

Brue leaned out the window. "How bad is it?"

"Oh, I guess it could be worse."

As Jo appraised the damage, the clomping of heavy footsteps grew louder until large black shoes encroached her peripheral vision. She looked up. Relieved to see Chief Stout, she let loose a big puff of breath. "Oh, thank you for coming. I'm not sure what to do here. I've never had an accident before."

The chief stared at the scene, silent with a deafening absence of expression.

Oh, no! It's his car.

The chief looked considerably more imposing now that she looked up at him and he wasn't sitting down. Thumbs tucked in his belt. Thickset chin jutted high into the air. Not the kind of man anyone would want to meet in a dark alley; that was for sure. He glared at the shattered glass and then took a long, discriminating look at his Packard's battered left headlamp.

With a mouth barely moving and a hardened jaw, he asked for her driver's license.

She fumbled through her purse and found it. "How much will this cost?"

"It won't be cheap, I assure you."

"Hey, Mom," Brue said excitedly from her perch on the front seat. "There's Mr. Howland."

"Where?"

"Across the street there."

Jo followed the invisible line drawn by Brue's pointing finger to find Tryg limping past The Copper Kettle. He stopped mid-stride and glanced at her, expressionless yet squarely, before disappearing into the brick building next door. The shingle above the door that read T.W. "Tryg" Howland, III, Attorney-at-Law, continued swaying in the quiet breeze.

And Big Ole was still sitting, huge as a house, just inside the restaurant's front window at his legendary table for two, party of one. Jo could swear his lips mouthed *women drivers!* He pushed to his feet and shuffled out the door. Jo glanced back at Brue who was sitting at attention, her eyes fastened on the old man as he disappeared around the corner. "Are you okay?"

She nodded.

Chief Stout crouched to the asphalt and carefully surveyed the damage. He picked up a shard of glass and held it high in the air, studying it as though it were a rare and fine diamond.

Not about to let a little humiliation keep her down, Jo took a step forward. "Look, I'm really sorry about hitting your car. My clutch slips sometimes, and I'm afraid I haven't had a chance to get it fixed yet. But I do intend to pay for the damage."

"You're lucky I'm not topping this off with a ticket."

He couldn't be serious. "For what?"

"A repair ticket," he said matter-of-factly. "That would be for your bad clutch that took out my fender."

A rush of indignation swept over Jo. If his car had been an old wreck, they wouldn't be having this conversation. But then her clutch should have been fixed by now.

At first Jo didn't see the car wheeling around the corner, but she heard the hum of its engine. The driver glanced at the disturbance at their side of the curb then jerked his '42 Oldsmobile to a halt in the middle of the street and cranked down his window. "What's going on here?"

It was Brady Malone.

Chief Stout didn't look up, and he didn't respond, but his cheeks tightened and flushed.

Brady ogled the broken chunks of glass lying at the chief's feet. A leisurely grin cut a horizontal line across the entire width of his face. He glanced at Jo but must not have recognized her. "You okay, ma'am?"

"I'm fine."

"That's swell. Sorry, Chief," he said, sounding overly sincere as his car crept on down the street.

Ignoring both the car and its driver, the chief jotted a few words down on a piece of paper and ripped it off his small pad. "The repair shop is a couple of blocks from here. That's the name and address you'll need. I'll bring my car in first thing in the morning."

Jo wasn't happy about the repair bill. Neither was she particularly happy when she turned and contemplated Brady's vanishing car. When she looked back, the chief's eyes were fixed on hers. "Something on your mind?"

"I take it you don't know Brady Malone."

"Can't say as I do. I assume you're referring to that pitiful piece of work that just drove off."

Tall enough to naturally peer down on her when he spoke, was it really necessary for the chief to lift his chin?

"Yes, but I don't think I'd be inclined to speak of him quite so disparagingly."

"Is that a fact?" he said irritably.

"He had three children. I went to school with his daughter. She was a couple of years ahead of me so I didn't know her all that well. She was a nurse with the Red Cross and his oldest son was in the infantry. I say *was* because Brady got word about a year ago that he lost both of them within a matter of days of each other. I thought you'd appreciate knowing there actually is a good reason for him to have little patience with the war."

Jo left Chief Stout moaning beside his car while she set off for home with Brue at her side. Her tires bawled against the pavement as she powered down the streets, completely lost in thought.

"How much will it cost to fix Chief Stout's car, Mom?"

"Hmm? Oh, I don't know, but like he said, it's not going to be cheap. That's a very expensive car."

Jo glanced at Brue, who was sitting at the edge of her seat looking troubled. "What are you thinking about?"

"Mr. Big Ole."

"And?"

"Why does he have to be so mean to little kids and old people?"

Brue touched on a valid point. From what Jo had witnessed, Big Ole freely showered his disrespect on the young and old alike. "I doubt he even knows. It's not right, is it? Why they make such a fuss over him at the O.M. Harrington House is beyond me. I wish I could protect you from all the people in the world like him. All of the bullies. But that's not possible, is it?"

Brue shook her head.

More strongly than ever, Jo felt the full weight of raising a child alone, her child, without Case's counsel and protection. But these days she was merely one of an enormous number of young widows facing the same plight. "About Big Ole being nasty, you need to know that he's nasty because of who he is, not because of who you are."

Brue looked at Jo, her expression blank. She wasn't making this easy.

"Look, regardless of how that man makes you feel," Jo said, "there's something I want you to do."

"What's that?"

"Just be kind to him. Show him respect."

"Why?"

"Because he's your elder, and we all need to show respect to our elders even when they're misbehaving. It may not make a difference to him, and you may not feel any better about him, but at least you'll feel better about yourself. Do you understand what I'm trying to say?"

Brue plucked at a loose thread on her sweater. "I think I do."

She continued to look unsettled. Bothered. It was going to take time for her to work through the Big Ole incident.

As Jo downshifted and headed down the brick-paved hill on Newton, she saw Big Ole again, this time in the distance, shuffling along, still beating his stick against the sidewalk. He crossed the railroad tracks by a small wooded area near the corner at Charles Street.

"And speaking of Big Ole," Jo said, "look who's there."

She reflected on the incident that had tipped her entire afternoon upside down. How frightened had Brue been? Big Ole occupied the bulk of the sidewalk as he ambled along. Actually, his presence swallowed up the entire landscape. With his focus fixed on the ground, the big man stopped at the curb. "Guess we'd better wait for him to cross the street."

Brue stretched her small chin above the dash. "He sure is nasty looking."

"How about if we call him interesting instead of nasty? I don't want you fearing people for no good reason, especially people like him."

"Do you respect him, Mom?"

"That's a pretty interesting question. I don't believe I do, but I'm looking hard to find something in him I can respect."

Or did she? His brush with Brue aside, for some odd reason, Jo felt drawn to the man, fascinated by him, and she wasn't alone. Questioning looks and murmurs from turning heads seemed to follow in his path wherever he went. She'd heard the townspeople whispered his name. Why?

The strain from the clutch nearly wrenched her leg into spasm. She clasped the steering wheel and pulled herself forward.

Her subtle movement drew a quick glance, but a glance he directed past her. She'd seen that look before. If the episodes with the children weren't mounting, she'd try to put her irritation behind her, but she couldn't, not with the tally of incidents on the rise.

Big Ole finally stepped onto the opposite curb and lumbered along, not bothering to look back.

Meanwhile, Jo shifted gears and drove on, determined for now to forget about the old man fading from sight in her rearview mirror.

CHAPTER SEVENTEEN

J ust over the hilltop, Jo turned right onto River Lane. Harrington Park loomed into view—a golden meadow on a hillside dotted with maples, oaks, and elms, and skirted with the still, blue waters of Amber Leaf Lake. She pulled to the curb in front of the O.M. Harrington House to gather another load of soiled linen, her car heaving and sputtering to a stop. Big Ole was barely a couple of blocks away. If she made a quick entry and exit before he returned, she could buy a few days' time to consider how to make peace with the man.

With Brue clipping at her heels, Jo hurried along the well-manicured lawn and immaculately trimmed hedges hemming the boarding house. Designed after a replica of a grand Victorian-style farmhouse, she never tired of the massive structure with its stately white columns, balustrades, cupolas, and multi-paned windows. It housed fifteen guest rooms. A wide wooden porch wrapped around its front and sides. Hanging flower baskets and potted plants trimmed the porch, which offered rocking chairs and a swing just large enough for two. The sight of Calvin Doherty on the porch fussing with several of the rocking chairs, nudging and aligning them just so, gave Jo pause. He glanced at her before taking a step forward. Was it her imagination, or did a hint of distress lurk behind his cautious smile?

"Hello, Mr. Doherty. You're improving on perfection, I see."

"Oh, I don't know that anyone could improve on it. Just helping Mr. Harrington maintain the place."

"I remember when this neighborhood was speckled with nothing more than a spattering of small, aging houses. Just look at it now."

"And Mr. Harrington bought up the entire block," Mr. Doherty said. "I understand he paid the owners twice their homes' worth and then leveled the houses to build this dream of his."

Jo smiled appreciatively. "That's right. And no one complained."

"So I've heard."

"We're here to pick up that load of laundry, if it's ready."

Mr. Doherty stepped back and extended his hand for Jo and Brue to take the lead.

Jo gave a last nervous glance up the sidewalk before entering the wide double doors of the O.M. Harrington. They opened into a vestibule displaying Mr. Harrington's memorabilia, which included a smartly framed picture of him during his younger days when he won a fencing competition, a framed certificate of his law degree, and framed news clippings of his ventures as a circuit judge up in the Cities. Jo hadn't met Mr. and Mrs. Harrington yet, but she hoped to during one of their rare visits to Amber Leaf.

Just outside the parlor, better known as the great room, Spitfire pattered up the hallway and jumped into Brue's waiting arms, lapping her face with his wet tongue.

"Brue, I think that dog is lonely. Would you like to play with him for a few minutes?" Jo asked, looking to Mr. Doherty for approval.

Grinning at the spectacle, Mr. Doherty nodded. "Thinks he's found quite the lollipop." But then he quickly turned back toward Jo. "We have a large load of soiled linen in the back room. Do come with me, please."

Jo's forehead tightened involuntarily. Calvin Doherty had never escorted her to the laundry room before.

Leaving Brue's scrunched-up and wet face with Spitfire, Jo followed

Mr. Doherty. Over the past months, a welcome friendship had blossomed with him in a fatherly sort of way, but today their conversation seemed to have lost its easy flow. His eyes scanned the walls as he walked, reflecting that hint of sadness more than usual.

"I appreciate your business more than you know," Jo said in an effort to break the subtle tension.

"I'm happy to keep you busy."

I, not we?

Inside the laundry room, she pulled on the light string dangling from the middle of the ceiling with a bit too much force. Relieved the string hadn't broken, she glanced at the near-empty shelves. "Dear me. You must have a full house again. I see Evelyn has gone through most of the linen already."

He nodded. "Between now and the holidays, it's going to pick up even more, I'm afraid. Even the waiting list is full." He patted the hamper with the flat of his hand. "This is it."

What an odd thing to say. Who could possibly know better than Jo where the boarding house stored its soiled linen? Calvin Doherty appeared to have more on his mind, but he also appeared to be holding back. Why?

As she transferred the load from the hamper into her basket, Jo had the unshakable feeling that Mr. Doherty was studying her.

When she finished, he said, "You might as well go ahead and exit through the front door. There's no one around."

No, but there will be soon enough with Big Ole lumbering up the sidewalk. "Great," she said politely.

"May I carry the basket for you?"

"That's not necessary, but thanks, anyway. It's awfully kind of you to offer."

Mr. Doherty stepped back to make room for her to lead the way.

As they walked up the hallway, the front door flew open. Jo bristled at the familiar sound of a cane tapping against the hardwood floor.

Big Ole stepped in and removed his hat, hanging it on the clothes tree immediately inside the door. When he turned and met her gaze, Jo's stomach constricted. "Good afternoon."

He gave a slight expressionless nod, his face contorted at the sight of Brue, and he disappeared into the coffee room, siphoning the air out of the room he'd left behind.

A strained expression trawled across Mr. Doherty's usually pleasant face, a look that magnified Jo's concern.

She quickly gathered Brue—it was well past time to go home.

CHAPTER EIGHTEEN

The porcelain cup clattered on the saucer from the stove to the table as Jo eased onto her chair, contemplating how many setbacks she could endure before getting crushed beneath their weight.

She picked up a thick pile of bills and slapped them against her hand once, twice, then plunked them back on the table and nudged them fastidiously into a neat stack. She then fanned them with her thumb while torturing herself with the text of the telegram one more time. No need to read it. She had it memorized.

NOVEMBER 9 1944

AUDIT COMPLETE STOP EMBEZZLEMENT OF ALL ASSETS FROM PAPER MILL CONFIRMED STOP CRIMINAL CHARGES FILED STOP

WITH SINCEREST REGRETS

Now what do I do?

Meaning to pick up her cup, she bumped it instead, spilling a few spatters of tea on the table. She wiped them away with the edge of her apron. If only the bills could be wiped away with such ease.

Jo had a real dilemma on her hands. Her job was becoming increasingly vulnerable; she sensed it. Her '31 Chevy needed new tires, a new clutch, an oil change, and gas. It was running on fumes. Brue was growing out of her clothes faster than Jo could replace them. Jo looked around the kitchen with its chipped cupboards, cracked window pane, and yellowing curtains. Her small, weather-beaten home needed a lot of work. It would be well into the hereafter before she could afford a better place to live. Overwhelmed with concern, she whispered an earnest prayer. "How do you move a mountain, Lord?" Then, knowing the answer, she looked up and let out a slow sigh. "One stone at a time, right?"

She knew what she had to do—keep her focus on what she could control. She would begin with the smallest bills and plow her way to the largest, paying them off one at a time until the last bill had been paid. Until then, she and Brue would have to make the best of what they had. Jo dropped her elbows onto the table and rested the full weight of her head in her hands. It was time to move on.

Through the paper-thin walls of the living room, the grandfather clock chimed, breaking her concentration. Two o'clock. She glanced out the back window. The sheets should be dry by now. She needed to get Brue's bed made before Brue scuttled through the door from school.

Opening the old Havana cigar box, Jo stashed the unpaid bills on top of an unopened envelope from Haskins & Sells, snapped the lid shut, and then placed the cigar box back on the uppermost shelf in the cupboard.

The bills temporarily out of sight, she went outside and gathered the sheets from the clothesline. Moments later, after tucking her daughter's sheets and woolen blanket snuggly around her mattress, Jo reached for Brue's patchwork quilt. The palm of her hand hit against something hard. She rifled through the tangled quilt and found Brue's well-worn book, *Cinderella.* "What in the world?" Jo muttered to herself and then clutched it in her arms, wondering. "What's this doing stuck in her bedding again?"

CHAPTER NINETEEN

Evelyn Tomlinson's front door rasped open in the mid-afternoon cold, and she blinked her olive eyes behind her wire rimmed glasses. With her hair the color of burnt toast set in pin curls and wrapped in a red and white polka-dot headscarf, she looked like a model for a Rosie the Riveter poster.

"I'm glad you called about the plums," Jo said. "I was looking for an excuse to come over."

"N-nonsense. You never need an excuse to visit. Come in."

"I wanted to ask you some questions about Big Ole." As Jo slipped out of her overcoat, Evelyn peered awkwardly down at her shoes. Something was bothering her. Taking care not to disturb the doilies veiling the back of Evelyn's sofa, Jo draped her coat lightly over its arm. "Before I do, we need to have a chat. What are you all worked up about?"

Evelyn slipped her hands deep into the pockets of her apron, her shoulders hunched forward. "Honestly, I can't keep anything from you. C-can I?"

"Nope. So out with it."

With no small amount of tripping over her own words, Evelyn filled Jo in about her son's looting a full winter's supply of canned plums from their root cellar.

No wonder Jo had seen Poke traipsing around the neighborhood with a splash of purple staining his lips and cheeks. "Now, that's what I call a golden problem." Jo smoothed her friend's shoulder. "Enjoy him."

Evelyn parked her hands on her hips as if it were possible for her to actually look authoritative. "Do you have any idea how much of this stuff he pulls?"

"I know." Jo fought back a threatening grin. "But he's just getting mischief out of his system while he's still young. That's healthy. Kids like him can grow up to surprise you. Come on, Evelyn. If anyone is incapable of harboring malice toward anyone, it's you. That includes harboring malice toward that precocious son of yours, and you know it."

Evelyn shook her head halfheartedly and with a blink she dismissed her frustration.

"Now about Big Ole—"

Evelyn quickly padded across her oriental rug, giving Jo her back. She headed straight for a cabinet positioned immediately beneath her living room window. Sunlight streaming through her hand-crocheted curtains mirrored off the cabinet as effectively as Jo's question about Big Ole deflected off Evelyn. "Say, your timing couldn't be better. Not only was I out of plums, something's gone amok with my sewing machine, and my eyesight isn't what it used to be. What do you think?" Evelyn pulled out a chair. "You wouldn't mind helping me, would you?"

Jo sidled up to the cabinet feeling uncharacteristically out of place in her dear friend's home. "Not at all. What seems to be the problem?"

"That boy of mine ... you know, the one who's going to grow up to surprise me? He used it to alter one of his dad's leather belts for a costume he rigged up for the Harvest Festival. When I sat down to sew a split seam in my blouse, I couldn't get the needle to budge."

Jo checked the course of the thread, the hand wheel, tension, and bobbin. "You wouldn't happen to have another needle, would you? This one's bent just a smidge at the end. I can't believe it didn't break." In no more than a minute, Jo had the machine purring. "Now, about Big Ole ..."

"Hmm?" Evelyn said weakly.

"What do you know about him?"

Evelyn pulled herself up, strolled to the window, and busily worked a kink out of her curtain, giving it an inordinate amount of attention. "Not much. Just that he showed up at the O.M. Harrington late this past spring. Everyone's been k-kowtowing to him ever since. I'm too busy to listen to gossip to know anything more than that, but I'm afraid I wouldn't be all that interested anyway."

Jo smiled at Evelyn's humble comment. "That's one of your more endearing qualities."

"Thanks for the kind words, but I'm afraid I don't deserve a halo. I hardly have time to be snoopy these days."

Not only was Evelyn a reluctant audience, she wasn't asking any questions. Jo sensed an ominous undercurrent. Needing to find out what was going on, she waded in by recounting the incidents that had taken place uptown, all springing from a Cinderella watch, a glass slipper, and an old curmudgeon.

"You've certainly had a rough time." Evelyn stepped away from the window. "Is Brue okay?"

"Her emotions took a bruising, but fortunately she wasn't harmed physically."

"What are you going to do about it?" Evelyn asked, her inexpressive face hard to read.

Jo's thoughts in a muddle, she shook her head and nervously wrung her hands. "I'm afraid I've already done it. But now I'm questioning myself. I may have overdone it."

Evelyn leaned forward, color fading from her cheeks. "Ho-oh. Overdone wh-what?"

"Let's just say that when I saw the size of the tear in Brue's dress, I found myself hovering over Big Ole in The Copper Kettle. With Chief Stout looking on, I might add."

Evelyn gasped, lightly seizing her throat with both hands. "You wh-what?"

"I had a chat with him," Jo said strongly.

"You need to be careful," Evelyn replied, her words sounding far more like a warning than a comment.

What a curious response. Why would Evelyn focus more on Jo's interactions with Big Ole than Big Ole's interactions with Brue? "Why are you saying that?"

"Well, for one thing I still haven't been able to figure out why people let that man walk all over them."

"I don't understand. What does that have to do with Brue?"

Evelyn shook her head. "You don't want to say or do anything that could put your j-job at risk."

Jo frowned. "That's my daughter he's trifling with. I have to protect her."

"It's just that ... what if Brue did something wrong?"

"Then I need to know that. If she did, she's going to have to make things right. But I don't believe for a minute that's true. You've seen Big Ole. Normal people don't get that riled unless they have good reason. He gets riled if the sun shines."

Evelyn let out a resigned sigh. "Be careful, Jo. I get the feeling you might n-not want to mess with that man."

"But I can't let this pass—"

"How was Miss Bickford?" Evelyn asked, cutting Jo off. "I haven't seen or heard a word about her in years."

"She's pretty feisty."

"Some people never change."

Jo nodded. "When we chatted in the alley outside earshot of Brue, she did mention that if I wanted to buy the watch I could put one on layaway."

"Are you sure you want to do that?"

"Why wouldn't I be?"

Evelyn hesitated, her gaze scanning the carpet. "How much did the store want to hold it?"

She hadn't answered Jo's question. Why?

"Only a dollar, but I remember squirming. I didn't need to bother with checking my cash. I knew exactly how much I had. I can't believe I allowed myself to feel pressured by a stranger."

Evelyn reached over and lightly touched Jo's arm. "Don't be so hard on yourself."

"I can't help it. That Cinderella watch and glass slipper would make the perfect Christmas gift for Brue. This year, short of a miracle, I don't know if it's going to be possible to buy them for her, but I have to give it a try."

Evelyn looked away. "Maybe it's b-best to let it go."

Jo massaged her forehead with her hand as if to wipe her worries away. Evelyn seemed distant, uncomfortable inside her own soul. She knew something. She was holding back.

Neither Jo nor Evelyn said anything for a long and awkward moment, but then as if feeling the need to make small talk to fill the quiet, Evelyn changed the subject. "I understand Tryg Howland has a new law office up town."

"He does. We saw him."

Evelyn's eyelashes fluttered, another nervous tic she had little control over. "Did he say anything to you?"

"No. I can't read him. He looked at me, but it didn't go beyond that. No hello. No wave. No nothing. And he calls himself Tryg now. The shingle above his office door said T.W. 'Tryg' Howland, III, Attorney-at-Law."

"You mean he's finally become one of us?" Evelyn shook her head in disgust. "Maybe getting wounded has softened him some. Honestly, when I think back to your wedding, I still can't believe he had the audacity to publicly object to your marriage just because he felt like it."

"I know. He makes me want to prove myself."

"But he's—"

"What? A high-powered attorney? And I'm a lowly laundry lady? I will be a success, Evelyn," Jo said with no small amount of determination.

"That's not what I meant. Give him time. He'll come around. Men always do. And when he does, you'll be able to ask him some of those questions you've been saving up."

Evelyn had that right. After the accident that had taken her husband's life one short year ago, Jo hadn't seen the remains of the car. She had no desire to see it. At the time she'd read the police report, she'd been in shock. The words meant nothing. But with the passing of time, the written words, once black on white, finally cried out for her attention, setting her to wonder.

Why would Case hit the window on the passenger's side of the car instead of the driver's side?

Why would Tryg *come to* behind the steering wheel of Case's car? He had to have been driving.

Whatever possessed him to get behind the wheel with a bum leg?

Would she ever find out? Probably not. He wasn't the type to speak of such things. But neither would she let him know how thoroughly he had destroyed her world—at least not until she built it up again, if then.

Jo glanced at the clock. Three-thirty already. She needed to get home before Brue.

As Evelyn led the way toward the door, Jo caught a whiff of a light fragrance. "Is that cologne I smell?"

"Blue Waltz."

Jo plucked her coat from the sofa and pushed her arms through its sleeves. "Evelyn, you're blushing."

Evelyn tucked a loose pin curl under her scarf. "I always dab on a smidge when I read Howard's letters. Makes them seem a little more special, if you know what I mean."

"Do I ever." Just yesterday Jo and Brue had tried on a sample of Evening in Paris at the perfume counter. Someday, when she could get her finances in order, she wanted to treat herself to a bottle, but that would not be possible for quite some time. "By the way, speaking of Howard, how's our soldier doing?"

Hurt seeped into Evelyn's olive eyes. "He misses a warm, soft bed. It can get pretty rough sleeping out under the stars for nights on end." She stared off, her voice fading. "Freezing on that rock-hard ground. I worry about him getting frostbite. I can always tell when he's numb with cold when he writes. It sure takes a toll on his penmanship."

The pain flooding Evelyn's eyes concerned Jo. But was it pain she saw or was it something else? Fear, maybe? It didn't matter, really. Jo had respect for both, praying Evelyn would not have to endure the loss of her husband, too—not for many years to come.

Jo opened the door, but then thinking better of it, she closed it again. "Evelyn, you don't stumble over your words unless you're excited or upset about something. Do you have any idea how many times you've had difficulty getting them out? And I get the feeling mentioning anything about Big Ole is out of bounds for you."

Evelyn didn't hesitate to cast her guilt-ridden gaze toward the floor.

"How about if we get right to it," Jo said. "Is my job in jeopardy?"

"No!"

"Evelyn, you said that way too fast."

"Probably," she said softly, correcting herself. "Maybe," she said, softer still.

Jo's pulse quickened. "Want to tell me about it?"

Evelyn lifted her chin, looking sympathetic. She wasn't particularly good at hiding hurt. She reached out and placed a light hand on Jo's arm. "You don't deserve this. You're doing a fantastic job. You're even better at your work than I thought you'd be, and I knew you'd be terrific."

Jo leaned her shoulder against the door, mechanically tying and untying the sash on her coat. "Thanks, but where has it gotten me?"

"Look, it's probably nothing."

"I don't think so. Calvin Doherty hasn't been himself lately, either,"

Jo said pensively. "Maybe if I understood the problem, I might be able to do something about it."

"I don't know. Maybe you're right. It's just that the other day when I asked Mr. Doherty if we could get more shelving in the laundry room, he got a worried look on his face. Said we needed to wait until after the first of the year."

"Really? Why? Did he say?"

Evelyn nodded. "He said some changes were probably going to be made."

"And?"

"He was looking at the shelves. Mumbling something about the laundry."

Jo's heart hammered the air out of her lungs. "What about the laundry?"

"I honestly don't know. I couldn't make out what he was saying. All I do know is that he looked extremely troubled."

CHAPTER TWENTY

The cool afternoon breeze nipped at Brue's cheeks, but she enjoyed the walk home from school just the same, that is until she and Poke reached the edge of Harrington Park.

"Look at Big Ole," Poke said with a sneer and a point of his finger. "Looks like he's been eating dill pickles for breakfast again."

Brue glanced over and, sure enough, there he was, sitting alone on a bench in the middle of the park. He was mashing his huge hand into a brown paper sack and tossing peanuts, one by one, to a couple of hungry squirrels. All of his attention stuck on the furry little creatures.

Brue swayed back and forth in her shoes, her feet squirming to run. "Shh! Don't be so mean," she whispered. "Besides, he might hear you."

"I don't care."

"You're bluffing."

"Am not. Come on," Poke taunted. "I dare you to walk past him."

Brue's heart jumped in her chest. Finding it hard to catch her breath, she swung around and backed into the cold wind. "No!"

Poke spun on his heel and followed her, trailing so close she could feel his breath on her neck. "Come on, chicken. I double dare you."

"No. You can't make me," she barked then tore off for home at a full run.

A minute and a half later, Brue tramped into the living room still chewing on her anger.

Hearing the slamming of the front door followed by the pounding of small feet, Jo peered through the kitchen doorway. "What's going on?" she asked as she wiped her hands on her apron. "What happened to hello? And, come to think of it, why the distressed look?"

Brue wrestled her coat from her shoulders and yanked the closet door open. "I'm suffering!"

Smiling at her daughter's dramatic announcement, Jo stepped into the living room and reached for a coat hanger. "So, tell me, why are you suffering?"

"It's Mr. Big Ole."

Jo gulped. Fearful of the answer, she reluctantly asked, "What's happening with him now?"

"He's sitting on a bench out there in the middle of the park again, and that mean Poke called me a chicken cuz I didn't want to walk past him."

Jo let out a relieved puff of air. "What did you do?"

"I took the long way around."

After hanging up Brue's coat, Jo closed the closet door, crossed her arms, and leaned against the wall. "Hmm, I see. And why did you feel you needed to take the long way around?"

"Because Mr. Big Ole doesn't like me. He doesn't like any of us kids. And Poke is being a real creep about it. What else was I supposed to do? Besides, I don't like going through the park when the men from the boarding house are there."

Jo straightened the barrette in Brue's hair. "That's a good thing. But about Big Ole, he doesn't appear to like grown-ups, either. I doubt the man even likes himself."

"That doesn't give him the right to be so mean."

"That's true, but do you really think he wants to be that way? I wonder if maybe he just wants to be left alone."

Jo laid a hand on Brue's shoulder and gently guided her toward the kitchen. "Come. The bread's hot out of the oven. Since we both like the heel, how about if we slice it from both ends? If it dries out before we finish the loaf, we'll just have to make some bread pudding."

Jo's offer was met with a wide grin.

Jo handed Brue a table knife and while they buttered their bread, she said, "You know, your idea of staying away from the park when the men from the O.M. Harrington are out there is a good one. But judging by how upset you were when you came through the door, maybe you need to make things right with Big Ole."

Brue slumped in her chair looking distressed. "But I don't want to make things right. It's too hard. Besides, what good would that do? He'll still be mean. I just want him to go away."

"Well, you do have a point there. But until you make things right, I don't think things are going to get any better. Every time you see him, I'm worried you'll feel agitated and uncomfortable. Besides, I think there's something you need to know."

"What?" Brue asked skeptically.

"Yesterday afternoon at the O.M. Harrington, I saw Big Ole walking into that double-doored room down the hall from the registration desk. I thought I might be able to have a chat with him about what happened uptown, so I called out his name, but he ignored me. Next thing I knew, he shut both doors behind him. When you told me your torn dress was an accident, I believed you. But something may have happened from his side that we didn't know about. I wanted to see if I could make things right, but that doesn't look like it's going to be possible. I'm afraid it's up to you now."

Brue looked frightened and confused.

Noticing the little wheels churning in her daughter's mind, Jo lightly touched her hand. "I would give talking to him another try if that's what you're wondering, but I'm afraid I don't feel comfortable pushing things any further than I already have. We need my income from the O.M. Harrington way too badly, so we've got to be very careful not to jeopardize my job. There is something you might want to think about doing, though."

Brue placed her untouched slice of bread on her plate then propped her cheek on her hand.

"Do you remember what your dad taught you about forgiveness and kindness?"

Brue snapped back and her eyes widened. "Hunh-uh! I can't do that. Nope! I can forgive him, Mom, but I don't want to go over there and apologize. That's way too scary."

The unchecked fear and the unhappiness in Brue's eyes tore at Jo's heart, but she couldn't back down. For as much as she felt a need to protect her little girl, the price for doing nothing was far too high. Brue needed to develop inner strength. Unfortunately, it would take facing down Big Ole to gain that strength. "You've got to do something, Brue. Look at what's become of you. You're bitter and unhappy."

"But I didn't do anything wrong."

"Did Big Ole?"

"He looked mean."

"I know he looked mean, but did he do anything wrong?"

"No, I guess not."

"Miss Bickford?"

"No."

"You?"

"No."

"I thought you said you didn't get out of his way when he shuffled up the sidewalk because you were too afraid."

Brue pressed against the back of the kitchen chair and jabbed stiff fingers onto the hard surface of the table. "I was, but he didn't get out of my way either."

Jo sliced another piece of bread while allowing a deafening quiet to descend on their small kitchen.

Brue twisted her plate around, staring at it. There couldn't be a child alive who looked forward to doing things the hard way.

"So, what am I supposed to do?" she asked finally.

"Oh, I don't know. Somehow I think you know precisely what to do." Jo reached over and lightly patted Brue's forearm. "Look, I'm not saying you have to make things right. That's just a suggestion. But think about it. If it feels right, do it. If it doesn't, don't."

Brue rested her elbows on the table and dropped her chin into her hands.

CHAPTER TWENTY-ONE

Jo glanced at the grandfather clock and then at Brue who was sitting cross-legged on the living room floor, hovering over her coloring book. She plucked a red crayon from her crayon box, her attention riveted on her unfolding work of art.

The clock struck four.

Squinting back at the clock, Jo wondered, *Would I miss it if I sold it?*

She loved hearing the peal of its chimes. Loved hearing its steady tick, tick, tick like the beating of a strong heart. She enjoyed competing with it by calculating how many pieces of laundry she could iron, fold, or mend within any given timeframe—anything to add interest to her work. But the clock needed to be sacrificed.

Jo tugged a dry sheet from the clothesline that extended across the living room. Folding it into her basket, she said, "Brue?"

"Hmm?"

"Our grandfather clock, it overpowers our living room."

Brue looked up, expressionless.

"What do you think?" Jo asked. "Would you be okay with our selling it?"

Brue returned to her coloring book, busily outlining a brown-haired lady's dress in red. "If you sell it, how will you know what time it is when you're working?"

"I'll have to see if I can get my watch fixed."

"But what if it can't be fixed?" Brue inquired matter-of-factly.

Jo plucked three clothespins off another sheet and stuffed them into her apron pocket. "Then I'll have to find an inexpensive watch or clock of some sort. If we sell the grandfather clock, we might be able to buy those shoes I promised you and also pay for the repairs on Chief Stout's car. Would you be okay with that?"

"Yup," Brue said without hesitation.

Jo gave the clock another thoughtful look, a twinge of regret seizing her midsection. "Are you absolutely sure? We won't be able to get it back if someone buys it, you know."

"You said I'd get new shoes?"

"That's right."

"Then I'm sure."

The moment Jo called *The Evening Tribune* and requested to run an ad in Thursday's paper, she felt a rush of relief. At least for a while, anyway.

Later that evening still basking in her happy feelings about the ad, she bundled several loads of freshly cleaned linen together. Her back aching from lifting one too many heavy baskets, the mere thought of pulling a load in Brue's little red wagon wore her to exhaustion. She loaded up the Chevy. With Brue at Jo's side, sitting far back on the bench seat with her feet extending straight out in front of her, the car headed up Charles Street, made a right onto Newton, chugged up the hill, and when Fountain Lake cropped up into view, Jo turned right on Fountain Street.

Taking a breather from her backbreaking labor, Katherine Island offered Jo her favorite respite. They stopped and took a leisurely walk out to the middle of the bridge where they stood and watched the slow lapping water beneath them. Here her thoughts slowed down. Here she found happiness. Here she found peace. She then took Brue by the hand. Together they walked out onto the island and gazed at the lights of town blinking through the barren limbs of the deciduous trees sprouting up here and there. Jo inhaled a deep breath of the cool night air. Feeling comfortably refreshed, they returned to the car and powered back down the streets. The car rose and fell gently as it crested the hill on Newton, its tires thundering against paved brick. She turned left on First Street, drove up over another small hill, and then left again onto River Lane where the car rolled to a stop in front of the boarding house.

Jo tensed the moment she noticed Mr. Doherty standing at the back door, holding it open. His serious expression re-awakened in her that unwelcome sense of foreboding.

"Brue, Spitfire is snoozing by the registration desk if you'd like to play with him for a few minutes," Mr. Doherty said.

As Brue headed on up the hallway to find the cocker spaniel, Mr. Doherty ushered Jo by the elbow to the laundry room again. Just inside the door, he turned and said, "By the way, you might want to give Big Ole—"

"Big Ole?" Jo's forehead pulled tighter than her tug on the light string.

He peered down at her over the tops of his bifocals. "Are you okay?"

Jo suddenly found herself longing to hop into her car and go back, back to that serene island where she had enjoyed, albeit briefly, a complete absence of tension. "Yes, I'm fine ... No, I'm not."

Mr. Doherty casually slipped a hand into his pocket. "You do know that he lives here."

"Of course, I do."

"Then it might behoove you to give him a twenty-four-hour turn-around on his personal clothing."

Jo bristled. "Excuse me?"

"I think he might enjoy twenty-four-hour turnaround service on his laundry," Mr. Doherty repeated. A flush of color crept up his neck and onto his cheeks. "I mean, the boarding house does give you plenty of business."

Jo stepped back and choked on a puff of air she'd inhaled too quickly. She looked past the laundry room door and out into the warmly lit hallway. The allure of the stately O.M. Harrington suddenly corroded to dross, and all it took was one well-intentioned, completely unreasonable request.

"I know it may look as if he's putting himself before others," Mr. Doherty said as if he could read her thoughts. "But I can assure you that even though he is in a position to make this suggestion, he didn't."

"What are you trying to say?"

"It's coming from me."

You're in on this?

Mr. Doherty looked embarrassed, as well he should have. "If you knew the circumstances," he went on, "you'd understand. I'm afraid he's a *very* affluent man."

Jo lifted a stack of sheets from her wicker basket and placed them on the lower linen shelf. "That may be true. But he doesn't seem to like who I am," she said, fidgeting unnecessarily with the sheets, "and I'm not so sure I don't feel the same way about him."

"I think you might want to come with me for a moment." He led her out into the hallway and with a wave of his hand said, "Do you see those double doors down the hallway there to the left?"

"Yes."

"That's Big Ole's office now. He took over management of the boarding house several weeks ago."

"He what?" Jo blurted. She stood in a frozen stupor before retreating slowly into the laundry room with Mr. Doherty following close behind. Not only was the boarding house account huge, it was her only account. She could in no way afford to lose their business. But to have to give special service to *that* man? How could she not feel compromised?

"I said—"

"I know."

Jo needed time to rein in her emotions. She returned to her basket, drew out a stack of pillowcases, and stacked them neatly on the shelf immediately above the sheets, all the while thinking. Things were beginning to make sense—Calvin Doherty growing increasingly guarded, Evelyn mentioning changes at the boarding house, Big Ole callously shutting his doors on Jo. No wonder he had walked into that room the other day. It was his office. And now Calvin Doherty had to mention Big Ole's affluence on top of everything else.

But something didn't add up. If Jo's job was in jeopardy, why in this war-torn world would she be asked to work harder for the man?

Ho-oh. To get me discouraged enough to quit my job so he won't have to fire me.

Jo swiveled around. "Mr. Doherty—"

"Calvin. We've known each other long enough," he said, his tone warm and kind yet tinged with a hint of regret. "Please, call me Calvin."

"Thank you, Calvin. I'll do everything I can to give him what he wants. You have my word. Besides, I don't believe I have any other choice."

A sudden look of relief washed across his face, further rekindling her concern.

"The twenty-four-hour turnaround is only for his personal laundry. There's no way you could perform that sort of service for the entire boarding house."

Jo nodded her agreement. "I appreciate that more than you know."

Calvin looked pensive. "Mrs. Bremley—"

"Please, call me Jo."

The tension in his face lessened slightly. "Jo," he agreed. "I really am sorry if this causes you any undue hardship."

She stood backbone straight. "Don't be. I'll handle it."

About to resume unloading the laundry, curiosity got the best of her. "You know, I have no idea what you did before coming to the boarding house."

He sighed and shifted his position, crossing his arms as he rested his shoulder against the side of the door. "World War I. Then the European Theatre."

"Doing what?"

"Chaplain."

Jo's forehead twitched involuntarily. "Really?"

"Does that surprise you?" he asked, his smile hesitant.

"Yes." Jo sensed a light fluttering as she shook her head. "I mean no, come to think of it. Not at all." It took no time at all for her thinking to catch up with her. Big Ole. That's what the fluttering was about. Who better than a former chaplain could give her insight about how to repair the damage with the old man and move on?

"I'm curious. You've done a lot of counseling, then, right?"

Calvin looked down at his feet, shuffling them briefly against the hardwood floor the way one would smash out a cigarette butt. "That's right."

Jo perked up. "What was it like? I mean, did you ever find any sort of common thread in the soldiers you counseled?"

"Actually, I did."

"And?"

"I think at the root of just about everyone's problems you'll find they're struggling with either anger or fear, if not both. Soldiers are no different."

Jo shoved her empty basket to the side and slowly pulled another full basket forward; her attention stayed on him. "How did you counsel them?"

"Oh, I don't know. Every situation was different." He hesitated and then with a lift of his brow, he asked, "My overall favorite counsel?"

"Yes. Your overall favorite counsel."

He grinned, understated yet confident. "If a man compels you to walk with him one mile, walk with him two. If he takes your coat, give him your cloak also."

Jo stopped and draped her arms over her full basket, leaning toward him. "I can understand how that helps when soldiers are feeling anger, but not when they're afraid. Isn't fear something you need to pay attention to and either stand up to or back away from depending on the situation?"

"That's right. Depending on the situation. With soldiers, though, when they're out on the battlefield facing imminent death, they don't have time to mess around. If they go forward resisting or with half a heart, they put themselves in a position of weakness when what they really need is all the strength they can muster. I know it sounds kind of strange, but in this case a soldier's cloak is his life. Think about it. If he marches forward accepting that his life is already gone, he's the one wielding the power." Calvin shook his head and dropped his gaze to the floor. "For as cold as that may sound, it makes sense, doesn't it?"

Jo nodded into the silence that followed. Noticing that Calvin suddenly looked pensive, she said, "What are you thinking about?"

"Hmm?" he asked distractedly, but then appeared to catch himself. "Faith, I guess. The Word. Sometimes it's like reading black on white. Other times ..."

"I know what you mean."

As Calvin drifted inside himself for another thoughtful moment, Jo drifted into thoughts of her own, thoughts about Big Ole. She was also feeling anger and fear—anger about his maddening demeanor and fear that she could easily lose her job. "Maybe it wouldn't hurt for me to do that, too."

"What's that?"

"Give Big Ole my cloak also, so to speak."

"Oh, that." Calvin nodded. "I thought that might have been the motivation behind your curiosity."

As Jo returned to replenishing washcloths and towels on the linen shelves, she paused, glancing back at him. "I'm surprised you're no longer a man of the cloth. It suits you, you know. As if it's your calling."

He removed his glasses, folded them, and slipped them into his shirt pocket. "I've completed my military obligations. I'm far from a young upstart according to military standards so when I got scratched by a bullet, they allowed me to return stateside earlier this year. I've given more counsel during the heat of battle than I care to remember."

As he lifted his gaze toward the ceiling, appearing thousands of miles away and still in the throes of the dreadful war, Jo couldn't help but wonder. Scratched by a bullet? Or laid up for months from taking a bad hit? It had to have been the latter, but it wouldn't be right to ask. "Why aren't you in the ministry now? That is, if you don't mind my asking."

"Oh, no. That's not for me," Calvin said with a defensive bite. "I walked away from it the minute my feet hit American soil. Let's just say I've had some issues with my personal faith for a mighty long time. Haven't been able to get past them. Now that I'm home, I'm finally free to be me." Calvin appeared to catch himself and didn't hesitate to add, "Besides, I'm doing just fine here at the O.M. Harrington," but Jo noticed that his voice had a hollow ring to it.

"What do you mean by issues with your personal faith?"

A strained look twisted Calvin's features, causing Jo no little amount of concern. "Forgive me. I really didn't mean to intrude on your privacy. It's just that ... what about the advice you gave to the soldiers? You believed that, didn't you?"

Please say yes.

Spitfire barked, interrupting their conversation and drawing them back into the great room. Disappointed to have to cut their conversation short, a wave of sadness descended on Jo as she dutifully sought out Brue. Calvin looked sad, too, but then he plunged his hand into his pocket and glanced dispassionately down the hallway. "Looks like Spitfire's been working overtime again."

Brue lit up. "Mr. Doherty, why do you call the dog Spitfire?"

Jo lightly gripped Brue by her shoulders. "I'm sure they named him after the fighter plane, dear."

Calvin nodded. "Technically, yes. The dog was a stray. Early one morning Jonathan heard a racket out in the back alley. Found the mutt nosing through our trash. Called him a little Spitfire. The name stuck."

"I don't see him around here much," Jo said.

"He seems to like it better out back. He's getting on in years and doesn't exactly bring honor to his name. Clocks in more time sleeping than he does being awake." Calvin smirked and nodded toward the hallway. "He's taken quite a shine to Jonathan. See those newspapers stacked in front of that door down the hallway there?"

"I do." Jo took a quick count with a glance. "There must be a half dozen of them."

"That's right. And that's Jonathan's door. Every evening that mutt plops newspaper upon newspaper there. After he gets a good pile going, he scratches at the door, whimpers, and keeps repeating the process until Jonathan decides to show his face. You'd think the dog knew how to read. I think Jonathan enjoys having the guests march to his room to get their copies of *The Evening Tribune*. Thankfully everyone's a good sport about it."

Spitfire lumbered toward Calvin and pawed up his trousers, scratching.

Calvin quickly crouched down and tousled the dog's fur. "You're gonna tear my threads here, boy." He then pushed to his feet and anxiously rubbed the nape of his neck. "Thanks for agreeing to the fast turnaround on Big Ole's laundry. I think it's the right thing to do."

Jo stepped out into the darkness and descended the stairs with another heavy basket of soiled linen in her arms, Brue at her side, and Calvin's words invading her thoughts.

As Brue crawled into the car, Jo rested the basket on the running board. Before heaving it into the backseat, she glanced back at the O.M.

Harrington. There had to have been something behind Calvin's suggestion about the twenty-four-hour turnaround. It came from out of nowhere. And of all of the people to have to give special service to, it had to be Big Ole. Oh, well. Things worked out over time. After getting enough complaints, one day Mr. O.M. Harrington would handle the Big Ole situation himself and all would be back to normal. She hoped the day would come sooner rather than later.

Jo slid onto the front seat and stopped short of closing the door when someone called her name. She turned and looked back to see Calvin scuttling down the porch steps, heading toward her in a dreadful hurry.

"I forgot to ask you," he said with no small amount of concern. "Big Ole's favorite shirt disappeared. It's white with pale blue buttons. I don't know why, but he's pretty attached to it. You haven't seen it in the laundry anywhere, have you?"

Noticing the alarm on Calvin's face, Jo gasped. "I saw it. I know I did. It had a button on it barely holding on by a thread. I remember thinking the shirt was probably a rag."

"It wasn't a rag, Jo."

"I know that now. Don't worry. I'll look through everything the minute we get home and get back to you."

Calvin kneaded his forehead with his thumb and forefinger. "You might want to make that a priority."

Jo fired up the engine and drove around the block toward home. After shoving the basket onto the porch, she reached into her pocket and pulled out her skeleton key. As she slipped it into the keyhole, she glanced back at the boarding house.

The look in Calvin's eyes and the concern in his voice over the loss of a simple faded old shirt did little to calm her fear.

CHAPTER TWENTY-TWO

J o bolted down the basement steps, the boards moaning in protest beneath her feet. The dim overhead light cast a shadow on some remnants spilling over the top of a musty box in the back corner. She rifled through the clothing. Tugging at the discards one at a time, she held them up to the light. There were shirts all right, but none with blue buttons. If she did throw Big Ole's shirt in the trash, it might be too late to retrieve it. She was sure her next-door neighbor, Sam Wilder, had hauled yesterday's garbage to the dump by now.

She scrambled back up the stairs, and after upending every place imaginable and coming up empty-handed, Jo drew back the kitchen curtain and gazed out the window. Unfortunately, no lights on at the Wilders.

Early the next morning, she wrestled her sweater over her shoulders and hurried outside to find Mrs. Wilder in her backyard busily spanking an oriental rug with an oversized carpet beater, plumes of dust billowing every which way. Her neighbor mopped a strand of coarse steely hair from her forehead and nudged a few more loose hairs back into her tight bun before joining Jo at the picket fence adjoining their properties.

"Has Sam gone to the dump yet?" Jo asked.

"I'm not sure. He drove off about an hour ago. Took his pickup.

Didn't say where he was going, but he should be back soon." Mrs. Wilder hesitated. "You look troubled, Jo. Is everything okay?"

"I'm afraid not," she said before expressing her concern about the whereabouts of Big Ole's shirt.

"Come with me."

When Jo met up with her at the far side of their home, Mrs. Wilder was already poking through their trashcan with a long stick. Even with her advancing age, her movements were as swift and fluid as her husband's.

Jo rocked nervously in her penny loafers. "I'm sorry to put you through this."

"Nonsense. I'm happy to help." Mrs. Wilder pulled up from the trashcan. "Doesn't look like it's in here. You must have it somewhere. It's not like you to throw things out."

"I know. Somehow, some way, I'll find it. I have to."

Mrs. Wilder's kind eyes were filled with concern. "You're really upset over this, aren't you?"

Jo nodded.

"If I were you, I don't think I'd fear losing that shirt any more than I'd fear my own shadow," Mrs. Wilder said, her smile warm, her voice kind and gentle. "It's only a shirt."

Who was right? Jo? Or Mrs. Wilder? True, it was just a shirt. But it was Big Ole's shirt.

After thanking her neighbor for her help, Jo made another thorough pass through her basement.

No shirt.

She checked the nooks and crannies of her back porch.

No shirt.

She headed into the living room where she foraged through her ironing basket.

Still no shirt.

Finally, she rummaged through her mending basket. There it was, at the very bottom. She let out a sigh of relief.

With Big Ole's shirt in hand, she pulled out a needle and thread and sought the brighter light of the sun porch.

Carefully positioning the button, she pulled a stitch up through the fabric and down again, securing it in place. The shirt looked familiar. She double checked the alignment before pulling through another stitch. Case. That was it. He used to wear a shirt with shiny blue buttons. When it hung on the clothesline, it looked no different than any other run-of-the-mill piece of clothing. But when he put it on, he looked richer than royalty. *Case.*

She folded the shirt onto her lap and quickly exchanged one set of upsetting thoughts for another. Evelyn's concerns. Calvin's reserved behavior lately. Honestly! Their fear was more contagious than the common cold and clung to her like leaves on a tree. Needing to shake it off, she immersed herself in her mending. After all, every problem had its own time frame.

Several stitches later, a cooling darkness advanced across the porch. Jo looked up. A thick, slow-moving cloud was blotting out the sun. Its vast shadow prowled lazily toward the shoreline and out onto the lake. Jo smiled inwardly. Mrs. Wilder was right about the shirt. Fearing losing it was a wasted effort, as wasted as fearing her own shadow. Could the threat of losing her job possibly be nothing more than a passing shadow as well? As she watched the heavy cloud move eastward, it was the strangest thing. She couldn't shake off, nor did she want to, a sudden deep and peaceful inner knowing. Everything was going to be fine.

When the rays of the sun once again brightened and warmed the porch, Jo resumed her mending. With the button secured properly in place she reached for her scissors, but then paused when she heard unexpected chattering. She glanced out across the park where the men from the O.M. Harrington were busily pressing wires into the ground, their croquet mallets in hand. Big Ole led their charge wearing a black street-length woolen coat and leather gloves handsomely offset with a hunter green neck scarf. She'd been noticing recently that he appeared to favor hunter green as an accent color.

Gazing at his coat, she mused about her chat with Calvin and revisited how she might give Big Ole her cloak also, so to speak. Maybe she could secure his personal laundry with something special like a dark, masculine colored binding of some sort that would set his items apart from the rest of the laundry. Why hadn't she thought of that before? Hunter green. That's what she would do—bind his laundry with hunter green ribbon. But he was a man. Would he even notice?

Calvin would be pleased, at least. No, by the way he'd been acting lately, Calvin would be relieved. She finished sewing the button and snipped the thread with her shears. She needed to make a special run to the O.M. Harrington. She had a shirt to deliver.

CHAPTER TWENTY-THREE

Brue punched her hands through the sleeves of her coat and strutted up the gravel road. The late afternoon was gray, dismal, and cold, just like the thoughts that hounded her. But some things were better done without thinking about them. Finally making peace with Big Ole was one of those things. So she marched on, refusing to pay attention to the taunting willies.

Hearing a faint whooshing sound, she glanced at Mrs. Tomlinson's lilac bushes. Was it her imagination, or had they just rustled? She listened closely and then inched backward toward the far side of the road.

It had to be him. It just had to be.

She planted her hands on her hips and with as much authority as she could muster, she said, "Poke Tomlinson, you come out of there right now."

Silence.

"Poke?"

The bushes rustled again. She nudged ahead a half step and leaned forward. As she raked the thick bushes with her eyes, she caught a glimpse of something or someone. She could feel her eyes getting wide as she softened her voice. "Poke, is that you?"

Suddenly the lilac bushes split apart and Poke crawled out. He drew himself up, held a thin finger to his lips, and looked all around. Slowly. Carefully. Up one end of the road and down the other.

"Shhh! Semper alertus," he whispered through a black licorice calabash pipe clamped between his teeth. He peered through an oversized magnifying glass. Dried petals and leaves tumbled down his forehead and cheeks like oatmeal out of a Quaker Oats box, but he didn't seem to care.

"What's semper alertus?" Brue demanded. "Why are you dressed like that? And why on earth are you whispering?"

"It means 'always alert', you half-wit. I whispered because I heard a strange noise, and if you must know, I'm dressed like this because I'm practicing to become a private eye. That's what I'm gonna be when I grow up, a private eye just like Sherlock Holmes."

"You're silly."

"Am not."

Brue swatted the air with her hand. "And stop looking at me through that silly magnifying glass."

"Why? I might find something interesting." He inspected her carefully from head to foot and stopped short at her shoe. "Hey, what's this? I thought you had a hole in your shoe."

"Did not."

"Did, too."

Poke could be so maddening. "It wasn't a hole. The sole ripped loose."

"So, what happened to the tear? You didn't have to get it sewn, did you? Those shoes are clunky. Why doesn't your mother buy you a new pair?"

"She's going to just as soon as she can."

"Sure, she is," he mocked.

Brue spun away from Poke and headed on up the road, but he rushed ahead and twisted around, skipping backward to keep pace with her.

"Hey, where you going?" he asked.

"Why do you want to know?"

"Because I wanna know, that's why."

Brue thought for a moment. Maybe she could take care of two bullies at the same time. "Would you like to come with me?"

Poke pulled the magnifying glass away from his eye and dropped it into the wide side pocket in his trousers. "Sure. Why not?"

"Good, because you and me are going to the O.M. Harrington House."

"No foolin'?" he asked excitedly. "What for?"

"We're going to talk to Mr. Big Ole."

Poke's eyebrows snapped together. He started breathing funny. Brue could see his chest heaving through his sweater.

"Poke, is that you?" Mrs. Tomlinson cried from the backside of the lilac bushes.

When he called back, "I'm over here, Mom," Brue was sure she heard the sound of relief in his voice.

"I'm looking for my magnifying glass," Mrs. Tomlinson said. "You didn't take it again, did you?"

"Coming."

He threw Brue a don't-you-even-think-of-breathing-a-word look and then retraced his steps through the bushes with a telltale bulge in his pocket.

Brue had a funny feeling Poke would much rather face his mother than the likes of Big Ole. She couldn't blame him, really. But having turned the tables on Poke's taunting, she fought back a grin. Maybe he wouldn't be so mean in the future.

As she turned to walk away, Poke shoved his nose back through the bushes. "You'd better watch out. Big Ole's gonna chew you up and spit you out!"

Far sooner than she wanted, Brue stood at the bottom of the steps of the O.M. Harrington and stared up at its chilling front entrance. After inhaling a few deep breaths, she clutched the railing hand-over-hand as she trudged up the steps, then crossed the porch, and slowly pushed the heavy door halfway open. Needing to be brave, she peeked inside trying to work up enough courage to go all the way in. Mr. Doherty wasn't at his desk. She slipped inside, the huge door closing behind her and pushing her farther into the room, but she couldn't close the door on Poke's taunting. What if he was right? What if Big Ole did chew her up and spit her out?

Hearing a staticky voice, she glanced over to the far side of the great room where a small group of men were gathered around a radio. They sat backwards straddling their chairs, listening to war news. Mr. Doherty was with them, leaning over, resting his foot on an end table with one hand in his pocket and the other draped lazily over his knee. As the voice drawled over the airwaves, Brue didn't hear any sirens going off in the background this time. The blare of sirens made her feel scared inside.

After the news was over, a man with an unlit pipe clenched between his teeth turned off the radio and said, "Doesn't sound good, boys."

Mr. Doherty straightened. "It was a bad move to ever go into that place," he said, sounding serious. "Hürtgen Forest is a trap. We can't take advantage of our air superiority in those woods."

"We'll never be able to get any heavy artillery in there, either," another man said.

Mr. Doherty plunged his hands deep into his pockets. "You're right about that. Not with thousands of trees there." He shook his head as if he was worried. "Too many tree trunks for the Krauts to hide behind."

The man with the pipe looked up and saw Brue then motioned to Mr. Doherty.

"Well, good afternoon, Miss Bremley." Mr. Doherty removed his foot from the end table and walked toward Brue. He squinted his eyes and wrinkled his forehead. "You're looking a bit apprehensive. Is there anything I can help you with today?"

"Yes, sir. I'd like to see Mr. Big Ole, please."

"*Mister* Big Ole, hmm?" A thoughtful smile slid across Mr. Doherty's kind face. He glanced down the hallway. "Wait here a moment," he said. "Let me see what I can do for you."

When Mr. Doherty walked away, the men around the radio headed toward the coffee room. As the man with the unlit pipe passed by, he gave Brue a reassuring pat on the top of her head and winked.

Brue glanced back just in time to see Mr. Doherty disappear into Big Ole's office. She turned and looked back at the front door. She wanted to run through it, to go home. But she wanted to get past her misery more. She thought about those soldiers in the forest protecting themselves behind tree trunks. Talking to Big Ole was like being in a forest of her own. She would love to have a tree to hide behind, too.

While she waited, she unbuttoned her coat and fixed her eyes on the threatening double doors ahead.

Was Poke right? What would she do if Big Ole yelled at her? She could run, but that wouldn't make her feel good about herself. She could speak up, but that might not be respectful. No, she was just going to have to say what she came to say. She might not like hearing what he had to say back, but at least she might be able to find out why he was so crabby all the time.

She jumped and could feel her back going ramrod straight when she heard a loud and deep voice ask, "Who?"

Mr. Doherty stepped back into the hallway and motioned for her to come. "He can see you now."

Brue forced her footsteps along, working hard to keep her knees from shaking.

She stopped in front of Big Ole's double-door entry and peered into his office. It was huge. It had a shiny wooden floor and a whole bunch of windows that covered the entire back wall. He was sitting in a black leather chair behind a wooden desk. Both he and his desk were gigantic. And he was blowing short puffs of smoke from a foul-smelling cigar while he twisted around in his chair. He pulled the cigar out of his mouth and smashed the end of it into a square glass ashtray. When he finally looked at her, one of his bushy eyebrows shot straight up.

"Come in," he said. He looked at the seat at the far side of his desk and gave her a nod. "Please, have a chair."

Brue took one look at that chair and her dinner squeezed back up into her throat. "That's okay. I can stand. I won't be long, sir."

"Is that so?" His voice sounded gruff and impatient when he talked. "Well, what can I do for you, then? Speak up." He picked up a small piece of paper and rubbed its edges like someone who made of habit of rubbing things. That's probably what nervous grown-ups do, Brue decided.

"I, uh, I wanted to apologize for getting in your way that day when you were walking by the five-and-dime," she said, making sure she looked him straight in the eye. Somehow, having the courage to face him made her feel like a grown-up, and she didn't feel as frightened. That was a surprise. The longer she spoke, the more the fear went away. "I was looking in the window at a Cinderella watch and glass slipper and was too afraid to move."

"Ah, yes," he said, nodding his head. "Now that you mention it, I do remember that day quite well. And why were you too afraid to move, might I ask?"

"I don't know." That wasn't really the truth. She did know, but not wanting the hard feelings between them to get any worse, she said, "I just was."

"And?"

Brue kneaded her hands together. "I didn't mean to bump into you, sir. Honest."

"I'm sure you didn't," he said, but the sound of his voice wasn't sincere.

"Anyway, I really am sorry. That's all I had to say."

"Apology accepted." He quickly shooed her away with a flap of his big hand. "You may run along now. Hurry on."

"Thank you, sir."

Maybe her mother was wrong. Maybe Brue shouldn't have apologized. Big Ole didn't look happy when she walked out the door. Come to think of it, he didn't look all that happy when she walked into his office, either.

As Brue scuttled past Mr. Doherty's desk, he glanced at her with a curious expression. "Did everything go okay?"

"It was fine," she said, but she knew that wasn't quite the truth, either.

Brue's steps clipped faster the closer she got to the outside door. She couldn't wait to get out of the boarding house. Buttoning her coat, she hurried along. But when she reached for the door handle, Mr. Doherty called her name.

Brue looked back. "Yes, sir?"

He took off his glasses and set them on his desk. "Are you sure everything went okay?"

Brue nodded weakly, forcing a smile. "Uh-huh."

"Well, okay, then," he said, but then he got a funny look on his face, the same kind of look her mother got when something was wrong.

Brue said a quick goodbye and hurried out the door. As she made her way across Harrington Park, a stone crunched on the sidewalk beneath her shoe. She kicked at it a few times and then turned around and took a long look at the boarding house. Making things right was supposed to make her feel better. At least she felt better about having had the courage to face Big Ole. But why did he have to shoo her away so fast? With her shoulders sagging, she kicked the stone aside and walked on. Evening shadows stretched out across the park. Like silent fingers, they inched along, slowly snuffing out the daylight. The air was cold and night falling fast.

Brue stopped on the frozen brown grass at the edge of the park and gazed at their home, a place where she knew she belonged. Her mom already had the lights turned on. The windows were all aglow.

She crossed the road, climbed the porch steps, let out a big puff of cold winter air, and, before turning the doorknob, she twisted around for one last good look at the boarding house.

It was done.

And Big Ole didn't even yell at her. Come to think of it, Brue did feel better—better about herself and better about the grouchy old man, too. She couldn't help but wonder if old men like him ever stopped being grumpy.

CHAPTER TWENTY-FOUR

C alvin poured two coffees, dreading the conversation he was about to engage. Carrying them down the hall, he stopped at the entry of Big Ole's office and indicated his intentions with a lift of a cup. "Mind if I come in? Thought I might interest you in a short break."

"Not at all." Big Ole swiveled toward him. "Please do."

"What does the advertisement say?" Calvin asked with a forced grin.

Big Ole's chair squawked as he sat back and briefly interlaced his large fingers. "'When I say coffee I mean Folgers'? That one?"

"That's right," Calvin said brightly. "The coffee could be fresher, I guess. Left over from this morning, but I poured it myself."

"Sounds good. Please, have a chair." Big Ole picked up an empty note card and tapped it mindlessly against his desktop. Looking troubled, he muttered, "Not everyone appears to like to sit there."

"Well, I'm not everyone." Calvin settled back and rested his elbow on the chair's arm. He glanced past Big Ole and out through the multi-paned windows behind him toward the darkened sky. Big Ole, he noticed, appeared more tolerant of a late afternoon break than amenable to one. "The days have gotten shorter, I see."

Big Ole turned and glanced briefly out the windows, too. "They have at that." But then with sharpness in his voice he asked, "Is there some reason you find the approaching winter solstice particularly interesting this year?"

Calvin ignored the question. "Say, that young Bremley girl—"

"Is that the reason for the break so late in the day, Calvin? To have an early evening chat with your boss about a little kid?"

No. It's to throttle you for your attitude toward a little kid. "I guess you might say that."

"I'm not sure we see eye-to-eye on that one."

"Really? Do you mind if I ask why?"

"Sure, I mind." Big Ole picked up his cup, blew at the hot liquid, took a small sip, and winced at its bitterness. "But I'll tell you anyway. I find her a bit too rude for my taste."

Calvin feared he might be balancing nitroglycerin on a tightrope. With Brue vulnerable with the loss of her dad and Jo especially vulnerable with the pending loss of her job, he needed to choose his words carefully, draw the man out, and help him see reason. "Really? Why would you say that?"

"Why would I say that?" Big Ole repeated as he set his cup down on his desk. "Let me tell you why. I've seen her and those little hooligan friends of hers dawdling around in the park and gawking at me one too many times. Either that or they back off and run away like wild animals from a crack of thunder. You'd think I was a mean old ogre or worse."

Calvin failed at holding his smile in check.

"You find that amusing, do you?" Big Ole asked, the creases in his forehead cutting deep.

"I wouldn't take it personally," Calvin said thoughtfully. "That's what kids do."

Big Ole rotated his chair and, looking out the window toward the park, he said, "Do they need to make that much racket when they're playing at the baseball diamond, too? Irritates me no end."

"But they're just kids."

"Just kids? The next time I see that young little whippersnapper come into the boarding house hiding behind her mother's skirt, I'm tempted to shout 'boo.'"

Calvin's brows rose involuntarily. "She must have said something that's gotten you upset."

"Absolutely not! It's what she does that's the problem."

This conversation was far more difficult than Calvin had anticipated. "Which is?"

Big Ole leaned forward and interwove his fingers, looking anything but happy. "I can't believe I'm actually having a conversation with one of my staff about a little girl over a stale cup of coffee this close to suppertime."

One of my staff? Calvin didn't like the sound of that. "This wouldn't have anything to do with the incident up at the five-and-dime, would it?"

"You heard about that, did you?"

"Small town."

"Too small."

Concerned he might be straddling the squiggly line between asking too many questions or too few, Calvin took a chance and ventured, "So that was it, then?"

"Part of it, I guess. Five, ten minutes before that, she actually pushed past me up on Main and elbowed me to the side like she owned the sidewalk. Then she came flying straight at me in front of the five-and-dime. Nearly knocked me on my keister. Of course, everyone in The Copper Kettle got an eye full. At my expense, I might add. No, sir, I don't care for that child. Don't care for her at all."

So that was it. "You're right. That was rude. Must have been embarrassing having a little girl humiliate you in front of your friends."

Big Ole looked taken aback. "Why, I wasn't humiliated. Felt a little discombobulated for a passing moment maybe, but definitely not humiliated."

Good. Child handled. Time to move on to Jo. "Her mother does an outstanding job with our laundry. Sure beats the starch lady."

"Her mother?" Big Ole asked far too quickly.

"Don't tell me you're having problems with Mrs. Bremley, too?"

Big Ole narrowed his eyes. "Now, why would I possibly have a problem with a young woman who comes storming into The Copper Kettle and, in front of God and the entire restaurant, instructs me to keep my distance from her daughter?"

Calvin shot up in his chair. "She did what? I find that hard to believe."

Big Ole nodded. "So did I."

"What did you say to her?"

Big Ole nipped the tip off of a new cigar, pulled out a match, and lit it with a flick of his thumbnail before inhaling a heavy drag. "Let's just say that I handled it. I wasn't about to get into a bun fight with a young woman in the middle of a restaurant with a bunch of busybodies around getting an eye full."

"Can't say as I blame you," Calvin said sympathetically.

Big Ole leaned back in his chair and spewed short puffs of smoke shaped like tiny doughnuts high into the air. "Love this rich tobacco," he said as he admired his vanishing artwork. "Too bad that Bremley woman doesn't raise her daughter as well as she does the laundry. And by the way, now that you've brought it up, I've been meaning to have a chat with you. I want her to continue doing laundry until the end of the year. Then I want to contract out with a new place come January one. There's an outfit uptown I'd like to give a try."

Calvin choked on Big Ole's words, completely blindsided before he could make his pitch. "Are you sure? Everyone here seems more than happy with her work."

"I couldn't be more sure, Doherty."

Doherty, huh? Calvin nudged forward in his chair. "You might want to rethink this. I'm afraid you may be making a big mistake. Mrs. Bremley has a real struggle on her hands raising that little girl by herself."

Too irritated to hold back, Calvin could hear the volume and pitch of his voice escalating.

"What does that have to do with me?" Big Ole asked incredulously.

"Everything. If she did approach you in The Copper Kettle like you said, it had to have been for a very good reason. You've been awfully hard on her."

"What?" Big Ole asked, his tone one of complete disbelief. "Where'd you ever get a crazy notion like that?"

"I've been noticing. You give her the cold shoulder whenever she comes anywhere near you. The other day I actually watched you slam your doors on her when she called out to you, and you weren't particularly subtle about it."

Big Ole's thick brows clamped together, his voice booming as he insisted, "I did no such thing."

"It sure looked like it from where I was sitting."

"You're wrong, Calvin."

Calvin thought back for a moment. He did recall seeing a scruffy half-gray-bearded stranger come walking up the hallway some time after that incident. "That may be," Calvin conceded, "but you just recounted your aversion toward her little girl. Am I wrong about that, too?"

"No. As a matter of fact, that you're absolutely right about."

"And now you want to fire Mrs. Bremley when she desperately needs her job."

Big Ole glared at Calvin. "Lay off. Not fire. There's a significant difference."

"Some difference."

With a few slow movements and without eye contact, Big Ole tapped the ashes of his cigar into his ashtray. And with the same deliberate movement, he turned toward Calvin again with narrowed eyes. "Are you through?"

"Forgive me—"

"I don't forgive you, and I most certainly don't forgive that miserable little girl or her mother, either. As for you, your job isn't going to get done by itself."

"I guess I deserved that." Calvin stood and gathered his cup. "I'd better get back to my desk, then. May I take your cup for you?"

"Certainly. And, Calvin?"

"Yes?"

"Thank you for the coffee." Big Ole paused, seemingly for dramatic effect. "And for the nice little chat."

Calvin left the room, feeling a hitch in his knees.

Now what have I done?

CHAPTER TWENTY-FIVE

A t half past one in the morning, weary of tossing and turning, Calvin rolled out of bed and shuffled to the registration desk. Nothing like a little work to help his worrying and restlessness subside.

But it didn't.

Too tired to work. Too awake to sleep. Too upset to concentrate on anything worthwhile. He traipsed into the kitchen and heated a cup of milk. Drank it. Went back to his desk and drummed his fingers. Looked at the clock. Drummed his fingers some more.

At three-thirty in the morning he was still wide awake, festering with agitation. Deep inside he knew what he had to do, made the decision to do it, and finally went back to bed where he continued tossing and turning until morning.

A few minutes before the sun made its daily break over the eastern horizon, he got dressed and prepared to take on the day. The smell of sizzling bacon and hot pastries didn't lure him the way they usually did. He shuffled into the coffee room long enough to pour a fresh steaming cup, then returned to his desk, pulled up his chair, and waited. Big Ole should be coming down from his upstairs bedroom any minute now.

Calvin didn't have long to wait. The wooden steps at the end of the hallway creaked and the rhythmic sound of a cane striking the hardwood floor grew louder. A moment later the big man appeared. Although he didn't say good morning, he did wield his walking stick with a wave. Without so much as a glance at Calvin, he walked on, disappearing into the coffee room.

Again, Calvin waited.

At eight o'clock straight up, Big Ole crossed the great room, shuffled down the hallway and through the double doors of his office.

Calvin followed.

After lowering his ample weight into his oversized chair, Big Ole shifted his gaze from matters at hand to Calvin. "I could swear you just followed me in here. Is it my imagination, or are you shadowing me? You wouldn't have something on your mind, now, would you?"

"As a matter of fact, I do."

Big Ole pushed back in his chair, stroking its black leather arms. "What I can do for you, then?"

"No," Calvin said, "there's nothing you can do for me. But there is something I need to do for myself."

"Well," Big Ole said impatiently, "spit it out."

"I want to apologize for my strong manner with you yesterday. I know my words weren't particularly offensive—but my attitude. It wasn't my place to take that tone with you. To be honest, I can feel myself getting agitated again. That isn't right. You're the boss; I'm the employee."

"Is that so?" Big Ole reached into his cigar box, acting as though Calvin weren't there. He then stopped and turned a penetrating eye toward Calvin, giving him his full attention. "You're the best thing that's ever happened to this place. Don't give it another thought. I like a man who speaks his mind. No offense taken."

"But about Mrs. Bremley ..."

"That subject, however, remains closed."

CHAPTER TWENTY-SIX

T
he morning started out too good to be true. Hearing the telephone ringing off the hook, Jo raced up the basement stairs.

"Mrs. Bremley," the man said, his voice deep and smooth,
"my name is Ellersby. Clayton Ellersby. I'm calling about your ad in *The
Evening Tribune.*"

A tremor of excitement surged through her. "Yes?"

"I may have an interest in your grandfather clock. If you haven't sold
it yet, I wouldn't mind stopping by to see it. I'll be in your neighborhood
this morning anyway, so I could stop by around ten or so. Would that
work for you?"

He arrived at ten o'clock sharp, accompanied by his well-muscled
son. Jo assumed Mr. Ellersby to be on the high-strung and shy side. He
looked past her when he shook her hand, and his right eye had a nervous twitch when he spoke. Jo thought it rude to stand over him and
watch his every move as he inspected the clock, but she couldn't help
herself. He made strange noises—a grunt here, a hmm there. Then, after
giving the timepiece a thorough going over, he straightened his muscu-
lar physique and announced, "This clock is worth an easy seventy-five
dollars. I wouldn't mind buying it—if you still want to sell it, that is."

He hadn't challenged the price. He must have noticed that he'd caught Jo by surprise because he answered her dumbfounded silence immediately with a toothy smile and a playful wink. "It's an anniversary gift for Mrs. Ellersby." Suddenly, his nervous twitch gave both eyes a rapid pull. "I'm a little short on cash at the moment. I was wondering if you'd mind taking a check. It's from our family business."

Caught off guard by his request, Jo hesitated.

He didn't hesitate to flip open his wallet. "This is my driver's license, in case you'd like to see some identification."

"That won't be necessary," Jo said, embarrassed that her candid emotions made the dear man feel a need to prove himself. "I have no reservations whatsoever about your integrity, Mr. Ellersby."

With the fat check in hand, Jo stood in the cool of the sun porch, drawing her sweater tight to warm herself. The sight of Clayton Ellersby and his son hauling the clock out of the living room, through the front porch, down the steps, and onto the back of their pickup finished the job, warming her inside and out.

Returning to the living room and seeing the empty space where the clock once stood, however, set off a surprising sense of loss. She hadn't expected that reaction. At least the clock found a good home with nice people who would appreciate and care for it well.

Surprised at how quickly the feeling of loss disappeared, she slipped the check in her purse. How soon could she get to town to cash it? More important, how soon could she get to the dime store? Fearing the watches might be sold out by the time she got there, she gave the store a quick call and asked if she could put one on hold.

"We'd be happy to," the kind clerk said. "But we do require a down payment first."

Jo contemplated the task before her and sighed. Big Ole. She would get uptown just as soon as she could, but for now she needed to get on with his laundry. After stoking the fire, she strung half a dozen clothes-lines across the living room. The fan propped in front of the oil burner would draw enough warm air throughout the room that all would be dry by sunup.

Later the following afternoon, she folded Big Ole's sheets, towels, and other personal items and bound them together with wide hunter green ribbon.

"What do you think, Brue? This should please the man, shouldn't it?"

Brue glanced at the basket. "Uh-huh. But aren't you going to put a bow on it?"

"I don't think so, sweetie. Not for Big Ole."

"Why not?"

"Because he's a man, and I don't believe a bow would be appropriate for someone as masculine as him."

"But you always say we need to find ways to be kind to people. And Dad was a man and he loved your bows. He said nobody could make them as beautiful as you do."

Jo grinned at the memory. "Well, okay, then," she said reluctantly. "I'll do it this time, but this one's for you." She pulled another generous-sized length of ribbon and crafted a huge bow, fastening it to the binding ribbon to polish off the basket with an organized and classy look. When finished, she managed a satisfied smile. Maybe Brue had a good idea after all.

Jo loaded Brue's wagon and together they hiked across the park.

Brue's friends, Poke, Heath, Em, and Holley, were playing at the baseball diamond. Jo and Brue paused for a moment and watched as Em threw a hard pitch. Heath's bat hammered the ball. All thin arms and legs, he tossed the bat and sprinted toward first base.

Brue looked up at Jo. "Heath says he's gonna be a professional baseball player when he grows up, Mom."

"I guess I'm not at all surprised." Jo looked at the young player. "He certainly appears to have the talent for it already."

"He can hit the ball really hard and far, and he can run fast, too."

"You can say that again," Jo said as Heath slammed into first base.

"Hey, Brue," Poke shouted from the outfield. "Come on out and join us, unless you're chicken."

Brue rolled her eyes. "Can I, Mom?"

"If you want to, go ahead. But just remember the rules. Watch on the sidelines and don't take any chances, especially with Heath's hard-hitting balls. And if any of the men from the O.M. Harrington come around, make sure you skedaddle. Understand?"

Fearing she might be too strict, Jo watched as Brue ran off to join her friends. Little Brue was definitely no match for Heath and Poke, of that Jo was sure. Serious players for their ages, those boys intimidated their peers. Best to leave well enough alone. Case would have, had he been here.

Jo trudged on, the wagon thumping at her heels. Hauling the little red wagon continued to embarrass her, but at least she felt better knowing she'd gone an extra mile with Big Ole's laundry. She couldn't wait to see the delight in Calvin's eyes when he saw her added touch.

Unable to see through the glare of the windows, she took a chance and entered through the front door, lugging the heavy, but tidy and visually attractive load inside.

Jo took in the great room with one fluid yet comprehensive glance. Calvin was nowhere in sight. Not so with the men. They were playing cribbage at the card table by the bay window. Big Ole shuffled a deck of cards while Jonathan dealt. By the reticent expressions on their faces and the softening of their voices, she had a hunch they'd heard well-embellished stories about the incidents uptown.

So be it.

After graciously acknowledging their presence with a slight nod, she hiked up her chin and walked confidently toward the registration desk, set the basket down, and rang the bell.

Calvin's familiar voice rose from somewhere behind the counter. "Be with you in a moment."

She peered over the top to find him busily rummaging through the bottom drawer of a filing cabinet. When he looked up and saw her, he grinned. "Jo. I didn't expect to see you back so soon. You mean you have the laundry done already?"

"As promised. I'll haul the basket to the back room."

Before heading down the hall, she hesitated and then peered over the counter one more time. "Oh, and by the way, Calvin," she said with a generous measure of confidence, "I mended that shirt of Big Ole's, the one you asked about, and left it in the laundry room several days ago. I assume that's the shirt you were looking for, right?"

"It sure was. You did a great job on it. Thanks."

"My pleasure. Oh, and by the way, I bound his personal items with a nice hunter green ribbon so it won't get mixed up with the rest of the laundry."

An immediate chorus of snickering, whispering, and repetition of the words *hunter green* drifted from the game table.

Calvin chuckled as he pushed to his feet. "Why, Jo," he teased in a quiet voice. "Are you wearing a bit more rouge today, or is that my imagination? You appear to have more color than usual."

"Calvin Doherty!"

The chatter behind her eased to a light snicker and then to muffled voices. Now she could hear them breathe. Her curiosity piqued by loud silence, she glanced toward the table where the men's heads quickly darted back to their cards the way dominoes fall in too-perfect order.

Jonathan interrupted the awkward quiet. "Gentlemen, why don't we take a nice little stroll out to the park?" he said with a smile still evident in his voice. "Maybe we can get in a good game of croquet yet before supper."

Their chair legs scraped against the hardwood floor as the men stood and shuffled past Jo, single file.

As Jonathan neared the registration desk, he stopped and craned his neck, anything but subtle about taking a good look at the laundry basket. "Hunter green ribbon, Big Ole. How do you rate? And a lovely large bow to boot!"

The men exploded into laughter. But not Big Ole. When they reached the door, he glared at Jo.

Her cheeks burned long after the door closed. "Looks like I won't be binding any more of his laundry with hunter green ribbon," she muttered beneath her breath.

Interrupted by the shrill ring of the telephone, Calvin held up a single finger indicating she should wait.

While he conversed on the phone, she delivered the basket to the laundry room, chiding herself all the while for doing something so half-baked. She ripped the bow from Big Ole's personal items, wadded it up, and tossed it into the trashcan.

On her way out the door, a stack of yellowed sheets piled against the wall in the far corner caught her eye. She glanced back at the shelving where someone, undoubtedly Calvin, had stacked a pile of new white sheets where the yellowed sheets had been. The O.M. Harrington wouldn't throw them away, would they? Not during wartime.

She returned to the registration desk just as Calvin hung up the phone.

"I'm sorry, Jo," he said with a restrained smirk. "Now, where were we? Ah, yes, I remember. I personally guarantee that if you don't individually bind the rest of the men's laundry with colored ribbon, they'll be miffed about Big Ole getting better treatment than them. Mark my word."

Jo didn't believe him. Not at all.

A moment later she plodded down the O.M. Harrington's porch steps, shuddering at the recollection of Big Ole's glare. She paused long enough to regroup and then picked up her wicker basket and placed it on Brue's little red wagon. Hearing the soft crack of a mallet against a croquet ball, she looked up and saw the men out in the park. Unfortunately, her passing shadow had just sprouted sharp teeth.

CHAPTER TWENTY-SEVEN

THANKSGIVING DAY 1944

At four o'clock in the morning, Jo rolled over and turned off the alarm. Yawning and stretching, she twisted to the side of her bed and slowly flopped one foot on the floor and then the other, her cold feet inching around until they found refuge inside her slippers. She lingered for a moment with her flannel nightgown gathered about her legs. The house was freezing at this hour, but not nearly as cold as the snow-packed trenches on the far side of the world where soldiers slept. As she pressed her hands through the sleeves of her heavy robe, she wondered if the servicemen would have an opportunity to celebrate Thanksgiving today as well.

All across her great country, the fortunate would feast in warm and noisy and wonderfully crowded homes. But as for Jo and Brue, they would celebrate alone. That was okay. Without Case at her side, Jo would prefer sleepwalking through the holiday, but that wasn't an option. She chose instead to make a good day of it and provide Brue with a festive Thanksgiving.

By seven in the morning, with a small goose in the oven and the washing machine chugging noisily in the basement, she pressed laundry at full speed. It didn't take long to fill her first basket. Keeping a lower-than-usual profile at the boarding house and an even more ambitious workload after her hunter green ribbon blunder, she decided she would quietly slip the baskets through the back door later in the afternoon. To his credit, Calvin hadn't breathed a word about the feminine bow incident, and she refused to bring it up until she could find a convincing way to redeem herself.

Brue got up well past sunrise. After breakfast, she fiddled around on the living room couch looking unsettled. She picked up a book and began reading, but then stopped and peered over the top. "Do you *have* to work today, Mom?"

"I'm sorry, sweetheart. I do."

"But it's Thanksgiving," Brue said, sounding unconvinced.

"I know, but the O.M. Harrington is booked solid this weekend so I'm afraid I don't have much choice." Jo glanced at the alarm clock she'd temporarily set above the radio. "Oh, dear. It's five minutes to ten already."

Brue placed her book at her side and sat to the back of the sofa with her legs straight out, clicking the soles of her re-sewn shoes together, staring at them. "Aren't you going to take your midmorning break?"

"No, not today. I don't want to take the time to brew any coffee."

Brue drew her knees up and wrapped her arms around them. "Mom, can we change my name?"

"What?" Jo's iron halted in midair. "That's certainly coming from out of nowhere. Why on earth would you want to do that?"

Brue shrugged.

"Let me guess. Poke, right?"

Brue stared across the room. "Yup."

Jo resumed ironing with one eye on Brue. "What's going on inside that kid's head now?"

"He said it was a dumb name. He said if he were me, he'd change it."

Jo managed a smile. "I see. And did he say why he'd do that?"

Brue nodded. "He said that whenever his mom says she wants to brew a pot of coffee he always thinks of me."

"Don't you like your name?"

"I did until Poke said that. Why did you and Dad name me Brue anyway?"

Jo released a satisfied sigh. "Well, since you were born in February, your dad said, 'Fe-*bru*-ar-y. Why don't we call her Brue?' I liked it. Brue seemed to flow well with Bremley."

"Dad liked it?"

Jo set the iron aside then grabbed a towel from the basket and shook it out with a snap. After folding it, she hugged the towel tightly. This wasn't the best day to be remembering Brue's father. "It was his idea," she said softly, "so yes, he definitely liked it."

"Okay. I'd like to keep my name, then, please."

From the oven, the aroma of a small stuffed goose and a bowl of scalloped corn baking at its side permeated the air. "It's beginning to smell like Thanksgiving," Jo said as she crossed the living room. "I think I'll turn the radio on. Maybe we can make it sound like Thanksgiving, too."

Brue frowned. "But there's only war stuff on."

"I know, but maybe they'll make an exception today." Jo hoped the radio stations would take a short break from their exclusive coverage of the Allied invasion.

Turning the dial, she stumbled across a Thanksgiving program. For the next half hour or so, Jo continued ironing while she and Brue listened to tales of the first Thanksgiving in Plymouth when pilgrims feasted with Indians after a bountiful harvest. The speaker drew a parallel between the years 1621 and 1944, expressing concern about the ongoing war, Nazi Germany, and Imperial Japan, as well as pride in the courage of the American and Allied soldiers.

At the conclusion of the program a choir sang an old Dutch hymn, "We Gather Together." As she listened Jo thought about the tremendous suffering throughout the world, the oppression, and how hard the Allies were fighting to contain it. She recalled the letter Case received from Tryg barely over a year ago telling how he'd been rescued on foreign soil. She mused about his wounds and how they had set the wheels in motion for Case's untimely death. Setting her ironing aside, Jo listened thoughtfully to the solemn music floating through the radio's speaker. The words penetrated deeply as if written today rather than in the sixteenth century.

We gather together to ask the Lord's blessing;
He chastens and hastens His will to make known.
The wicked oppressing now cease from distressing;
Sing praises to His Name; He forgets not His own.

As the choir went on to sing the second and third verses, she folded the linen. At noon she set the laundry aside and reached for her daughter's hand. "Come, Brue. Time for dinner."

They gathered together at their small Thanksgiving Day table and Brue offered up grace. As they filled their plates, a sudden breeze disturbed some dry leaves and spattered them against the back window. Hearing the scraping leaves reminded Jo of the many times they had heard that very same sound as they ate at the table with Case. Although many long and lonely months were behind her now, the words, *He forgets not His own,* from the hymn she'd heard earlier occupied her thoughts.

Jo would forget not her own, either. Case would remain alive in her heart, always.

CHAPTER TWENTY-EIGHT

The stone-faced, raven-eyed clerk at the First National Bank flinched when she looked at the endorsed check.

"Anything wrong?" Jo asked.

The clerk didn't answer. "I'll be right back." Her high heels clicked against the marble floor as she sashayed to the desk of a distinguished-looking middle-aged gentleman at the far corner of the room. The clerk leaned forward and whispered. The man, appearing totally absorbed in her words, murmured something back and then stole a glance at Jo, the expression on his face inquisitive.

Jo felt strange standing alone, waiting, as if she had unwittingly become involved in something shady. She lifted her purse from her side and clutched it to her chest. There couldn't be a problem with the check from Mr. Ellersby. He was a gracious and kind man. By the way he opened his wallet to reveal his identity, he had to be the epitome of honesty.

It didn't take long for the clerk to return with the man from the far corner at her heels. The scent of Old Spice swirling on the air about him hinted at pleasantness, while the look in his eyes hinted that he was about to share some rather unpleasant news.

"This is Mr. Robertson, our bank manager," the clerk said, looking contrite.

Mr. Robertson waved the paper in midair. "I'm afraid this is a bad check, Mrs. Bremley."

Jo seized the legitimate-looking piece of paper from his hand. "There's got to be some mistake," she insisted. She held the check up toward the light and carefully examined it. "It certainly looks valid. It can't be bad. Are you positive?"

"I wish I could tell you what you want to hear, but I'm afraid there's no mistake. You see, the Ellersby account has been closed for quite some time. I'm sorry, Mrs. Bremley."

Jo pushed through the heavy door, its weight nudging her awkwardly out onto the sidewalk. She stood for a moment feeling dumbfounded and violated, as though her intuition had suffered the delicate blow of a jackhammer. Not liking the feeling, she hurried home and headed straight for the telephone.

"Operator, I'd like the number of a Mr. Clayton Ellersby, please."

CHAPTER TWENTY-NINE

The front door flung open and ushered in an icy breeze. What chilled Calvin more than the cold air was the sight of Reverend Collver rolling an upright wooden barrel into the great room, weaving it from side to side—a large, empty, hollow-sounding wooden barrel. A plea for Christmas gifts for the poor, no doubt. Even more disturbing was Calvin's suspicion that the minister had rolled it all of the way from Village Church. The charming house of worship where Reverend Collver had ministered for years sat on the crest of the small hill bordering Amber Leaf Lake, immediately to the south of Harrington Park and a good block and a half away from the O.M. Harrington.

The redness at the base of the minister's nose, glassiness in his eyes, and rumpled handkerchiefs spilling from the pockets of his overcoat did little to lessen Calvin's aversion.

"Hello, Mr. Doherty," Reverend Collver said a little too cheerfully for Calvin's taste.

Judging by the hoarseness resonating from the minister's vocal cords, the man belonged in bed.

"Reverend Collver," Calvin acknowledged with measured indifference.

"I was wondering if the boarding house would consider sponsoring a gift barrel for the needy again this Christmas."

Calvin gaped at the barrel, though briefly. If the man merely wondered, why did he bother to roll the thing in? The word *presumptuous* entered Calvin's mind and stayed there. "I'm sorry, but I'm afraid you have me at a disadvantage. Not only was I not here last winter, I haven't heard any mention about a gift barrel, either."

"That's right." Reverend Collver stifled a sneeze. "You are relatively new here. The boarding house has sponsored it in past years, but I'm afraid it hasn't done that well. I thought it couldn't hurt to give it another try."

Calvin contemplated the barrel, repelled by the thought of looking at it day after day. He'd gotten roped into this sort of thing in the past and wasn't about to have any part of it again. Not if he could help it. "We have a new manager now," Calvin said in a valiant effort to discourage the preacher. "I'll be sure to check with him and we'll get back to you. Until then, I'd be more than happy to help you roll it back outside."

Calvin heard Big Ole before he saw him, sounding far too pleasant as he broke into view outside his doors and shuffled up the hallway. "Is that Reverend Collver's voice I hear? Why, yes, it certainly is. How nice to see you."

The Reverend rushed forward, pulled off his gloves, and vigorously shook Big Ole's hand. "It's nice seeing you again, too. You're looking dapper as usual and the height of good health."

"Thank you very much. So, what brings you here this fine day, might I ask?"

Calvin watched in amazement as the two grown men gushed over one another—and so shamelessly.

"The gift barrel. Thought I'd drop it off. I asked Mr. Doherty here if the O.M. Harrington might consider promoting it again."

Big Ole shot a disapproving glance at Calvin before re-engaging the minister. "Yes, I do believe I overheard that."

Big Ole's keen hearing in his advancing age astonished Calvin, but his disdainful glance had little effect. After all, Big Ole wouldn't be the one being leaned on to request donations.

Reverend Collver stepped back and quickly held up a finger while he turned his head and let loose a sneeze. "Pardon me. I'm afraid I've picked up quite the cold, but I have way too much to do with the holidays closing in to dawdle around in bed."

Calvin didn't respond to the sneeze, but Big Ole did. "We're sure sorry to hear that ... aren't we, Calvin?"

Calvin nodded halfheartedly.

Big Ole approached the barrel and gave it a good looking over. "We hope you get over it quickly. And about this barrel—why, we'd be delighted. We can place it up against that far wall there near the fireplace." Big Ole pointed out the location with a sweep of his cane. "Calvin, do give Reverend Collver a hand with the barrel, would you, please?"

Calvin caught his chin before it dropped too far. "Yes, sir."

"And, Calvin?"

"Yes, sir?"

"You're in charge here," Big Ole said, a smirk in his tone. "I'm sure you'll be happy to keep Reverend Collver well informed as to the barrel's progress."

No, but I'd be more than happy to shove it out the door, up the road, and back to the church. "Certainly."

Feeling as though he were back in grade school taking orders from a strict schoolmarm, Calvin dutifully rolled the empty wooden barrel from the minister to the far wall.

"Thank you, Calvin," Reverend Collver said, his voice warm and sincere.

Calvin's gait stiffened. He resisted making eye contact with the preacher and nodded toward nothing as he returned to the registration desk. His new assignment gave him no pleasure whatsoever.

CHAPTER THIRTY

As November gave way to December and Christmas drew near, Jo pushed harder. Multiple trips to the O.M. Harrington had become, by necessity, a daily routine. Although relieved to announce the day's final delivery, she stumbled across a scene in the great room that stopped her mid stride when her eyes rested upon the backside of a man crouched over, of all things, a rough-hewn wooden barrel.

At first glance she thought it might be Calvin—all elbows and arms, banging lightly against the sides of the barrel. Totally absorbed in his task, he poked around rearranging bulky gifts, a few wrapped in red, others in green.

"Calvin, is that you?"

He jumped at the sound of her voice then drew up his shoulders and stretched his back. "Oh, I'm sorry," he said cheerily. "I didn't hear you come in."

"Calvin Doherty, what on earth are you doing poking around in that barrel?"

He pointed toward a large sign above it. Written in flawless calligraphy were the words *Noblesse Oblige*. "What do you think?" he asked, his eyes shining.

"The penmanship is beautiful. Noblesse oblige. That's Latin for nobility obligates, isn't it?"

"No. Actually it's French. In the past when Reverend Collver brought in an empty barrel, I understand that all he got in return for his trouble was the same empty barrel. That's not right. It's embarrassing for a well-to-do place like this to be less than generous during the holidays."

"I can see that." Jo restrained a coy grin. "So you're putting pressure on everyone to give?"

"Pressure? Ouch! I don't particularly care for that word."

"Sorry." Jo's smile broke loose. "What word do you prefer?"

"Encourage."

"I guess that does sound better," she conceded.

With the heel of his hand, Calvin gave the barrel a few quick pats, lines of concern creasing his forehead. "I'm afraid I didn't handle myself all that well when the preacher rolled the barrel through the door the other day."

"Why? What happened?"

"Oh, it wasn't so much what I said as how I said it. So I decided I'd better plant some seeds if I want to live with myself. Anything to appease my guilt."

Stunned, Jo couldn't take her eyes off Calvin. For a man who spurned the ministry, he continually heeded its principles in spite of himself. "Plant seeds?"

"You know. The law of sowing and reaping. If I don't bother to buy gifts, why should anyone else? Someone's got to take the lead to get this thing going."

Jo's heart warmed toward Calvin's sudden burst of conscience. "That's very noble of you."

"I don't think so. Pure and unadulteratedly manipulative maybe, but definitely not noble."

Calvin leaned an ear toward the sound of footsteps treading up the hallway. Holding a finger to his lips, he whispered, "That Jonathan I hear?" He raised a brow, a smile wrinkling the corners of his eyes, and then quickly dove back into the barrel throwing in a few well-timed grunts as he reorganized the presents, spilling them generously over of the top.

Jonathan rounded the corner, entering the great room with the percipient and calculated movements of someone trying to sidestep an overly obvious trap. With his overcoat draped over his shoulder with one hand, he plucked his pipe from his thin lips and cradled it close to his chest with the other. "What's going on here? Where'd all those presents come from?"

Calvin drew himself up. "Oh, Jonathan, it's you."

Jonathan's dubious glance found its way toward the barrel. "Of course, it's me. And okay, I'll take the bait. What's going on here?"

"The poor," Calvin said pridefully. "Making sure the little tykes have a good Christmas this year. Everyone's being a real sport about helping out, especially with the war raging overseas."

Jonathan drew his coat from over his shoulder and draped it over his forearm. "Everyone? Who do you think you're kidding?"

"Excuse me?"

"I've lived here the past couple of years. Maybe you forgot about that."

Calvin ignored the remark and shot Jonathan a wily smile. Tapping a light finger against the barrel's side, he said, "You might want to step up to the plate, too. This barrel is going back to Village Church next week. Trust me, there's nothing that could give you more pleasure than putting a sparkle in the eyes of some destitute little kids come Christmas Eve."

Jonathan took a step toward the barrel and peered over the top. He hesitated, and shooting Calvin an accusing look, he took another step forward and peered deep inside. "Wait just a minute. You're setting us up."

"Why, Jonathan, how unkind. How could you even think to say such a thing?"

Jonathan's brows cinched together. "These presents."

"What about them?"

"They all came from the same person."

Jo stepped back, stifling an explosion of laughter.

"Look at them," Jonathan prattled on, sounding incredulous. "They're all wrapped with the same paper. You bought them, didn't you? You bought every last single one of them!"

Calvin chuckled. "You're right. This is a set up. Thought I'd start with a gentle nudge first and see how that worked."

The resigned shake of Jonathan's head obviously did not get lost on Calvin. "Seriously, though," he said, "I am concerned about the kids. Kids who've lost their dads. Dads who've been badly injured. And what about the dads missing in action? Can you imagine what the holidays are going be like for those kids this year? Now, those kids could use some help."

Caught up in the moment, Jo reached for Calvin's arm. "I don't mean to interrupt—"

"Please do."

"I know it's not much, but I have some jars of applesauce and apple butter that I could wrap and bring in if you think that would be appropriate."

"Would you, Jo?" Calvin asked, appreciation surging through his voice. "That would be wonderful."

They exchanged warm smiles. Jo knew her contribution couldn't be more humble, but she also understood the depth of Calvin's gratitude. She was helping him grow the number of gifts, and that's what pleased him most.

Jonathan tapped his pipe thoughtfully against his hand. "These barrels have been distributed to businesses all across town. I hear Trygve Howland offered to match the number of gifts that get donated."

Jo took a step back as the air whooshed from her lungs. For a moment there, she had actually felt useful being able to contribute something. Now, even from a distance, Tryg wielded the power to make her feel puny.

"Trygve Howland? That new attorney uptown?" Calvin asked skeptically. "How can he afford that? He's an upstart."

"Comes from big money," Jonathan said. "It's a family thing."

To Jo's relief, the door flew open and Doc hurried in looking frazzled, the tip of his nose crimson from the chilly outdoors. "Hey, we're waiting on you, Jonathan. The croquet mallets are collecting frost." He paused long enough to toss a curious glance Calvin's way. "We were hard-pressed to knock the wires in the ground. It's rock solid." His gaze then found the barrel, and he took a few steps forward. "Say, what's going on here?"

Jonathan passed his pipe from hand to hand as he slipped his arms through the sleeves of his overcoat. "I'll tell you everything you want to know over our game of croquet. Suffice it to say we've got some shopping to do."

"We do, do we?" Doc's eyes widened. "So what are we gonna buy?"

"I have not a clue. How about if we let the clerks up at Skinner Chamberlain's make that decision for us?"

When the door clacked shut, Jo set her injured pride aside and said to Calvin, "You were brilliant."

He shook his head and looked and pointed upward. "No, but He doesn't do too badly."

Jo took note of Calvin's gesture and his words. "Regarding planting seeds—"

"Yes?"

"I believe I recall a conversation we had recently when you mentioned something about having left the faith. Is it my imagination or is your faith deeper than you care to let on?"

Calvin's gaze locked with Jo's, but not for long. He looked away, dismissing her question with a self-conscious chuckle. "If I don't think this cause is worthy of a donation, why should anyone else? It doesn't get any deeper than that."

Jo felt as though she'd stepped across a fence and onto private property.

CHAPTER THIRTY-ONE

Jo mopped the perspiration from her forehead. She'd been awake since five and already felt the full weight of exhaustion. As she maneuvered her ironing board close to the window to take advantage of the outside light, she nearly jumped out of her loafers when a loud jangling sound startled her.

Brue was sitting cross-legged in the middle of the living room, vigorously shaking her piggybank, coins battering the linoleum and rolling in every direction. She popped up, busily gathered her coins like a hen gathering her chicks, and hovered over them, totally preoccupied, lining them in straight and meticulous rows of pennies, nickels, dimes, quarters, and one fifty-cent piece.

Jo peered over her ironing board for a better look. "That's a lot of money you have there. Any idea what you plan to spend it on?"

"I don't know yet." Brue carefully nudged the edge of her coloring book against her rows of coins, aligning them even more perfectly, if that was possible, and then grinned approvingly. "I'm still thinking about it."

The rhythm of Jo's heart accelerated. If Brue bought the Cinderella watch with the coins from her piggybank, Jo could pay her back. But if Jo could gather enough of her own coins, she could still buy the watch in plenty of time for Christmas. She'd called periodically to check on their availability only to find a dwindling supply. What should she do? With the sights and sounds of Christmas filling the air, time was anything but her friend.

Suddenly, Brue's face lit up. She dropped her coins back in her bank and disappeared into her bedroom. Returning with three books in one arm and Shirley Ann tucked in the crook of her other arm, she hopped up onto the couch. Thoroughly pleased with herself, she flipped open one of her books, and began reading. What was that all about?

Brue hadn't been reading for more than ten minutes when she bounded off the sofa and settled in on the floor. With a slow and careful toss, a handful of jacks spilled onto the linoleum. After a few bounces of the soft rubber ball, she hesitated.

"What's on your mind?" Jo asked.

"The Christmas Eve program."

"Any ideas about what you want to say yet?"

"Nope. That's what I'm thinking about."

Jo ran her iron across a sheet and then pulled another length toward her. "Fortunately, Christmas brings out the best in people, doesn't it?" she mused.

"Why are you saying that?"

"Oh, because of Mr. Doherty and the Christmas barrel, I guess."

As Jo folded the freshly ironed sheet, she thought about Calvin and the gift barrel. She longed for what he had if only for a moment—that confidence, that feeling of being alive, of doing something that really mattered. She thought about Tryg and swatted aside a jolt of envy that he was able to share so generously, even if it was from his family's fortune and not his own. She wanted to do something more meaningful than sharing her canned apples, but what? With the war raging on, the wants and needs in everyone's lives were nothing short of overwhelming.

Reaching into her basket, she pulled out another sheet, this one discolored with worn edges. She rubbed its sides together, and held it loosely in her hands. The sheets were unraveling, going bad.

She recalled the yellowing sheets in the laundry room at the boarding house, but wished she hadn't. She looked up. *I don't mean to be disrespectful, but this isn't fair. When I wished I could do something meaningful to help the poor, I was thinking in terms of my own assets, not the O.M. Harrington's!*

She wasn't about to put a further strain on her job by asking about them.

At two minutes before ten, Jo set her work aside for a quick mid-morning break. She enjoyed few pastimes more than leafing through the colorful pages of a magazine with a hot beverage in hand. She picked up a well-read copy of *The Saturday Evening Post*, and as she placed it on the arm of the easy chair, she heard a muffled sound. "Do you hear that, Brue?"

Brue nodded. "Sounds like the chimes of our old grandfather clock."

"That's what I was thinking." Jo walked out into the porch. Clayton Ellersby's well-muscled son was ascending her front steps. Through the window she saw the clock hidden beneath a thick blanket on the back of his pickup and well secured with a tight rope. No wonder the chimes had sounded muted.

Ellersby's son was alone. He asked if he could back his truck up to her porch, assuring her he could easily maneuver the clock with the help of his dolly. Like his father, he didn't make eye contact. He merely went about his work. When he positioned the clock near the south wall in the living room, Jo couldn't help but feel sorry for him. For all of them, really. Mrs. Ellersby couldn't have been kinder when Jo spoke with her on the phone. She had said that her husband meant well, but also mentioned that he had problems. Jo would have loved to give them the clock, but unfortunately she couldn't afford it.

As the young man drove on up the road, Jo gazed at the clock, suddenly realizing just how much she had missed it. Ten minutes past ten. Still wanting a break, she cozied up in the easy chair and thumbed through the pages of her magazine.

As a rule, she paid little attention to advertisements; however, a full-page ad highlighting one of "The Top Ten Boarding Houses in the Country" not only caught her eye, it also seized her breath. The boarding house boasted of fine food, overlooked a picture-perfect park and lake, had fifteen guest rooms, and offered complete laundry service. The public rooms included a great room, a dining room, a library, a card room, and it had a coffee room where breakfast was served in the morning, fresh-baked cookies in the afternoon, and coffee throughout the day.

Jo fanned her face.

"What's the matter, Mom? Are you okay?"

Jo nodded weakly and, without so much as a glance her daughter's way, she continued reading. The name and address of the O.M. Harrington House in the lower right-hand corner were as understated in the ad as the boarding house was in Amber Leaf. Built on a lightly traveled road, how many of the locals knew it existed in their own hometown?

Jo mulled over the words "one of the top ten boarding houses in the country." No wonder they had such high standards. No wonder she received so much business from them. A sinking feeling plunged to the bottom of her stomach, a feeling of being unequal to her task. If only she hadn't read the ad.

She set the magazine aside and paced to the window. Nervously thrumming her fingertips against the windowpane, she stared out across the park.

"Mom? What's wrong?"

Not wanting to concern Brue, Jo said, "I just read an ad in *The Saturday Evening Post* about the boarding house is all."

When Jo had nothing, she had nothing to lose. But now she understood what she had and what she could not afford to lose.

Complete with laundry service. *That would be me.*

Jo needed to iron the wrinkles out of her thoughts, and fast. She flicked on the lights to brighten their living room. If nothing else, she could at least see the creases in the linen better. Knee-deep in work, she pulled her overflowing basket closer, scraping it noisily against the linoleum. In an effort to redirect her thoughts onto something more productive and less upsetting, she resumed pressing, beginning with the larger pieces to pare down the basket faster. Worrying was a waste of time.

But she couldn't help herself.

She was worried sick.

A hint of pipe tobacco floated on the air down the long upstairs hallway. The doors on all of the second-floor rooms were closed. No sign of Evelyn anywhere. Then an intriguing movement caught Jo's eye. At the far end of the hall, her friend emerged, pacing back and forth slowly waving a wet towel to and fro at arm's length.

"It's going to take a month of Mondays to get your towels dry that way," Jo ribbed.

A blush found Evelyn's cheeks as she lowered it and grinned. "Don't be unkind, dear friend. It works. These wet towels absorb the smell of smoke better than anything else I've tried, other than scrubbing down the walls and floors, that is, and I certainly don't have time for that these days."

"I wondered how you kept this place smelling pristine."

"So, what brings you up to the high country, anyway?" Evelyn asked. "I haven't seen you on this floor before."

Jo restrained a grin. "Don't worry. I can handle the thin air. And I'm here because I just came from the laundry room and noticed you ran out of these." Jo placed the stack of towels on an accent table at the end of the hall. "I thought you might need a fresh supply."

Holding the wet towel loosely at her side, Evelyn nodded her warm-eyed thanks. "You didn't happen to notice anything else when you were in the laundry room, did you?"

"You mean the yellowing towels, washcloths, and bedding stacked up in the far corner? Yes, I noticed. They aren't going to throw them out, are they? What does the boarding house do with them when they've seen better days?"

"That's not what I was referring to. I was referring to the ad in *The Saturday Evening Post*. Everyone's pretty excited about it. A framed copy is hanging on the wall."

"I saw that ad at home this morning. Makes me feel a little intimidated."

"I think you should feel proud. But in answer to your question about the yellowing linen, I'm not sure what they do with them. Why are you asking? Do you need them for something special?"

"Not at all." Jo raised a brow. "If they're being tossed out anyway, I was just thinking what a shame it would be to waste them."

Evelyn's face lit up. "Ask Calvin. You'll be going past the registration desk anyway."

"Oh, no. I'm not comfortable approaching him about it."

"What's it gonna hurt?"

"Evelyn, you don't understand. I'm not the one who should be asking about them. I'm already treading on shaky ground with my job."

"Okay, then I'll ask him."

Lifting and stretching for another round of smoke absorption, Evelyn resumed waving the towel back and forth. "Say, I've been meaning to ask you. Did you ever get your clock back?"

"As a matter of fact, yes. Just this morning." Jo leaned her shoulder against the forest-green-and-ivory-striped wallpaper. "Much as I hate to, I'm going to give selling it another try. I still need money for Brue's shoes and Chief Stout's car repair, but more than anything I want to buy that watch for Brue for Christmas. I just have to."

"You might want to hold off on selling it, at least until after payday."

Jo stepped away from the wall and realigned the already straight stack of towels she'd set on the table. "Why's that?"

"Because I overheard Calvin Doherty mention something about bonuses with our December fifteenth paychecks, that's why."

Stunned, Jo looked down the long hallway, her hopes soaring.

"Look at this thing."

Jo glanced back. Evelyn was holding up her towel and grinning.

"It's filthy!" she said. "Come on. I might as well go with you. I need to rinse the smoke out of this anyway."

Jo fell in step with Evelyn as they headed down the staircase.

When they approached the registration desk, Jo stopped dead in her tracks. Big Ole stood leaning his heavy weight against the counter, lost in the daily paper and quiet as usual. Either he was completely engrossed in the words on the printed page or deliberately ignoring them. Jo reached for Evelyn's arm. This was not a good time to speak with Calvin.

"What are you ladies up to?"

Why did Calvin have to call them out?

"Jo, I'd better get this anything-but-fragrant towel to the laundry room. Go ahead. You ask him."

Jo turned to see not only Calvin, but also Big Ole watching. Big Ole remained expressionless.

"Okay," she said, slowly taking a step closer. "About the old linens that are wearing out." Her words passed awkwardly from her lips. "I was wondering what happens to them when they go bad."

Looking surprised, Calvin gave Big Ole a quick glance. "We generally let our employees take what they want first and the rest we throw out. Why are you asking?"

Although heat rose in Jo's cheeks, she pasted on a smile. "If that's the case, when you return the gift barrel, would you consider passing them along as well? I mean the linens that are being tossed out anyway.

Mothers are practical. I'm sure the sheets and pillowcases could be put to very good use."

Calvin looked more uncomfortable than Jo felt. Not only did she feel overwhelmed with intimidation, this wasn't the time to be asking about discards no matter how honorable the cause.

While she waited for him to respond, the front door flew open and a cold draft swept in. A stout, middle-aged woman entered, heading directly toward the desk as though she was in a hurry, but the men appeared oblivious.

Calvin looked to Big Ole for approval. Fortunately, he nodded.

"We'd be happy to give them to you," Calvin said, sounding relieved. "Feel free to help yourself. And by the way, this is for you." He handed her an envelope.

"Thank you very much," Jo said to Calvin and then she directed her attention at Big Ole. "My thanks to you as well, sir."

"Jo?" Calvin said.

"Yes?"

"Thanks. For helping the poor, I mean. That's a brilliant thing to do. Just wish I'd thought of it."

Jo made her way down the hallway toward the back door, grateful she'd received a positive response and even more grateful for the extra thickness of the envelope in her hand, but stopped when she overheard the stout woman's loud and confident voice.

"Hello. My name is Martha Hansen. I have lots of experience with laundry and wondered if you could use some help with your linen service."

Had Jo not known better, she could have sworn the woman was singing.

Big Ole took no time whatsoever to respond. "I think that might be possible."

Jo meshed gazes with Calvin. He looked the way she felt. Shocked.

She fought for deeper breath to suppress the fear that was building up inside of her.

Feeling defeated, she turned and stepped out into the bitterly cold wind. Walking down the path toward home, she gazed back for a better look at the stately structure behind her, viewing it through far more aware and appreciative eyes.

Calvin sat at his desk dumbstruck. Why would Big Ole hire a stranger to help with the laundry when he planned to use a new service come January one? If Martha Hansen was merely backup, why wouldn't he bother telling Jo? With Jo losing her job at the end of the month, the poor woman needed every nickel she made between now and then. Why would Big Ole jeopardize that? Was this a temporary assignment? If so, why wouldn't he bother to tell Mrs. Hansen?

Calvin nervously rubbed the back of his neck. From the moment he challenged Big Ole about his attitude toward Jo and Brue, he had noticed a change in the man, a change not necessarily for the better. Easily agitated, Ole spouted off about something every time he turned around. Calvin could handle his agitation. He was used to it and always cleared out of the old man's way until he got to the other side of whatever it was that he was going through. Maybe he was having second thoughts about Calvin's cheekiness when he stood up to him. Or was he conflicted about something else? Unfortunately, it took only a few days for the man's anger to plunge into sadness. Calvin could handle Big Ole's anger, but his sadness? Now, that was something else.

CHAPTER THIRTY-TWO

The bat cracked and the ball whistled.

Brue stood at the pitcher's mound gaping at Poke's fly ball as it hurled toward an elm. It snapped and splintered a number of small branches then whacked a thick limb before thudding on the frozen ground.

"Don't pitch the ball so slow," Poke whined. "You pitch like a girl. Gimme a fast one with a little spin on it. I wanna ball I can clobber."

Brue glanced across the park toward the windows of home. What if her mother was watching? She'd been awfully quiet the past couple of days. Something bad must be upsetting her. She'd be even more upset if she saw Brue playing baseball with Poke and Heath. With only a few players, they kept switching positions—Poke was currently at bat, Em in the outfield, Heath playing shortstop, Holley at the catcher's mound, and Brue pitching.

As Em hurried from the outfield to hunt down the ball, Brue heard a commotion at the edge of the park. Her insides twisted. She couldn't look. It had to be the men from the O.M. Harrington. She could tell by their deep voices. Her mother would really be angry if she knew Brue was in the park at the same time they were. Brue needed to get out of here. Why did she let Poke goad her into playing in the first place?

Just because he'd called her a sissy and chicken didn't give her the right to disobey her mother. This wasn't fun anymore. She shivered, getting colder by the minute. She wanted to quit playing, but how?

"Aw, come on," Heath shouted. "She's doing swell."

"Sure. Easy for you to say," Poke sneered. He scraped the tip of his bat against the hard ground. "You're the only one creaming good balls today."

"Don't be such a spoilsport."

"Am not!"

Brue's insides squeezed tighter. *Come on, Em. Hurry.*

Em dug through a hedge of dead bushes, looking high and low for the ball, while the men from the boarding house set up a game of croquet. Brue snuck a peek and saw Big Ole glancing past her, not at her. And to think she'd apologized for what had happened up at the dime store. What good did it do? Maybe if she pretended he wasn't there, she'd feel better. She looked away. All she wanted was to get this dumb game over with so she could go home.

"I found it," Em shouted. She prodded the ball out of the thorny brush and tossed it to Brue. "Don't listen to Poke. You're doing swell."

Poke rolled his eyes. "Girls!"

Lifting the ball up to eye level for good aim, Brue threw it toward home plate.

Poke took a swing and the ball hurled out of bounds again.

"That was strike two," Heath shouted as poor Em huffed and tore off after another foul ball.

The men's mallets popped against balls of their own that rolled smoothly through hoops alongside the baseball diamond. Every now and then they glanced over at Brue and her friends like they were keeping an eye on the kids or something. The men's voices were growing louder. And Big Ole? He sat on a park bench, twirling his cane, probably waiting for his next turn. It looked strange to see him being playful. Only fun people twirled things, and he wasn't any fun at all.

Em picked up the ball and tossed it. "Here you go, Brue. Catch."

Brue caught the ball then sized up Poke, who was crouching down at home plate, bobbing slowly up and down, his hands squeezing his bat so hard his fingers were white.

"Now pitch me one faster this time," he demanded.

Holley rammed her fist into her catcher's mitt and squatted down. "Come on, Brue. Give him what he asked for."

"Yeah, Brue. Throw the ball as hard as you can," Heath chimed in.

Brue didn't think that was such a good idea. Poke could hit balls even harder and farther than Heath. But maybe if she caved into the pressure, they could get the game over with faster. "Okay. I'll try."

Brue concentrated real hard. She wound up her arm the way she'd seen the boys do and threw the ball with all her might.

The ball cut loose from her hand.

"This one's for the Gipper!" Poke yelled. He took a powerful swing, his bat exploding on another high flier.

Brue kept her eyes on the lightning-fast ball as it whistled out of the baseball diamond—and headed straight for Big Ole. Her hands shot up and cupped the sides of her mouth. "Look out!" she shouted.

Big Ole ducked just in the nick of time, leaped to his feet faster than she'd ever seen him move before, and then he shot out his cane. "Hey!"

Brue gasped. The ball missed his ear by an inch, if that.

All of the color drained from Poke's face, his eyes widened to three times their normal size, and he tore out of the park in a blur.

Brue was so frightened, she wanted to cry. She ran to Big Ole's side. "I'm really sorry, sir," she said breathlessly. "Are you okay? It was my fault. I shouldn't have pitched that ball so hard."

The huge old man glared at her and then sat back on the park bench and shook his head. He looked totally disgusted. As he rested his hand on his walking stick and moved it slowly back and forth, the men from the boarding house rushed to his side.

If only Big Ole would say something to her, anything. But he wouldn't. She looked for Em, Heath, and Holley for help, but they scattered off in a blur every bit as fast as Poke.

With nothing more for Brue to do, she wandered across the park toward home with her gaze glued to the ground and her shoulders sagging. How many more things could possibly go wrong with that awful old man?

When Brue finally looked up, she slowed to a stop. She was in real trouble now. Her mother was standing on their front steps watching in disbelief. The disappointment and anger in her eyes nearly brought Brue to her knees.

"Now what have you done, young lady?"

Brue clambered up the steps too ashamed to speak.

"I saw you talking to Big Ole. Did you apologize to him?"

Brue nodded. At least there had been a hint of kindness in her mother's voice.

"We'll discuss this later," she said, laying a hand on Brue's shoulder.

Brue glanced up. Her mother was staring off toward the park. "What are you looking at, Mom?"

"I'm looking at Big Ole. He watched you walk home. He's looking at me now, too, but not the way people normally look at people. He's almost reading us the way one would read a book. Honestly, sometimes I find that man far more interesting than frightening."

Brue didn't feel the same way. She looked back and saw him heave to his feet. He set off toward the boarding house slowly tapping his cane. Even though the other men walked alongside talking to him, she watched him glance her way with a hard-to-read look.

What if he got all of the kids kicked out of the park for good?

CHAPTER THIRTY-THREE

Although crushed by Brue's disobedience, it was the unseen ramifications of her actions that made Jo shudder. Had Big Ole been gravely injured, Brue would have worn that scar for the rest of her life.

"I've never been so angry," Jo said. "You need a serious time-out, Brue. Get a chair from the kitchen and face it toward the wall next to the oil burner. You will sit there and think about what you've done until I tell you to leave."

Jo quickly busied herself with daily chores. For the longest time, the only audible sounds in the house were the ticking of the grandfather clock, her occasional footsteps, the swish of her broom, and the flutter of her feather duster.

"Mom?"

Jo glanced at Brue, saying nothing, as dust shook loose from places even she didn't know could be dusted.

"What?"

"Oh, nothing."

"Nothing?"

Jo set the duster down and marched to the sofa. "Come here, young lady."

When Brue hesitated, Jo patted the cushion. "Come on."

Brue backed onto the sofa, sitting at an angle, appearing too embarrassed to make eye contact.

"First you made a big scene with Big Ole uptown," Jo said, "and now this. Not only did you blatantly disobey me, you kids just sidestepped something that could have been disastrous, and I mean disastrous to the extreme. What if that ball had hit that man? He could have gotten seriously injured. And of all of the people in this troubled world to be the recipient of your careless behavior, it had to be Big Ole again. Honestly!"

"I'm sorry, Mom."

"I'm sorry?" Jo shook her head, her insides ripping. She wanted desperately to calm down, but the stakes were too high. "I'm afraid that's just not good enough. Do you have any idea how hard I've been fighting to keep my job? We need it for our livelihood and now you're risking it even more. This time you're going to have to do a lot more than just say you're sorry."

Brue's eyes widened. "But it wasn't all my fault. Poke—"

"Poke, what? Forced you to play with those kids?"

Jo refused to allow Brue to blame her friends. She squeezed Brue firmly by the shoulders and leveled her gaze. "This wasn't an accident. You deliberately disobeyed me, didn't you?"

Brue studied the floor. "Yes, ma'am."

Furious, broken, and on the verge of tears, Jo sighed. "Sweetheart," she said resignedly, "I just don't know what to do with you. I don't know how to make you understand. And I don't know how to stop these insane incidents from happening. If you have any ideas, I'd sure like to hear them."

Tears pooled in Brue's eyes.

"You need to find a way to put a stop to this," Jo said.

"But, how can I stop my problems with Mr. Big Ole, Mom? They just keep happening."

"No. They don't just keep happening, and you know it." Jo shook her head. "I need some time to think of an appropriate punishment, and you can mark my word there will be punishment."

"But—"

"No buts, Brue. Don't you understand what's happening here? The first incident happened when you went to town without asking for permission. This incident started the instant you didn't stand up to Poke. You caved in to his bullying. You wanted his approval—even if it meant disobeying me. If you'd said no to him in the first place, we wouldn't be in this mess. I can't just stand by and let you continue doing the wrong things."

Brue looked down at her hands and stifled a sob. "I know I shouldn't have thrown that ball so hard, Mom. But I can't do anything about it now."

"Oh, yes, you can," Jo said. "You can start by thinking about how you want to handle this with Big Ole *again*. You will handle this, and you will handle this well."

"Yes, ma'am."

"One other thing."

"What?" Brue asked, sounding completely worn down.

"I doubt I need to tell you that I don't want to see you playing ball with those boys again. Ever. Do you understand?"

"Yes, ma'am."

"And Brue?"

"Hmm?"

Jo exhaled a sizable breath. "Thank you," she said, her voice warm and sincere.

That evening after tucking Brue into bed, Jo worked into the wee hours mending, darning, and sewing on buttons. During those hours, she had time to think. Things were getting harder, not easier. With her desperate need to keep her job, she felt helpless as she watched her only means of income spiraling farther downward. And now Brue had jeopardized her job even more with a willful act of disobedience.

Too weary to sew another stitch, Jo set her mending aside. There had to be a way to stop the negative flow of events and get her job back on strong footing. She had no choice but to find it.

CHAPTER THIRTY-FOUR

Brue peered out the window and across the park toward the O.M. Harrington House. The afternoon sun hid behind the thick cloud cover making the sky look every bit as dark and dismal as her insides felt. How she dreaded the task before her. She turned and looked up at her mother. "I suppose you're wondering if anything's the matter with me."

Her mother clutched her iron in midair. "Now that you mention it, I guess I am. What's going on?"

Brue rested her hands on the windowsill and slowly shook her head. "This could possibly become the most awful day of my life."

"Really?" her mother asked with a smile in her voice. "And why's that?"

Brue didn't want to say anything more about it or think any more about it or face it. She just wanted it to be nighttime, because by then her awful day would be over. "Are you going to the boarding house today?"

"Yes. When I finish ironing. Why?"

"Can I go with you?"

"Of course, you can. But why?"

Brue looked down and played with her fingernails. "There's just something I need to do."

"You're suffering, I take it," Brue's mother said with one of those funny grins of hers. "Could this have anything to do with Big Ole?"

Brue nodded.

In the wee hours of the afternoon, Brue helped her mother carry two baskets of fresh linen through the back door of the boarding house. She nearly dropped her end of the second load when Spitfire jumped up on her. Thankfully, Mr. Doherty whistled for the dog, opened the back door, and turned him loose. When Mr. Doherty came back in, her mother told him she'd brought the gifts for the Christmas barrel.

"Swell," he said. "The barrel's gotten pretty full. We sure wouldn't want the jars to get broken. Why don't you go ahead and set them on the floor near the base?"

Brue felt a little worked up, but since it wouldn't take her mother long, she decided she could handle the wait.

As Mr. Doherty turned and headed toward Big Ole's office, Brue's mother stopped him. Again. "Calvin?"

"Yes?"

Now Brue's insides were beginning to churn.

"Has Doc heard anything from Charlie yet?"

Mr. Doherty stopped in the middle of the hallway and grinned. "He sure did. Got his first letter the other day."

"How's he doing? I've been worried about him."

Brue rocked restlessly in her ugly re-sewn shoes. Why did her mother have to stop and talk so long?

Mr. Doherty took a few steps back like he didn't have time to talk but wanted to anyway. "Doc says he thinks he's probably in Belgium by now. Charlie wasn't specific with the tight censorship, but he did tell Doc he's doing great. I heard on the radio this morning that between the fog and heavy snow the planes have been grounded. It's mostly the infantry that's out and about. Doc was happy to hear that, but I'm sure Charlie's pacing."

Mr. Doherty slipped into Big Ole's office while Brue and her mother finally made their way into the great room. Brue headed for the front windows where she walked in small circles while her mother carefully placed the jars of applesauce and apple butter on the floor and butted them up against the barrel.

A long moment later they headed toward the laundry room. Brue slowed down and took a peek as they passed by Big Ole's double doors. They were wide open. He and Mr. Doherty were making a fuss over some papers. Big Ole looked up at Mr. Doherty and asked, "What's with Mose Chamberlain? We've sent him at least a dozen notices if we've sent him one. You'd better get on it, Calvin, and the sooner the better."

Mose Chamberlain? Heath's dad? Brue wondered if they knew about his problem.

She trailed her mother into the laundry room and watched her stack the shelves with linen and gather another large basket of soiled laundry. It was taking forever. Brue wrestled with the same tortured feelings she'd had the last time she asked to speak to Big Ole. She also remembered how good she felt afterward. If only her mother would move faster. Brue wanted to get past this. Maybe it would go better this time.

As they headed out into the hallway, Mr. Doherty stepped out of Big Ole's office. Her mother quickly picked up her pace and started talking to him about the linens.

Not wanting to wait this conversation out, Brue slipped past them and into Big Ole's office. "Excuse me, sir. Would you mind if I came in, please?"

Big Ole didn't say anything at first, but then he said, "If you must." He didn't trouble himself with looking at her, either. Instead, he pulled open his top desk drawer and reached for something. Probably a cigar.

"Would it be all right if I asked my mother to come in with me, too?"

"That will be fine," he said, still not looking at her and sounding anything but fine.

Brue stepped back into the hallway. "Excuse me, Mom, but would you mind coming in while I speak to Mr. Big Ole for a minute, please?"

Her mother got a worried look on her face. "Be happy to." She placed her heavy basket outside his door and slipped into the room. Brue couldn't blame her if she didn't want to come all the way in. Her mother crossed her arms and her face turned serious. Maybe that was because Big Ole had closed his doors on her before.

"Come in." He waved his big hand toward the chairs opposite his desk again. "Have a seat."

Brue remained standing, as did her mother. "This won't take long."

She glanced from Big Ole to her mother. They were looking at each other with big questions on their faces.

"Well, what was it you had on your mind this time?" he asked gruffly.

Brue sucked in a giant breath then quickly let it out. Her heart pounded all of the way up to her ears. "I did a bad thing in the park the other day when I threw that ball so hard. Mr. Big Ole, you could've really been hurt bad."

"As I recall, this is the second time you've come in to apologize for your negligent behavior," he said to Brue, but he scowled at her mother and anger danced in his eyes. "I hope we aren't developing a pattern here." He peered down at his cigar, swiped a match against the sole of his shoe, and lit it. Then he sucked in a few short puffs to draw in the flames before bothering to look back at Brue.

"I know, but it's more than that," she said, too ashamed to look at anything other than the top of his desk. "I disobeyed my mother. She warned me about playing in the park when you and the other men are out there, and she warned me about playing ball with Poke and Heath, too."

"And?" Big Ole said.

This was much harder than Brue thought it would be, even with her mother in the room. What made it worse was that Big Ole didn't look happy about them standing around in his office.

"My dad told me to come to him whenever I did something wrong. If it was really bad, and this is, he said I should apologize and then I should ask for the right sort of punishment."

Big Ole choked on a puff of smoke and almost dropped his cigar.

Brue glanced back at her mother for support, but her mother was too busy watching Big Ole to notice.

"I see." He leaned forward in his chair. "So, help me understand this. You want me to dole out some sort of punishment that your father would approve of. Is that what you're trying to say here?"

"Yes, sir. I asked Poke to come with me. He's the one who hit the fastball, and I'm the one who pitched it too hard, but Poke said he couldn't come. I think he was too scared."

"I see." Big Ole picked up a small piece of notepaper and tapped it lightly on his desktop.

Brue wondered if that helped him think better.

"And how do you know any punishment I decide on won't be too severe?" he asked.

Brue suddenly wanted to run. "That's why I brought my mom with me, sir. I knew she wouldn't let the punishment be too bad."

"I see."

He sure says "I see" a lot, Brue thought.

Still scowling, Big Ole said in a booming voice, "Just make sure it doesn't happen again."

"Yes, sir. Thank you, sir."

As soon as Brue and her mother reached the door, Brue stopped. She rested her hand against the doorjamb and looked back. "Mr. Big Ole? About Mose Chamberlain—"

Big Ole's eyes widened and he got a baffled look on his face. He then glanced at Brue's mother, looking very hot under the collar. "What about Mose Chamberlain?"

"Mr. Chamberlain can't read. His wife gets mad at him all the time because he hides his mail."

Big Ole slumped back in his big chair. "And how do you know about that, if I might ask?"

"He's my friend Heath's dad. Heath said he thinks his dad is too embarrassed to let his mom know he can't read, but Heath figured it out."

A full two minutes later as they walked across the park toward home, Brue asked, "Why are you so quiet, Mom?"

"Oh, I don't know" she said, her voice warm and thoughtful. "I guess I was just thinking about how proud I am of you. You handled Big Ole like a real grown-up, and you certainly showed him respect. Your dad would have been very proud of you, too."

Brue had given a lot of thought to the respect her mother had shown her when she thanked Brue in advance for making things right with Big Ole. Her mother believed in her. Knew she would do the right thing. Brue hadn't deserved her kindness or her trust, but it sure touched her heart. It gave Brue the courage to do whatever it took to please her mom, even if that meant facing down Big Ole.

"Thanks. I feel better now. I really am sorry."

Liking the way it made the bottom of her feet feel, Brue purposely reached out and stepped on the cracks on the sidewalk all along the way. "You still haven't given me my punishment. Have you decided what it will be yet?"

"No, I haven't. But I think we've both been through enough this past year. Maybe we'll let it go this time, if that's okay with you."

Before Brue could respond, she noticed her mother glancing back at the boarding house. She still looked bothered. "What are you looking at?" Brue asked.

"Oh, I just have a feeling Big Ole wants to be mad at us for some reason, but I can't for the life of me figure out why. I don't think it has anything to do with our clashes with him. He was cranky long before any of that happened."

CHAPTER THIRTY-FIVE

What's that whacking sound? Calvin sat in his usual spot at the registration desk. He lifted his head, did a double take, and couldn't help but grin at the spectacle. Big Ole was snooping around the Christmas barrel poking at the gifts with his cane. "Good selection, don't you think?" Calvin asked with a fair amount of pride.

Big Ole glanced back at him inquisitively. "Very impressive. How'd you pull this off? I understand in previous years this barrel's been a disaster."

"I have my ways," Calvin said matter-of-factly.

"I don't doubt that."

Big Ole poked his cane at the gifts lying at the base of the barrel. "What's in these?"

"I believe those are jars of apple butter and applesauce," Calvin said as he casually tapped a pencil on his hand.

"Hmm." Big Ole leaned down and nudged one of the jars closer to the barrel. "You don't say. Any idea who donated them?"

"Jo Bremley."

"The laundry lady? Is that a fact?"

"Yes, sir."

Big Ole ambled across the great room and asked, "How could she afford that?"

"If I'm not mistaken, the apples were from her tree."

"I see," he said, but then a curious warmth radiated from his eyes.

"What are you thinking?" Calvin asked.

"Oh, I was thinking about yesterday, I guess, when the Bremley woman and her little girl stopped by my office."

"I saw Brue poking her head in and wondered what she wanted with you."

Big Ole looked contented with the world for the first time in months. Resting both hands on his cane, he shifted his weight from one heel to the other. "The little girl asked me to dole out some sort of punishment for her misbehavior in the park the other day."

"You mean when you nearly took a good hit from that lightning-fast ball?"

"That's right." Big Ole broke a half smile. "She asked her mother to come in with her to make sure the punishment wouldn't be too bad. Imagine that."

With Big Ole's formidable presence, Calvin couldn't begin to imagine how much courage it took for Brue to face the man down. "I guess I can, actually. What did you say to her?"

Big Ole tapped his cane lightly against the floor and stared off. "Told her to make sure it didn't happen again."

Calvin smiled. "That was mighty kind of you."

"Little girl has chutzpah, just like her mother. By the way, speaking of her mother, I've given some thought to the breakfast and supper tables. How about draping some white tablecloths over them and pulling out our best linen napkins and finest silverware? During the long, dark, and bitterly cold months of winter, it also might be a good idea to illuminate the tables with the warm glow of candlelight." Big Ole hesitated. "Why are you grinning?"

"I didn't know you had it in you to be so flowery with your words."

"There's a lot about me you don't know. I just thought it might be a good idea to spruce the place up a bit. You know. Make it a bit more elegant and inviting. Do you think the Bremley woman could handle the extra workload while we try out the idea?"

"I don't know," Calvin said, holding back a relieved and hopeful smile, "but I'd certainly be happy to ask her."

"You do that."

"By the way," Calvin said with a smirk, "Word's out that you've been getting standing ovations every night at supper and that you don't look all that happy about them."

"That's a bunch of hooey." Big Ole flashed a sheepish grin. "I'm surprised no one has bothered to challenge my rules."

Calvin chuckled. "You mean the ones about no hanky-panky?"

Big Ole didn't grin, but his eyes did as he slowly drew out the words, "They all just fall into line."

Calvin knew better. He'd heard one too many grumbles about Big Ole's rules—grumbles braided with unsullied admiration for Big Ole's exceptionally high standards.

"What they do under their roof is their business," he said. "What they do under my roof is mine. Maybe if I start coming to the parlor for the social hour, they'll get used to my presence and back off. Those standing ovations are wearing me out."

"You might want to do that. The hors d'oeuvres are terrific, and I know you of all people would have plenty to contribute to the conversations. Everyone loves discussing the news, especially the war news these days. And the atmosphere around here certainly lends to a warm camaraderie."

Big Ole nodded and shuffled on down the hallway. When he disappeared into his office, Calvin shook his head.

Now, what do you make of that?

Suddenly, the front door opened and in walked the scruffy

half-gray-bearded stranger, the same stranger Calvin had seen leaving Big Ole's office the day he'd closed his doors on Jo.

"I have an appointment with Big Ole," the man said. "He phoned about an hour ago. Asked if I might stop by."

"Fine. I'd be happy to tell him you're here. Your name, please?"

"Pritchard. Ernie Pritchard."

CHAPTER THIRTY-SIX

J o picked up the book that slapped on the floor. She eased onto the edge of Brue's bed and plucked mindlessly, repeatedly at a strand of thread protruding from the bare mattress, a spot where a button used to be. Wondering. What was going on?

It had started weeks ago with Brue's book, *Cinderella,* sitting on her dresser and then laying on the floor next to her bed. Last week after Jo stripped the sheets, she'd found the book tangled up in Brue's patchwork quilt. But now, concealed deep inside her bedding, it had tumbled onto the linoleum. Brue couldn't be using it as a security blanket, could she?

But then, why not? What better way for a child to crawl back into the safety and warmth of her dad's heart than through memories—memories of nestling in his arms and listening, soothed by the sound of his masculine voice as he read her favorite stories.

Jo smiled at the memories of Case and Brue cuddling in the easy chair. She could still see them as clearly as if it had been just yesterday. Case often held a book off to the side, resting his chin on top of Brue's head as the words on the pages leaped to life, his total attention focused on her. But Jo's heart had warmed most when she'd heard the tenderness in his deep and velvety voice at the end of each story when he clapped the book shut, always kissing Brue lightly on the top of her blond head and throwing in a warm and sincere, "I love you, pumpkin."

Jo clutched the book, holding tight to the bittersweet memories.

I love you, pumpkin.

Suddenly, the shadow-filled room grew dark and eerie. A gust of wind rattled the windows, demanding her attention. She got up and peered out into a sea of billowing clouds. No wonder it had gotten darker. The early onset of the snowstorm forecasted for later that night must have caught even the weatherman by surprise. The first snowstorm of the season. The vivid recollection of last year's first snowstorm tore through Jo's heart like a sharp claw—the knock on the door, the lone policeman standing on the porch steps, the ominous timbre of his voice.

Forcing her thoughts aside, she bolted to the living room and quickly spun the radio dial until a scratchy and muffled voice broke through. "Ladies and gentlemen, we interrupt this broadcast with an important—"

A loud burst of static obliterated the transmission.

Jo gave the radio several forceful strikes and leaned closer to the speaker, spinning the dial again, hoping to find the sound of a voice, any voice, until a faint one emerged.

"Severe blizzard conditions have swept across the Upper Midwest. Please be advised that all schools in Freeborn County will close at ten thirty this morning."

Jo glanced at the clock. Twenty past ten. Brue was at school without her boots, and Jo had little time to get there.

As she rushed to the closet to snatch her coat, the telephone rang, causing her to jump. She rushed over and grabbed the receiver after the first double ring.

"Jo?"

Through the heavy static, Evelyn's voice sounded like it was a hundred miles away instead of a handful of footsteps up the road. Jo envisioned her friend pacing nervously as she spoke.

Evelyn, you worry better than anyone I know. And it's catching.

"D-Did you hear about the school closings?"

Pressing her arm through the sleeve of her overcoat, Jo said, "That's where I'm heading now."

"That's why I called. Poke's mittens and boots, they're still in the closet. He tore off for school this morning without them. I'm on my way to p-pick him up. I can pick up Brue, too, if you want."

Jo sighed the moment she heard the welcome rumbling of Evelyn's Hudson. She watched as it backed out of the Tomlinsons' driveway and roared on up the road, steam billowing from its tailpipe.

Brue would be cold when she came through the door, cold in more ways than one, so Jo busied herself. She placed a blanket near the oil burner to warm. She then fired up the stove and heated the teakettle to fill a large basin with warm water. She also searched the pantry for a can of Brue's favorite soup, Campbell's tomato, to warm her insides.

Before Jo knew it, the clock chimed at the three-quarter hour. *That's odd.* Ramsey School, a mere handful of blocks away, closed fifteen minutes ago. Backhanding a wild wisp of hair, she nudged back the curtain and gazed out at the bank of inky clouds still tumbling through the sky. They cast an eerie darkness on the late morning hour. No sign yet of the Tomlinsons' Hudson or of Brue. Suddenly, she heard a familiar roar and sighed with relief. The snow-caked grill of Evelyn's Hudson wheeled around the corner and into full view from River Lane onto Charles Street, her windshield wipers slapping at full speed.

Jo dashed into the kitchen, listening for the familiar bang of the outer screen door followed by the welcome sound of pounding feet stomping off snow. She poured the steaming water into the basin and strained as she lugged it into the living room. It took no time at all for Brue to charge in from the outer porch with her teeth chattering and her hair dripping.

Jo placed the heavy basin on the floor. "What took you so long?"

"Poke and I took the shortcut. We got halfway home before Mrs. Tomlinson could find us."

Jo slid the warm water to the foot of the easy chair and helped Brue yank off her wet shoes and socks. She reached for Brue's pink cheeks and felt her forehead. "You're a little on the cold side, pumpkin. We'd better keep an eye on you. I don't want you getting sick. Here's a toasty blanket." Jo wrapped it snuggly around Brue's shoulders then grabbed a towel and blotted the moisture from Brue's hair. "As soon as we get you all warm and dry and fill you up with hot soup, you'd better get into bed. Just in case."

Brue swished her feet slowly back and forth in the basin, her shivering slowly subsiding as she relaxed from the warmth.

Shaking the towel with a snap, Jo noticed Brue staring into the flames of the oil burner. From there Jo shifted her focus to the flow of water where Brue skimmed her toes through the warm basin, lost in her thoughts.

"You look sad, sweetie. Are you all right?"

Brue nodded, but the look in her eyes told a far different story.

"It's your dad, isn't it?"

Brue nodded again.

Jo laid the towel aside and held out her arms, drawing Brue into a tight embrace. "I know," she said softly. "I miss him, too."

Jo gently stroked Brue's hair and then glanced down at the placid water. "Hold your dad tight in your heart, just like I'm holding you now," she whispered, "because one day when we finally get to heaven, we'll both be able to wrap our arms around him and hold him tight forever."

A teardrop plunked into the basin, forming a ripple on the surface of the water.

CHAPTER THIRTY-SEVEN

O pen up," Jo said, sliding a thermometer into Brue's waiting mouth. As she read it, she could feel a smile form that
wanted to break across the entire width of her face, but
wasn't quite ready.

Bing Crosby crooned *White Christmas* on the phonograph. The
tree was up and decorated, and although not much to look at with its
spindly branches, it still looked and smelled like Christmas. Brue was
the picture of health again. The blizzard moved eastward. And with her
Christmas bonus tucked away in her wallet, the empty space beneath
the tree was about to be filled.

Adding to Jo's good fortune, *Cinderella* happened to be the story of
the week at the library. Jo would walk Brue there for the Saturday morning reading and then hurry on to town.

Jo had phoned the dime store again earlier in the week to inquire
about the watches and was relieved to learn they still had four left. Now
not only would she be able to finally buy one, she would pay for it in full
as well.

Jo peered through the window before venturing out. Although the
outdoors looked inviting, better things filled her mind—things like
checking back issues of *The Saturday Evening Post* to research the ads

for the O.M. Harrington. How long had they been running? Had the ads been Big Ole's idea? Was he expanding his vision for the boarding house? More importantly, was there any possible way for her to fit into his future plans? The fact that she'd gotten a call at his request asking if she could handle an extra work assignment gave her the first inkling of hope that things had a chance to turn around. With their troubled relationship percolating behind the scenes, she couldn't say no to his request. She had thought about it, though. The additional workload might help pay the bills, but it was exhausting.

Jo smiled at the freshly shoveled sidewalks generously banked with snow as they trudged up the road. The sky was filled with clouds too heavy to hold their weight; light flurries tickled her cheeks.

Brue reached for Jo's hand. "I wish Dad was here with us."

"I do, too. Very much."

"Mom?"

"Yes, dear."

"How come Dad didn't go into the Army with Mr. Howland?"

Jo slowed her pace, her stomach constricting at the mention of Tryg's name. She flicked away a snowflake that landed on her eyelash and asked, "What made you think of that?"

"You said you were going to stop uptown. Isn't that where Mr. Howland is?"

A weak "yes" passed from Jo's lips.

Brue gazed up at Jo, her eyes a question.

"Your dad tried to get into the Airborne, but he couldn't pass the physical."

"Why not?"

"Well, he wasn't sick really. He had a kind of silent disease and you can't fly in airplanes if your blood isn't flowing right."

"Why didn't his blood flow right?"

"I don't know, sweetie. It just didn't. Then he tried to get into the infantry, but they wouldn't take him either because foot soldiers have to carry heavy loads for long distances. Combat duty can be pretty strenuous.

"I never saw your dad so low. In the end, he decided to stay home and help the farmers." Jo gave Brue a nudge. "Do you know what they call the farmers?"

"Hunh-uh."

"They call them soldiers without uniforms."

"Really? Why?"

"Because they help feed the world even if it means plowing by the dim light of lanterns and harvesting by hand. When your dad found out his health would keep him from doing what he wanted to do most, he threw himself into working the fields. He got up in the wee hours of the morning and headed out while it was still dark to help cultivate and plant crops. He weeded onions and helped with the harvest. Remember how he used to come home and pull off his cap to show off his farmer tan? His forehead was so white it looked like his sun-browned face was frosted with icing."

"Yeah," Brue giggled. "He really looked silly, didn't he?"

Jo smiled. "Yes, he did. But he also looked very, very handsome."

The sky washed from gray to white. A complete absence of wind allowed snow to collect beneath their boots, muting the sound of their footsteps as if they were walking in stocking feet across a pure white carpet. With squinted eyes and snow-coated hair, they pressed on until they saw light glowing through the windows of the library. They hurried up the tall, wide concrete steps and, once inside the door, stomped the snow from their boots and dusted themselves off.

After removing Brue's coat, mittens, head and neck scarves, and boots, Jo guided Brue into the reading room where the dry smell of radiator heat and the hollow sounds of old books crashing on the hardwood floor, hushed voices, and uncovered coughs filled the air.

The librarian walked up behind them. "Good morning."

Jo jumped at the sound of her voice. "I'm sorry. I didn't hear you coming."

"I was in the back room. You didn't happen to bring any cake or cookies, did you? We could be here for a while. The weatherman was certainly off the mark again today. I wouldn't doubt but we'll get a good foot or more before it stops snowing."

"Look!" Noticing the room brighten, Jo nodded toward the windows. "Just like that, I believe it's slowing down. The worst is probably over, at least for now. Are you still having story time?"

"Yes, ma'am. But if the snow picks up again, I'm afraid we'll have to close for the day."

"I'll keep an eye on it. Meanwhile, I need to run a quick errand. I should be back easily before you finish."

After getting Brue settled in, Jo stepped out onto the front steps of the library and headed on toward the heart of town.

When she entered the auto repair shop, its front doors stretched open like the wide doors of a barn. A man dressed in grimy coveralls glanced her way. "May I help you, ma'am?"

"Yes. My name's Jo Bremley," she said, peeling off her gloves one finger at a time. "I'm here to pay for the repairs on Chief Stout's Packard."

The man's oil-streaked face registered surprise. "There must be some mistake." He wiped his hands roughly on an old rag as he approached her. "That bill was paid a few days ago." He then added as an afterthought, "In full."

"Are you sure? Why would anyone bother to do that?"

"We have no idea, ma'am, but I'm absolutely sure. We found an envelope under the door the other morning. That's never happened before. Whoever slid it under there must have been in a big hurry. The envelope was beaten up pretty badly. There was a hand-written note on the outside. It said, 'For the repair of Chief Stout's Packard,' but it wasn't signed. There were two twenty-dollar bills in it. Since that amount more than covered the cost of the repairs, I'm afraid we owe you the difference."

Jo took a step back and shook her head forcefully. "No. Absolutely not. I can't take that money. It isn't mine."

"I would consider it a gift, if I were you. It certainly wasn't given to us. If and when you find out who paid for it, you can always give the difference back to them." He dipped his hand into the cash register and counted the money into Jo's reluctant hand. "And, by the way, have a very merry Christmas."

"Are you sure? I really don't feel comfortable accepting this."

"Of course, I'm sure. We'll be on the lookout. If we find out who dropped the envelope off, we'll be sure to let you know."

Jo shook his hand, enthusiastically wished him the best of holidays, and hurried out the door. Her feet felt as if they were walking on a cushion of air as she rushed on to the five-and-dime, wearing a smile as wide as her strides were long.

Breathless from her fast pace, Jo stopped briefly at the display window for one last glimpse at the Cinderella watch before buying it.

No watch. Only an empty space. That couldn't be.

Unnerved, she raced inside to find Miss Bickford standing behind a counter, rearranging small bottles of perfume.

"The watch and glass slipper," Jo said, floundering for breath from the walk as well as the shock of not seeing them, "they're not in the display window. Please tell me the store didn't sell the last watch set."

Miss Bickford's thin eyebrows rose. "You aren't serious?"

"I'm sorry to interrupt you," a nearby clerk said, "but I couldn't help overhearing. We sold the last set the day before yesterday. You were off that day, Miss Bickford. I remember, because there were two boxes left and we sold both of them within minutes of each other. And of all the unlikely people, Big Ole from the O.M. Harrington House bought the last one. He mentioned something about a Christmas barrel for the poor. Imagine that."

"Oh, no. Big Ole." Jo refused to give up hope. She'd come too far. "I'd like to pay the full amount in advance on the next shipment that comes in and get it then, please," she announced confidently.

"I wish you could, but we received the last delivery the Friday after Thanksgiving and won't be getting any more in."

"Please tell me that isn't so," Jo said, desperate to believe she still had a chance.

Miss Bickford shook her head regretfully. "I'm the one who placed the order. I'm afraid our store got the last boxes that were manufactured. I really am sorry."

Jo's shoulders slumped and her heart ached.

"But, what about another watch?" Miss Bickford asked. "We have one here that's definitely been a favorite."

"No, but thank you anyway."

CHAPTER THIRTY-EIGHT

J o stood on the corner watching idly as a stream of cars drove by, their windshield wipers thumping at full tilt, the steam puffing out of their exhaust pipes and dwindling into oblivion. She then gazed up at the sky. Still smarting from the sting of disappointment, she looked away. Why would God care about a silly Cinderella watch, anyway? He certainly had better things to do than worry about that sort of nonsense.

She walked across the street with a listless gait. With a half hour to spare, she headed toward The Copper Kettle. Might as well treat herself to some time alone. Time to think and regroup. That would be a decent place to retreat from the weather, anyway.

Just inside the door she noticed a large man leaning over to pick up a hat from the floor. At a glance and from an odd angle, she could only see the top of his head. As he straightened, something fell from his coat pocket, but he didn't appear to notice.

Jo quickly sidestepped the tables and scooped up a wallet-sized photograph of a well-dressed woman. She had soft features with short-cropped, fluffy gray hair and dark, deep-set eyes that radiated happiness. The picture looked remarkably frayed around the edges, frayed by nervous and empty hands.

Captivated by the stunning face in the picture, Jo looked up and said, "Excuse me, sir."

When the man turned around and towered over her, Jo stiffened.

Big Ole.

How could she not have known he was Big Ole?

"I believe you dropped this."

He seized the picture from her hand, not taking his eyes off of it, and gave her a nod of thanks. "It's the missus," he said mournfully and shuffled out the door.

The ice in Jo's heart melted. As she stood in stunned silence, a waitress stepped up from behind. "Is anything wrong, ma'am?"

"I'm fine," Jo said, her voice barely audible as her eyes lingered on the closing door.

A brief moment later, she slid onto a tall barstool at the counter. When the young waitress reappeared with a menu, Jo shook her head. "That won't be necessary, but thanks, anyway. Just a cup of hot chocolate would be fine, please."

Jo sat in a daze. She slipped her gloves into her pockets, unbuttoned her coat, and pulled her scarf from around her neck and draped it across her lap. She had misjudged Big Ole. No wonder the poor old man had been so wretched. He was grieving the loss of his wife.

The waitress reappeared, plunking a steaming cup in front of Jo a bit too hard. "Oh! I'm sorry about the spill," she said and quickly reached for a cloth. "Guess I'd better slow down. I'll bring you another cup."

Glancing at the young lady's name badge, Jo's lips curved into a smile. "Don't give it another thought, Alice."

Jo warmed her hands on the sides of her cup as she glanced around, uplifted by the restaurant's pleasant ambience. Its polished oak counters, wooden tables and chairs, and small clusters of booths at the center and far side of the room reminded her of happier times when she'd dined in pleasant restaurants with her grandparents up in Fort William and Port Arthur.

The cash register jangled at the far end of the lengthy counter, and a bell rang for an order to be picked up. As Alice busily dashed back and forth balancing large platters of steamy food, Jo twisted on her barstool—thinking about Big Ole, thinking about Brue, thinking about that almost-perfect Christmas with the ultimate gift under the tree that could no longer be. Thinking about what to say to Brue or if she should say anything at all.

Jo barely paid attention to the long and narrow mirror hanging above the lunch counter and running the entire length of the wall, that is, until a sudden movement caught her eye. Several gentlemen were sitting at a corner table undoubtedly discussing business. One of the men bent down and searched through a black leather briefcase.

Tryg again.

Jo slouched on the barstool, but couldn't slouch far enough to escape the mirror's broad range.

The men stayed in sight.

Not up for handling another one of Tryg's dismissals—not today, anyway—she took slow sips of the hot chocolate, hoping her unhurried movements wouldn't draw his attention. With plenty of books to thumb through at the library, she wanted to finish her hot chocolate and make a quiet exit.

Before she had a chance to take her last sip, Tryg and the other well-dressed gentleman got up to leave. They would have to walk past her to get to the cashier.

Good. If one of them would cower, let it be Tryg. She lifted her shoulders and raised her chin just high enough to feel a pull.

As he approached the cash register, her eyes sought his in the mirror. Although he acknowledged her presence with a noncommittal you-can-bet-I-see-you-too gaze, he didn't hesitate to make a quick exit.

Good going, Tryg.

The door swung open and Chief Stout entered, crossing paths with him. They greeted one another, engaging in a short but serious conversation, both nodding their heads in agreement. Then Tryg turned and stole a quick yet unreadable glance at Jo before stepping outside.

CHAPTER THIRTY-NINE

When he caught sight of Jo, Chief Stout's face brightened. He eased onto the barstool beside her, his mood upbeat. "Why, if it isn't Mrs. Bremley. Mind if I join you?" He was sitting beside her before she had a chance to respond.

Jo laughed lightly. "I'd like that very much. Does this mean you're still talking to me?"

A grin cut a becoming dimple deep into the chief's left cheek. "My car looks brand spanking new again, so, yes, you bet I'm talking to you."

A regular at The Copper Kettle, the chief no more than sat down when the waitress came and poured him a cup of coffee.

"Thanks, Alice." Lifting his cup, he turned toward Jo. "Here's to a very merry Christmas and a happy New Year, Mrs. Bremley."

She clinked her cup against his. "Thank you. That's awfully sweet."

"Say, you're empty."

"I was just about to leave when you came in."

"Nonsense. Alice, how about bringing Mrs. Bremley here another cup of whatever it is she's drinking."

Before Jo could protest, Alice placed a new hot chocolate on the counter.

"By the way, I've been meaning to thank you for giving me the heads up on Brady Malone," the chief said, speaking to Jo as warmly as if they'd been friends for years.

"You mean about his losing his son and daughter?"

The chief nodded. "What a tragedy."

Jo drew her cup close and smoothed its stem, staring down at the counter. "Any idea how he's doing?"

"As a matter of fact, yes. Tryg Howland and I just had a word about him when I came in. He's been checking in on Brady." The chief broke a thoughtful smile, but then his eyes turned sad. "That Tryg sure is a good man. They don't come any better than him. But he's also a broken man, just like Brady Malone."

Jo could see Chief Stout's lips moving, but his words? She lived on the other side of that reality, and Case was enduring an eternal rest beneath the underside of frozen tulips because of they-don't-come-any-better-than-him Tryg.

"Mrs. Bremley? Are you okay?"

Startled, Jo looked up and forced a nod. "Of course. I'm fine."

As if suddenly aware of his blunder, the chief rotated his mug and redirected the conversation.

"I went to have a visit with the unusually outgoing Brady Malone about a week ago. I swear that man stood in his doorway rigid as a telephone pole. Wouldn't invite me in. The arctic in the dead of winter couldn't freeze as solid as the chip on that man's shoulder. I'm not too proud to tell you that I humbled myself right there on the steps of his front porch. Told him how wrong I'd been, how bad I felt about his loss. You should've seen him. His hard shell cracked quicker than a raw egg on cement. Never thought I'd see the day I'd feel compassion for a grown man sobbing like an infant. Tears streamed down his cheeks so hard he could barely talk." Chief Stout shook his head. "That sure was a sight I don't care to see again, but I think we're friends now."

Jo touched her fingers to the warmth of her cup and stared at the swirling steam, listening intently.

"I also made a call on Reverend Collver," the chief added. "I'm sure you knew he lost his only son about a year ago."

Unnerved, Jo looked up. "No. I hadn't known. What happened?"

"Jeep hit a land mine."

"How awful. The tragic stories just keep coming."

The chief gave Jo a slow nod. "The reverend said he'd be happy to visit with Brady. I understand they've already shared their stories and their grief. I get the impression Brady's doing much better. Still has a ways to go, though. That's something you never get over, not in a lifetime."

Jo gazed into the silence while the chief lifted his cup, swirling it a bit before taking a sip. Noticing that the weight of his words had subdued him, she picked up the conversation.

"As I recall, the last time I was in The Copper Kettle, you were engaged in a private chat when I interrupted you and Big Ole."

Chief Stout chuckled. "As I recall, you're absolutely right."

"Tell me. His run-in with my daughter, that was an accident, wasn't it?"

"From where I was sitting, it sure looked like it. That's why I didn't involve myself."

"I see. And a short while ago, I stopped by the auto repair shop to pay the balance on your car and found out that someone had already paid for it. Anonymously. You wouldn't happen to know anything about that, would you?"

Chief Stout's eyebrows hiked several inches. "No, ma'am, but I can't tell you how relieved I am to hear it. With you struggling with your finances and all, I felt like a bona fide numbskull insisting you pay for the damages. But with the audience we had watching through the windows here and the passersby listening in, I'm afraid I was stuck and needed to assert my authority." He flashed a disarmingly sheepish grin. "I hate to admit it, but I was a bit miffed about my car, too."

"I can understand about your car. But how could you possibly know I'm struggling financially?"

"Ma'am, anyone who drives a beat-up old wreck like yours, is a young widow with a small daughter to raise, and takes in laundry just to make ends meet can't be doing all that great."

Jo choked. "How do you know so much about me?"

"I'm the chief of police, remember?" He shrugged, sadness stealing the joy from his eyes. "Small town. Besides, it's my job. It's really more than that, though."

"What do you mean?"

"Well, with so many men getting their lives wiped out during the First World War and now this one, I feel a need to keep a watchful eye on all the widows, young and old alike."

Jo's sigh succumbed to a relieved smile. "That's very kind and I assure you, we do appreciate it. But I wish you had an idea about who paid for your car repair. I can't imagine who would want to or why."

"Let me think on that a minute." Chief Stout slid a thick thumb across his stubbly chin. "Come to think of it, the men at the O.M. Harrington House take up collections every now and then for good causes. They definitely have the means, and that Calvin Doherty is the only man I know of who could talk you into giving away your entire family fortune for any cause whatsoever and make you believe you actually wanted to do it."

Jo grinned at Chief Stout's colorful way of speaking. But after giving his words some thought, they didn't ring true. "Why would anyone want to take up a collection for repair work on a brand-new car?"

"That wouldn't be why they'd do it. Their motivation would be to help you."

"I doubt that." Jo raised her cup, stopping short of her lips. "I don't think they feel all that comfortable around me. But if you're right, how can I find out for sure?"

"I doubt you ever will."

"I may not, but I'm certainly going to try." She hesitated, lightly setting her cup back on the counter. "By the way, since we're talking about the O.M. Harrington House, what do you know about Big Ole?"

"Big Ole?"

"Yes, sir. When I came in a little while ago, I caught a glimpse of a picture that fell out of his pocket. When I handed it back to him, he told me it was his wife. He looked sadder than I've ever seen anyone look."

"Big Ole Harrington—"

Jo's eyes widened and her jaw dropped. "You don't mean *the* O.M. Harrington?"

"Yes, ma'am. The one and only."

Jo shifted on her barstool, catching her breath on what felt like a thimble full of air.

As Chief Stout continued talking, Jo watched his lips form words, but they deflected off her ears. Why had Big Ole bothered to let her keep her job? Why hadn't anyone mentioned his last name before? But then, how could she not have figured it out? No wonder she walked on thin ice with the man.

Chief Stout reached out and lightly touched Jo's arm. "Mrs. Bremley, are you okay? I've seen shock before and you definitely show all the signs of being in it."

"I'm sorry," she said, breaking out of a stupor. "But am I ever in trouble. I can't seem to get on track with that man. And now I find out that I work for him. You wouldn't believe how ill-fated we are. My daughter keeps having accidental run-ins with him, and you were actually privy to mine right here in this restaurant. Unfortunately, that one wasn't an accident. Try as I may to do everything right, whenever he's anywhere near me something humiliating seems to happen—every single time."

"I'm sure it's not as bad as you say."

"Oh, yes, it is." Jo pushed her mug back a few inches on the counter. "Tell me. Why do people whisper his name?"

The chief smiled. Wide. "Because it has so many zeroes behind it. You don't stumble across too many people like him in a lifetime."

"I see. No wonder Calvin Doherty pointed out how wealthy he was. What about his wife? Do you have any idea what happened to her?"

Chief Stout twisted on his barstool and hooked his thumb on his belt. "Now that's a tragic story. Big Ole lost her this past spring; I believe it was last April. It all happened so fast. I heard she had an appendicitis attack. Wasn't diagnosed on time. He hasn't been the same since. Resigned his post as circuit judge and moved into the boarding house right away. He's lost without her. Used to be a great guy, but now I'm afraid he spends most of his days exercising bad manners. He's not the same Big Ole."

"So, that's it," Jo said. "Mark my word, the anger will pass. I'm sure he'll be his old self again as soon as he's through grieving."

"I sure hope you're right." Chief Stout picked up his mug and gripped it in his hands. A smile played across his firm lips.

"A penny for your thoughts."

"Oh, my dear Mrs. Bremley, I do hope they are worth far more than a penny." His large fingers combed a tuft of graying brown hair off his forehead. "About Big Ole, I'd be hard pressed to recall how many times I heard him refer to Mrs. Harrington as his bride. They had a presence together that very few people have the privilege of enjoying."

Jo glanced up at the clock on the far wall. A quarter past the hour already. How she wished she could move back its hands of time. "Oh, no. I really hate to be rude, but I've got to get back to the library and pick up my daughter. Promised I'd be back before the librarian finished reading the story of the day." She reached over and lightly touched the chief's arm. "You have no idea how much I've enjoyed chatting with you, Chief Stout."

"The pleasure was all mine, I assure you. Be careful out in the elements, now, you hear? And a merry Christmas to you and your little girl, by the way."

"A very merry Christmas to you, too."

As Jo reached into her purse to pull out some change, the chief cupped his large hand over hers. "Don't worry about it. I've got it covered."

Jo smiled, said a warm thank you, and quickly made her way out the door.

The temperature outside had dropped a few degrees, and the wind had grown appreciably colder. She hugged her coat tightly at her waist, lost in a hodgepodge of conflicting thoughts. Before she realized it, she was opening the door of the library.

As she entered, the story of the day ended. She checked out several recent issues of *The Saturday Evening Post* then headed home with Brue at her side.

"I saw Big Ole up at The Copper Kettle," Jo said, resting her hand on Brue's shoulder as they walked along. "And I chatted with Chief Stout for a while. I also saw Tryg."

Brue looked up at her mother. "Was Mr. Big Ole mean again?"

"No. This time I actually felt sorry for him."

"You did? How come?"

Jo finger-combed a loose lock of blond hair away from Brue's forehead, tucking it under her woolen headscarf. "Because I found out that he lost his wife earlier this year."

Brue looked straight ahead, kicking thoughtfully at the loose snow blanketing the sidewalk. "Is that why he's so mean?"

"I'm beginning to think he's not mean. He's just very, very sad."

"What about Mr. Howland? Did he talk to you this time?"

"I'm afraid not."

Brue stopped and rubbed her boot along a thin patch of ice buckling through a thin stretch of snow. "Why doesn't he like us, Mom?"

"Unfortunately, I think it will be a very long time before Trygve Howland is able to like anyone." Jo picked up their pace. "Pumpkin, there's something else I think you should know."

"What?"

"The Cinderella watch and glass slipper. I hate to tell you this, but there aren't any left. That's the real reason I came uptown today. I wanted to buy them for you for Christmas. I know how much they meant to you."

Brue looked straight ahead, responding with silence rather than words.

"I really tried. I've been calling at least once a week to make sure they still had them in stock. The store wouldn't let me put a set on hold without a down payment, and today was the first time I could get to town, only to find they were all gone. Including the one in the display window."

"That's okay," Brue said.

"What do you mean by that?"

"Santa will bring me one for Christmas."

"No, Brue," Jo said, maybe a bit too strongly. "Please don't get your heart set on them. That's not going to happen. Like I told you, the last Cinderella watch and glass slipper have been sold. The store won't be getting any more in. Santa can't possibly bring them to you now."

"It's okay, Mom. Santa Claus *will* bring them to me for Christmas. You'll see."

CHAPTER FORTY

The silence closed in on Calvin. It had been uncharacteristically quiet for most of the day, but then again it was that either-or time of the year—either the O.M. Harrington bustled with activity or emptied of life when its guests slipped off to town for Christmas teas and shopping or ventured out to the parks and frozen lakes to participate in varying kinds of winter sports. Although happy when it bustled, when the boarding house emptied of life, Calvin also emptied of life.

He stoked the flames in the fireplace and heaped another log on the fire. A warm distraction. A happy moment. He then straightened the magazines on the coffee table into a ruler-straight line before strolling to the window to absorb the view of Harrington Park.

I need to get out more.

He glanced back and considered his living quarters—a small room directly behind the registration desk, ideal for being available for early- and late-arriving guests. He took pleasure in spending the bulk of his time at the boarding house when people were around, but lately he found himself feeling increasingly uncomfortable. Too many quiet hours alone. As the days rolled on, a depleted, restless, and, although he would never admit it to anyone, downright lonesome feeling settled over him. The holidays could do that to a man when he walked through life alone.

He looked back again toward the park, letting out a relieved sigh when he saw Big Ole tramping up the sidewalk. Calvin whistled lightly as he made his way back to his post.

He listened for the footfalls and smiled as the door swung open. Big Ole sauntered in, accompanied by a gust of air with a good nip to it that flowed through the great room, giving Calvin a chill. He didn't mind, though. The presence of another person warmed him and made him feel better.

Big Ole stomped his feet, the snow melting into small puddles near the entry. He appeared self-absorbed, not saying anything as he yanked off his galoshes. He stuffed his gloves into a pocket and hung his coat and scarf on the clothes tree, lightly resting his hat on top of them.

"Pretty rough out there, is it?" Calvin asked.

"Sure is. Brr."

Big Ole strolled deeper into the room and hesitated before giving Calvin a thoughtful glance. "I just came from The Copper Kettle." Then, almost as an afterthought, he said, "Ran into the laundry lady up there."

"The young widow Bremley?"

A pained expression blanched Big Ole's face. "Widow?"

"You didn't know, then?"

"No, I sure didn't." He ambled closer to the desk. "I recall your having mentioned something about her raising her daughter alone. I just assumed her husband was overseas."

"I'm sorry. I was sure you knew."

"What happened? To the widow's husband, I mean." Big Ole's voice grew warm with concern. "And how long has she been a widow?"

"Car accident. A little over a year ago."

"Oh, my." He shook his head and took a step back. "How dreadful. And she's so young. I'm sure sorry to hear that."

Calvin nodded his agreement, but he would have to think about Big Ole's response.

As Big Ole disappeared through the doors of his grand office, Calvin busied himself with paperwork. He plucked a letter opener from his drawer and sliced open a stack of envelopes that arrived in the afternoon mail run. One of the letters addressed to him was from Village Church. Feeling some reluctance, Calvin set it aside and then opened it last. Inside the envelope he found a hand-written note from Reverend Collver thanking him for helping with the Christmas barrel. Calvin read the note, feeling little more than indifference. However, there was an adage at the bottom of the page, which resonated with him, a thought he needed to consider. It said, *God loves making harmony; He loves getting our hearts in tune with others, our hearts in tune with His.*

Calvin set the letter aside and then got up and headed for the coffee room, wondering in spite of himself if there might be hope for Big Ole and Jo yet. Was God making things right with them? Making harmony? Getting their hearts in tune with one another? Their hearts in tune with His? Even as he permitted himself some small belief in fulfillment, he knew it was wisest to keep his hope under wraps ... just in case.

CHAPTER FORTY-ONE

E vening gave way to night, heavy snowfall gave way to a howling wind, and drifting snow piled higher than the windowsills.
Say hello to the dawn, Jo.

She tended the fire in the oil burner before peering outside where
Harrington Park sprawled into a winter wonderland. Powdered snow
covered its walking trails, which curled around well-spaced elm, oak,
and evergreen trees, park benches, and coach lamps. If time had been
more plentiful, Jo would have reveled in the sight longer, but her workload needed attention and Brue needed something to eat.

Jo stopped by Brue's bedroom. "Time to wake up, sleepyhead."

A few long minutes later, Brue climbed up to the kitchen table,
yawning. "What's for breakfast?"

"Cream of wheat. Did you make your bed?"

"Uh-huh."

Jo poured a scant spoonful of sugar on the hot cereal. Placing it
in front of Brue, she heard the first shout. Thinking nothing of it, she
resumed her chores while the washing machine chugged away like an
uphill freight train in the basement below.

Not five minutes later, she heard another shout, and then another,
intermittent against a background of excited chattering. She drew back

the living room curtain and looked outside. "Brue! Come here a minute. You're got to see this."

Brue scrambled to Jo's side and nudged her nose up to the window.

"Look." Jo pointed toward the park. "Big Ole and Jonathan."

Brue let out a slow, "Wow! What are they doing out there?"

"Looks like they're playing shuffleboard."

"With brooms?" Brue asked with a tone of unmistakable disbelief.

Jo nodded. "Who needs shuffleboard sticks when you have brooms to clear the snow off the court? Isn't that something?"

Midmorning, Jo headed out to the front porch with a shovel in hand only to find the door blocked by drifted snow. She pushed up against it until she could wedge an opening large enough to force her shovel through and then spent the next ten minutes or so shoveling the steps clean.

Exhausted, she leaned against the house to catch her breath only to hear more excitement out in the park. Jonathan was leaning on his corn broom, appearing to take issue with Big Ole's push broom.

"I can't get any traction with this thing," Jo heard him complain.

She called into the house and asked Brue for their push broom, then Jo took a chance and waded out into the park. Big Ole stepped back and quietly looked on as Jo handed Jonathan her broom. "Thought you could use this."

Jonathan's eyes sparkled. "I believe I could at that. Thank you, madam!"

A warm feeling filled her. A short walk later, she rested her shovel against the side of the house then went back inside, where she returned to her ironing by the light from the window and glanced out every now and then to enjoy more of the outdoor happenings.

Suddenly, another shout rang out.

"On guard!"

Brue glanced up from her book. "What's that, Mom?"

"I can't believe it," Jo said, craning to get a better look. "Big Ole is standing with his broom held high in the air like it's a sword or something. No wonder. He won that fencing competition when he was young." Not realizing she held her iron in midair, too, Jo said, "I wonder what's happened to him."

"Why?"

"Oh, I don't know. It's like he's springing to life or something."

Since Big Ole moved to Amber Leaf, Jo had only been honing in on the bad in the man. The fine hairs on the back of her neck had stood at attention when she considered his offenses. But seeing the good in him now and that tragic sadness in his eyes at The Copper Kettle undermined her resolve. She sensed his warmth even if it did emanate from grief.

She pressed the hot iron hard across a cluster of resistant wrinkles in a cotton sheet, sprinkled a generous amount of water on the troublesome creases, and pressed again. She trod on fragile ground with her job. She was sure of that. She couldn't allow it to slip through her hands. The flicker of a weakening standoff, slight though it might be, raised her hopes. If she wanted job security, she needed to make peace. There had to be a way to erase the past and build a new series of pleasant memories with him. But would Big Ole Harrington ever stand for it?

CHAPTER FORTY-TWO

Later that afternoon, Jo manipulated the radio dial, turning up the volume. She structured her work around Edward R. Murrow's broadcasts, which would break over the airwaves again in a few minutes.

Snatching her handkerchief out of her apron pocket, she polished a few specks of dust from behind the control knob. The moment Ed Murrow pronounced his signature "*This* is London" greeting, the door flew open and Brue rushed in.

"Mom, Mom, come look!" She grabbed Jo by the sleeve of her sweater and pulled her out onto the sun porch.

"Look," Brue said, pointing toward the park's edge. "Poke, Heath, Em, Holley, and me, we made that snowman."

"Well, I'll be." The snowman had a carrot nose and two large black stone eyes, one decidedly larger than the other, but that only added to its charm. A half-moon of small brownish stones formed its mouth and a maroon woolen scarf loosely encircled its neck. Two twigs poked out opposite sides of its shoulder area, one pointing down and the other straight out.

Meanwhile, Big Ole sat at his bench in the middle of the park.

Rather than feeding the squirrels, he appeared absorbed with the snowman as well.

Despite her interest in Big Ole's presence, Jo returned her attention to Brue. "Whose neck scarf is that draped around the snowman's neck?"

Brue let out a giggle. "It's Heath's. He was teasing Poke because he didn't have anything to put on the snowman."

"Let me guess. That's Poke's mitten, right?"

"Yup. He packed it real tight with snow so the thumb would point out better. Then he fitted it on the end of that twig there, the one pointing straight out. He wanted it to look like it was thumbing a ride. He said we should call the snowman *Hitch*."

Jo pulled Brue into a half hug. "You did a wonderful job. That certainly was clever, and I have to admit that he definitely looks like a hitchhiker. No doubt about it." She looked out across the park. "Where'd all your friends go?"

"That's what I wanted to ask you about," Brue said, her eyes pleading. "We're all invited to Heath's house. His mom said we could play musical chairs. Can I go, Mom?"

"I don't know. It's getting kind of late."

"Please!"

Jo grinned and gave Brue's chin a loving nudge. "Oh, okay then. Just make sure you're home in plenty of time for supper."

As Brue reached for the doorknob, Jo quickly seized her shoulders, holding her back. "Wait just a minute. Something's going on with Big Ole."

Brue snapped around in a half turn. "What?"

"I don't know yet, but I want to see."

He plodded toward the snowman, his expression inquisitive. Stopping in front of it, he turned and glanced around like a guilt-ridden kid making sure no one was watching. Jo doubted he could see her and Brue through the glaring reflection of their front windows. He smoothed his chin with his gloved hand and observed the snowman from various angles as though it were a sculpture and he an artist. Removing his hat, he held it in his hands and examined it for the longest time before reaching up and carefully positioning it *just so* atop the snowman's head, tilting it slightly at the brow. He took a single step back and inspected his workmanship before fussing with it one more time, making another small adjustment.

Jo folded Brue in her arms and rested her chin on the top of Brue's head. "Well, for heaven's sakes," she said. "I can't believe what I'm seeing."

Big Ole took another step back. He stood for a drawn-out moment, just looking.

Jo watched in amazement as he twirled his cane and set off, bare headed, toward the boarding house, glancing back after a handful of steps as if to admire one last time the snow art still standing at the side of the road.

When he disappeared from sight, Brue flew out the door and headed for Heath's home, and Jo returned to the broadcast only to hear Edward R. Murrow's sign-off, "Good night, and good luck." She'd missed the bulk of Ed Murrow's words, but she hadn't missed Big Ole's actions, actions she would not have wanted to miss for anything.

She turned off the radio and thought about Big Ole's loss of his wife and how crabby and sad he'd become. She then thought about the Christmas barrel and how he'd bought the last Cinderella watch for some other unfortunate little girl, a youthful stranger he didn't know. Jo was happy for the poor little girl who was about to have a very nice Christmas, but then she thought about her own daughter and let out a slow and weighty sigh.

With Brue away from home for a few hours, Jo reached for her knitting basket. She had work to do, Christmas gifts to knit, knowing it would be impossible to knit or make anything that could possibly compare with a little black box containing Cinderella's watch and her gleaming glass slipper.

CHAPTER FORTY-THREE

J o stood in front of the O.M. Harrington like a lost and empty soul suddenly recognizing something familiar, like someone hoping to find her way. Calvin Doherty. She needed to have another chat with him. She couldn't ask him about the upcoming changes that were going to be made at the boarding house; that needed to come from the O.M. Harrington without interference from her. But he might be able to offer insight on ways to improve her relationship with Big Ole. Maybe Calvin would also have a few words of encouragement about Brue. Jo could give him a try at least. What did she have to lose?

She entered through the back door. All appeared quiet. She looked around. Not seeing anyone, she made her way down the hallway and into the great room where she found Calvin crouching in front of the fireplace, stoking its flames.

"Well, hello there," he said, glancing up at her. He did a double take. "Say, what's going on? You don't look your usual chipper self. Anything I can do to be of help?"

Jo nodded apprehensively. "I'd like to revisit your having been a man of the cloth. You wouldn't mind putting on your chaplain's hat for a few minutes, would you?"

Calvin positioned another log on the fire and pulled back as a flash of embers sputtered and burst. With his attention fixed on the dancing flames, he said, "You know I'd do just about anything for you." He gave her a sidelong glance. "Anything, that is, other than that. I haven't felt comfortable performing the duties of a man of the cloth for quite some time. That's why I walked away from it."

Jo shrugged. "Oh, well, thanks anyway," she said then turned and walked away. "I thought it was worth a try."

"Wait," he cried out after her. "Okay. Come back. Why do you need me to put on my chaplain's hat?"

Jo hesitated, but only for a fleeting moment, then joined Calvin, resting against the side of the settee nearest the fire. She took in the entirety of the great room in one slow sweep. Disheartened, she loosened the sash of her coat. "I see the barrel is gone."

Calvin looked confused. "Yes, it is. We returned it to Village Church late yesterday afternoon. Why the sudden interest in the barrel?"

"I figured as much."

"What's this all about, Jo?"

"The last Cinderella watch. It was purchased from the five-and-dime a few days ago."

"You've lost me here," he said, reaching for the poker. "The last Cinderella watch?"

Jo nodded. "I'm sorry. Yes. They've been on display in the window there for months now."

"And?" he asked, returning his attention to the logs and carefully prodding them as more of the bright embers flared and hissed.

"And I understand they were purchased for the gift barrel."

"Really? The gift barrel we had here?"

"Yes."

He arched his eyebrows. "That's a good thing, isn't it?"

"Under the right circumstances, yes. Unfortunately, it was the last one they had. I wanted to buy it for Brue for Christmas. She had her heart set on it."

"I understand." He shook his head. "That is a problem. Any idea who bought it?"

Air pressed out of Jo's lungs in a rush. "Of all of the unlikely people in the world, it just happened to be Big Ole."

A glimmer of astonishment flickered in Calvin's eyes. "Really? Well, maybe there's something I can do to help then. It's not like I didn't work hard to make that barrel a success."

Clasping her hands together, Jo brought them to her lips then closed her eyes for a brief moment. Could it still be possible to get the watch for Brue? But as quickly as hope surfaced, shame tore it away. What was she thinking? She shook her head. "It's too late. Besides, that wouldn't be right."

"Why not?"

"Taking from one poor little girl to give to another?" she said, unable to hide the distress in her voice.

"But—"

"No. Absolutely not. I couldn't do that. I had my chance."

Calvin mindlessly twisted the poker around and around in his hands. "What do you mean you had your chance? What could you have done differently?"

Jo told Calvin about a plant down in Des Moines that manufactured armor-piercing and incendiary bullets for the war effort, and how seriously she had considered going down there. And then there was always New York or Minneapolis where her cousins Shirley and Margaret lived. If she had ventured off, she and Brue wouldn't be in the financial mess they were in right now.

Calvin stopped twisting, but he kept his attention fixed on the poker. "For our sake, I'm glad you didn't go, but I'm curious. Why did you decide to stay here?"

"A lot of the work these days is temporary. When the war is over, a good number of jobs are going to be eliminated. The ones that aren't will go back to the soldiers when they come home. The women knew that going in. I couldn't take a chance on losing my job when the workforce gets flooded again, not with having to raise Brue by myself."

"I understand," he said thoughtfully. "Your point is well taken."

Jo flinched as another ember wheezed and exploded. She had taken so much for granted—Case, the inheritance from her grandfather, even the effort required to hold on to a job. How she regretted not having paid better attention.

"I think you're being a little hard on yourself." Calvin's voice was kind and gentle.

"That's where you fit in," Jo stated matter-of-factly. "I was wondering if you might have a few words of wisdom. A string of sleepless nights is wearing me down. Brue is still lonesome for her dad and here I missed the perfect opportunity to buy her the one thing that could have made her life a little happier. I hadn't realized it, but she's been using her *Cinderella* book as a security blanket."

"A book?"

"That's right. Can you believe it? Case read the story to her so many times I swear the two of them had it memorized. Now I've been finding it in her bedding. She sleeps with it. I also found out by accident that she's been going up to the five-and-dime without asking permission and standing in front of the window ogling that Cinderella watch. And of all of the people to buy the last one, it had to be Big Ole. It's just unbeliev-able. I also found out that he owns the boarding house, that he is O.M. Harrington. I had no idea. I nearly fell off the barstool at The Copper Kettle when Chief Stout spilled the beans. How could I have not known or at least figured it out?"

"Don't beat yourself up," Calvin said softly. "He wanted to keep it quiet. Didn't want people fawning over him because his wife died. He's private about that sort of thing. Just needed some time to work things through."

"I understand only too well. I needed time to work through Case's death. In fact, I'm still working it through." Jo leveled her gaze on Calvin.

"I have to make things right with Mr. Harrington. I've got to keep my job. I need it, Calvin. And I also need to find a way to provide better for Brue."

"That's a tough one. Let me think on it."

Refusing to let him see the tears threatening to splash down her cheeks, Jo turned away.

"These things happen to all of us, Jo," Calvin said as if he could read her thoughts.

"I know, but still, there's got to be something more I could have done."

He reached over and lightly touched her arm. "No," he insisted. "You're wrong about that. You've done everything you could. I'm sure you made every attempt to buy that watch for Brue. I know for a fact you couldn't possibly do a better job for us here. And as for Brue's run-ins with Big Ole, you even handled those beautifully."

Jo let out a disbelieving chuckle. "How can you possibly say that? The run-ins keep happening. Did you hear that I even confronted him up at The Copper Kettle in front of Chief Stout and the entire restaurant only to find out that his incident with Brue really was an accident?"

Calvin smirked. "I'd wager a bet that Big Ole, Chief Stout, and everyone present respected you for it. Not many have people have the chutzpah to take on Big Ole Harrington. Besides, there's no question you've been coaching your daughter on the sidelines. No kid steps up to the plate the way Brue does without someone looking over her shoulder, providing direction. You're doing the right things. It may be too late to give her the ultimate Christmas gift, but you are giving her something that's far more valuable."

"Really? Like what?"

He smiled confidently. "Like an excellent example, that's what."

Jo shook her head. "I'm afraid I'm not very good in that department these days."

Calvin got up and, balancing the poker against the hearth, he sighed.

"These are troubling times. No one has it easy. Brue is bright, reasonable, and loving. If you have the courage to face a cold and hard reality, she will, too. It doesn't have to be a bad thing."

"But what about Big Ole? What do I do about him?" Jo reached for the sash of her coat and unthinkingly tapped its ends together. "It amazes me how much can go wrong in my relationship with him. Or should I say lack of relationship? How can we possibly move forward? Here I thought he was just a disgruntled old man. I had no idea he was grieving for his wife. Now I'm seeing a side of him that warms my heart. I want to reach out, but I think it's a little late for that. Too much damage has been done. And having to worry about losing my job every time I turn around is taking its toll on me."

Calvin sighed. "I know what you mean."

Was Calvin confirming her fears?

"It seems that just when I think there's even a flicker of hope that the ice will thaw between the two of you," Calvin said, sounding regretful, "something unexpected happens and the chill comes back."

Her heart sank. He was verifying her worst fear.

"He's been going through a pretty rough time," Calvin continued. "Maybe he'll snap out of it on his own. At least that's what I'm hoping for. I don't know if it's my imagination or not, but he seems to have perked up the past few days."

"I've noticed that, too." Staring into the fire, Jo combed her fingers through her hair. "Look, I'm taking up too much of your time here."

"I don't know that I've been much help."

"Sure, you have."

"You know, come to think of it," he said with a thoughtful tilt of his head, "there is something you may not have tried."

"What's that?"

"I'm playing man of the cloth here, okay?"

Jo caught his wink and smiled. "Okay."

"Have you tried giving thanks?"

As disbelief registered, Jo drew her gloves out of her pocket and simply held them. "Excuse me?"

"You know, as in, 'In every thing give thanks: for this is the will of God in Christ Jesus concerning you.' That giving thanks."

Calvin was quoting scripture again. He just couldn't stop himself. "But I'm not grateful for these trials. I'd be a raving hypocrite if I thanked God for them."

He shook his head. "Who's talking grateful for? I'm talking grateful in."

"Aren't you splitting hairs?"

"Not at all. It would be ludicrous for you to give thanks for your trials. But to give thanks while you're in the midst of them changes your focus. You begin to look for good things rather than dwelling on the bad. Think about it. Much needed rain falls from the darkest clouds, doesn't it?"

Jo hesitated. "Do you give thanks in the midst of your trials, Calvin?"

"Sometimes."

Her jaw tensed. "Not *all* the time?"

Calvin appeared to ignore her question. "Don't give up, Jo. Most peoples' feet are formed from clay, but then there are those few whose feet appear to have been forged from steel. You strike me as one of those rare people. Give thanks and then keep an eye out for the good. You'll find it. I know you will."

Calvin stared at the door long after it closed. Jo's words "not *all* the time?" stuck in his craw. She certainly could dish it out.

He then considered his words to her. She'd gone through some pretty rough times this past year and certainly didn't need any added pressure from him. Was there anything else he could have said to help her, or would he have only made matters worse? As he walked back to the registration desk, he decided to give it more thought.

Suddenly, the boom of a husky voice gave him a jolt.

"Mr. Doherty, might I have a word with you, please?"

Ho-oh! I was sure that man had gone to town.

"Coming, Mr. Harrington. Coming."

CHAPTER FORTY-FOUR

When Jo returned home, Brue was sitting precisely where Jo had left her—in the easy chair hidden behind the pages of yet another book. The house creaked in the afternoon's quiet like dry hinges on the doors of a well-weathered barn.

"Brrr! It sure is cold out there."

Brue's nose remained buried. "I hope it gets warmer soon," she said absently.

Jo peeled off her boots and tucked them away in the closet. Calvin's words weren't sitting right with her. In *everything* give thanks? The man wasn't thinking. He had the wrong audience. Young widows didn't give thanks when their husbands were killed. Nothing could bring Case back. And even if giving thanks in the middle of her trials could change her focus, what good would that do? It sure wouldn't change her circumstances, not one little bit.

"Mom, can I go sledding?"

Jo glanced at Brue, who sat waiting for a response. "Of course, you can."

"Mom?"

"Yes, dear."

"Nothing."

Nothing.

Brue clapped her book closed, set it aside, and then picked up her doll and cuddled it, looking as though she was protecting herself from impending doom.

"What's wrong?" Jo asked.

Brue's mouth bent downward. "You look sad again."

Jo moaned. "Oh, sweetie, I don't mean to worry you. I just have some stuff I need to think about. Everything is going to be fine."

Brue picked up Shirley Ann and repositioned her on her lap. She twisted the doll's arms into various positions and then walked the doll along the arm of the easy chair. Returning her to her lap, she looked up at Jo with worry-filled eyes. "Poke said you're going to get fired from your job at the boarding house."

Jo gulped. "He what?"

"He said everyone's talking about it. Is that really true?"

"Laid off, maybe, but not fired. That's an awfully strong word. When did Poke tell you that?"

"Yesterday."

"Oh, dear. I hope I don't get laid off." Jo let out a hefty breath of air. "But we can never be sure, I guess. Don't worry. If I do lose my job, I'll just have to find another one, won't I?"

Jo placed several worn stockings and one of Brue's dresses on the sofa. As she picked up her sewing basket, Brue got up and padded toward the coat closet.

"Brue?"

"Hmm?"

"I don't feel good about your going outside while your insides are unhappy. First the watch and now my job."

"I'm okay, Mom. Honest, I am. Even though the last Cinderella watch and glass slipper were sold out, at least looking at them made me happy for a while. And Poke could still be wrong about your job. But even if you do lose it, at least you had one for a while."

Out of the mouths of babes.

After Brue left for the park, Jo slouched back and toyed with the cro-
cheted doily dangling over the side of the end table. She had difficulty
dismissing Brue's response. So quickly with childlike faith, Brue found
things to be thankful for. But as Jo returned to her mending, knotting a
length of thread and pulling the needle through the heel of Brue's sock,
a bothersome thought struck her. Brue was thankful for things after
they happened, not during, not before. How could anyone give thanks
while they were in the midst of staring up at the dark underside of their
worst nightmares? That seemed disingenuous. If Jo did lose her job, it
wouldn't be for lack of trying. She'd been knocking herself out being
thorough and timely, saying nothing of working excessive hours, many
at no cost to the O.M. Harrington. And she was tired—tired of trying,
tired of the long and hard hours, tired of the struggle.

Jo caught herself. Fretting wouldn't save her job. What could it hurt
to heed Calvin's advice? She might as well give thanks. After all, she'd
given everything else. If she did lose her job while trying to put a smile
on God's face, so be it. If Brue could find things to give thanks for, so
could Jo. Brue was right about one thing. Jo had received a year's income
from the O.M. Harrington. How would she have survived without it?
More importantly, she had Brue. She had her friends, her health, and
a roof over their heads. As she considered her blessings, the emotional
load she'd been carrying evaporated like ground fog under a warm summer sun.

She thought about Case. If he were alive, he would have told her
to fight for her job. But that's what she'd been doing all along—literally
toiling with hard work and not a small amount of perspiration.

She then thought about Big Ole. Jo understood the reason behind
his moodiness and he had, in fact, softened somewhat. Maybe she
should reconsider going to the boarding house to have that chat with
him after all. Yes. That's what she would do. Break the ice. Make peace.
But what could she say that would make a difference? How many times

had Case said, "the answer is in the problem; look for the answer in the problem"?

Needing a pair of scissors, she pulled her sewing box closer.

In retrospect, color-coding a grown man's laundry with ribbon and a bow had been a laughable idea on her part. Had the laundry belonged to a woman, the act might have been okay. But even then, there's little question the bow was over the top.

Looking inside her sewing box, she shuddered at the roll of hunter green ribbon lying on top of the spools of thread. How could she do such an embarrassing thing? But the damage had been done.

Suddenly, an idea struck her. Dynamite the iceberg. If God wanted her to have her job, no one could take it away from her. And if He didn't, she might as well find out and get the misery over and done with.

Mid-afternoon, she loaded the wagon for another trip to the O.M. Harrington while Brue huddled near the oil burner red cheeked and still drying off from her sledding adventure.

"I'm on my way to the boarding house. Would you like to come along?"

"Nah, that's okay. You won't be gone long, will you?"

"Nope, just a few minutes. There's something I need to do."

"What?"

"Save my job, that's what."

"Huh?"

Jo feigned a grin that may have been too confident. "I'm not going to let anyone take my job from me. If anything, I'll throw it away first. And if I'm going to lose it anyway, I'm going down in flames. Spectacular flames. Big Ole has been taking himself way too seriously. He's been taking us too seriously, too, and I haven't been much better. That's about to change."

"But what if you do lose your job?"

"Brue, I thought about what you said. Poke was right. I've as good as lost it anyway. I think Big Ole has already hired my replacement. Things can't get much worse. At this point, I refuse to worry about it any more. I need to let it go. It's in God's hands now."

Jo bundled up Big Ole's personal items with unusual care and penned a note. She couldn't get to the boarding house fast enough. The back door was locked, so she marched through the front lugging in a full basket, said a quick hello to Calvin, and then hurried on toward the laundry room.

Calvin gave her a strange look. "What are you up to?"

"What makes you think I'm up to anything?"

"Jo?"

She kept walking. She deposited the basket in the middle of the laundry room where it would not be overlooked, turned sharply on her heel, and scooted past Calvin again with a strong and confident gait.

"Jo, what is it?"

"Just saving my job," she said as she breezed by.

Once outside the boarding house, her short-lived confidence plummeted, and all the way home she flailed herself.

What have I done?

Curiosity got the best of Calvin. The latch had no sooner clicked and the front door closed when he hurried off to the back room. The basket was sitting on a folding table, prominently displayed in the room's center. On top he found a full-page, hand-written note in generous feminine penmanship that read:

To: Big Ole

From: Jo Bremley

My sincerest apologies for tying a feminine hunter green bow on your masculine laundry. I do hope you will find this more to your liking.

Calvin lifted the note from the top of the basket and exploded with laughter.

Suddenly, Big Ole appeared in the doorway. "You shot down the hall like you were heading for a fire. What's going on in here?"

Calvin took a step back and, with a full sweep of his arm, said, "I think you might want to take a look at this."

Big Ole picked up the note. After reading it, he lowered it to his side. Peering at the basket and looking as though he was unable to take his eyes off of it, he said, "Well, I'll be. The next time Mrs. Bremley comes in, would you ask her to stop by to see me, please?"

"Be happy to."

Early the next morning, Calvin saw Jo walking past the windows, making her way toward the back door. He jumped up, hurried down the hallway, and held the door open. "Big Ole has requested an audience with you."

Jo looked visibly shaken. "Is everything okay?"

"I don't know. Is it?"

CHAPTER FORTY-FIVE

The double doors to Big Ole Harrington's office were wide open. He was alone, sitting in a leather chair behind his massive desk fidgeting with the edges of a note-sized piece of paper.

Jo tapped lightly on the doorframe. "I understand you wanted to see me," she said, trying to restrain the wild heaving in her chest. *This is it. If I'm going down, at least I'm going down fighting.*

Big Ole quickly stood with uncharacteristic energy. "Certainly. Come in."

Jo was surprised to see that he had that much life in him.

"Please, have a seat."

Not knowing how to read his mood, she lowered herself carefully onto the overstuffed black leather chair at the far side of his desk, fearing a good tongue-lashing or, worse, the swift and unbearable loss of her job. She'd heard horror stories about powerful men firing employees at Christmastime just to prove their manliness. Those stories couldn't possibly be true. He wouldn't do that, would he?

Before she could form a word on her lips, words gushed from Big Ole's mouth like water surging from a spigot.

"What's with women, anyway?" he asked, his voice unnecessarily loud and gruff.

"Pardon me?"

He clasped his hands behind his back and paced. Jo noticed he was pacing without his cane. She had never seen him walk without it appended to his hand before.

"That new lady I hired to help you—"

Jo disciplined herself to quickly close her mouth, which had fallen wide open. "What?"

"The new lady," he said, his voice still coarse. "You saw her. She came in the other day asking for work. This morning she brought in her first completed load of laundry. You'd think she'd give it her best shot. Not only was it not bound with any sort of whatever that funny stuff is you bind it with," he said, irritation seeping through his words as he slapped the air with his powerful hand, "nothing was sorted, and I swear she's even more starch happy than your predecessor."

Jo burst into shocked laughter. "I'm so sorry."

He turned to face her. "What's so funny?"

"Are you telling me I'm not being fired? I came in today to try to make things right, to plead my case, and to even offer to lower my wages if that would soften the rift between us. I can't tell you how relieved I am."

"Well, don't be too relieved," he scoffed. "I'm not sure I want to keep her. If I decide not to, we may need to find someone else for back up."

Jo couldn't believe her ears. "I think I can handle that just fine."

He strolled toward the windows and looked out across the park. Then after a seemingly endless moment of silence, he glanced back at Jo. "Incidentally, you may be in the wrong profession, young lady."

"Sir?"

A smile played on his lips as he rocked forward on his feet. "You've quite an artistic flair, Mrs. Bremley. Binding my clothing with suspenders and a bow tie made out of—what is that color, anyway?"

"Hunter green?"

He nodded. "Hunter green ribbon was really quite clever. But, I assure you, it's not necessary to go to that much trouble."

"But I want you to be a satisfied customer, Mr. Harrington."

Big Ole walked back to his desk, flipped open the lid on his cigar box, and pulled out a new cheroot, taking his time peeling off the cellophane wrapping. He lowered himself onto his chair and, sitting back heavily, finally made eye contact.

"I can assure you, Mrs. Bremley, I am."

CHAPTER FORTY-SIX

Brue emptied the money from her piggybank and stuffed the coins into her mitten. She slipped on her woolen coat, scarf, and boots, shoved the mitten into her pocket, and headed toward the door. At a quarter past four, it was already dark outside. Brue often played with her friends in the park during late afternoon hours, so she doubted her mother would suspect a thing.

"I'm going outside, Mom. I'll be back in time for supper," she said, her hand resting on the doorknob.

"Wait a minute."

Brue stiffened and looked back. "What?"

"Look at your legs. Come here, please."

Brue held her pocket close to her side so her coins wouldn't make any noise.

Her mother examined Brue's legs. Twisting her from side to side, she said, "Look at you. These boots are so stiff your legs are going to get chafed. Where are your knee-highs?"

"In my drawer."

"You'd better put them on before you go outside. I don't want your legs getting red and sore."

Relieved that her mother's only concern was chafed legs, Brue hurried to her bedroom, tugged on her long socks, and dashed out the door. She should easily make it uptown before closing time. With a bounce in her walk and crusts of ice crunching beneath her boots, she found herself lost in a world of Christmas. She stopped near the railroad tracks and drew in a deep breath of the cold dry air, gazing off into the vast night. At the far end of the horizon, the long and straight tracks narrowed before dropping off into nowhere at the edge of the sky. Frost sparkled on everything everywhere she looked, reflecting the bright light of the moon and the star-studded sky.

When she reached town, Broadway's glistening lights dazzled her. Red plastic bells moaned above the streets, swaying in the cool evening air. Light posts trimmed with pine branches, pinecones, sparkling lights, and huge red ribbons lined the sidewalks. Bells jingled at distant Salvation Army kettles, and Christmas music drifted out of shops along the way. An occasional whiff of freshly cut pine floated on the air.

She couldn't stop smiling.

As Brue entered the five-and-dime, a quick gust of wind slammed the door behind her. She scanned the store searching for the kind clerk with the wrinkled face. There she was. Behind the perfume counter.

"Excuse me, please," Brue said.

When Miss Bickford recognized Brue, her face fell.

Why did she look so unhappy all of a sudden?

"Well, little girl, it's certainly nice to see you again, but I'm afraid you've come too late."

"I have?"

Miss Bickford nodded. "The Cinderella watches. We're all sold out. Didn't your mother tell you?"

"Oh, no. That's not why I'm here."

The wrinkles across Miss Bickford's forehead got deeper and her eyes got big and wide. "It's not?"

"No, ma'am. I'd like to buy a bottle of Evening in Paris perfume, please." Brue smiled proudly. "It's a Christmas present for my mother."

"For heaven's sake. I guess I did have that wrong, didn't I? Well, let's see what we can do for you, then."

Miss Bickford slipped behind the counter and pulled out a small blue bottle of perfume. "Would you like to have this gift wrapped? There's no extra charge."

"Oh, yes, please."

Miss Bickford carefully wrapped the bottle of perfume and rung it up on the cash register. "Aren't you the lucky one? Evening in Paris just happens to be on sale today."

Brue pulled a wad of coins from her mitten and counted out the exact change. After giving the money to the kind clerk, Brue held her hand out flat, happy to see that she still had a few coins left over. Although she knew she was wearing a broad smile on her face, the bounce in her walk felt even more striking as she hugged the package with both hands close to her heart all the way home.

CHAPTER FORTY-SEVEN

L ate the following afternoon, Jo and Brue lifted their first laundry basket onto Brue's little red wagon. Jo had hauled enough baskets to and from the O.M. Harrington by now that she was numb to what anyone might think when they saw her towing the humble transporter. She drew her shoulders up into the nippy afternoon air, and together she and Brue set off.

"Can I pull it, Mom?"

"I don't know. It's awfully heavy."

"Let me try. Please?"

Stepping back for Brue to take the lead, Jo walked alongside the thudding wagon, holding a tight grip on the basket. It wasn't the heavy basket that held her attention; it was the man they were transporting it to that did. Yesterday Big Ole, with nothing more than a few kind words, had lifted an enormous load she feared would never be lifted. Her most threatening problem appeared to be behind her, at least for now. But when she glanced at Brue, who proudly pulled the wagon like a staggering old workhorse, she realized she still had plenty of work to do—find a way to make Brue's Christmas special, get out of debt so she could provide better for Brue, and make peace with Tryg to be a better example for Brue. In that order.

When they reached the curb near the far end of the park, Jo asked Brue to stop. Not only did the sounds of Christmas drift on the air, through the windows of the O.M. Harrington, a crowd gathering around the tree caught her eye.

Brue stood on her toes and pointed toward the great room. "Look, Mom! Everyone's singing the words to 'Deck the Halls,' but Mr. Big Ole's singing the *fa-la-la's* all by himself."

And that he was. He appeared to enjoy the exchange every bit as much as his guests.

"Doesn't he sing good?" Brue asked.

"You mean doesn't he sing well. And you're right. He sure does. I don't know that I've ever heard a deeper or more magnificent baritone."

"Can we go inside, Mom?"

"We'd better not, not with a Christmas party going on. I need to keep a gentle presence. Besides, I wouldn't want to dampen their partying mood with the sight of towels and sheets, even if they are fresh."

Jo left Brue outside with the wagon and quickly slipped around to the far side of the building. The basket she carried no longer weighed her down. And now that the rift with Big Ole had eased, she could easily acknowledge changes underway at the O.M. Harrington, remarkable changes under his management. Not only had he enhanced the appearance of the breakfast and supper tables, she recalled the day the cook retired. Rather than hiring another cook, Big Ole hired a world-class chef who happened to enjoy hunting. On his first day off, the chef went out with a bow and arrow only to have Big Ole add venison to their Christmas menu, compliments of the chef.

With the back door unlocked, Jo slipped in, unloaded the basket, and returned to Brue. They trekked home for their next load. Their first two trips were uneventful. Laughter and music flowing from the great room added warmth and nostalgia to their deliveries.

After placing their third and final basket in the laundry room, however, Jo glanced up the hallway one last time to see if the way was clear for a quiet and final exit.

The way was anything but clear.

Calvin jutted his head around the corner. "So, it's you, Jo. I thought I heard something back there." He waved her forward, extending an out-stretched hand. "Big Ole is hosting our First Annual Christmas Party. Please, come and join us for some holiday cheer."

Jo took a small step back and pulled at the pockets of her haggard woolen coat. "Oh, no, I wouldn't want to intrude. Besides, I'm hardly dressed for it."

"Nonsense. You look lovely as usual, and we'd be delighted to have you."

Although Jo was tempted, she really did need to get back to Brue. Along with her heartfelt regrets, she informed Calvin of the three baskets they'd delivered and the shelves she'd just replenished.

Suddenly, Jonathan swept into view with a perky grin and Doc at his heels. "Mrs. Bremley's here? Oh, my dear Mrs. Bremley."

By the looks on their faces, Jo sensed something might be up ... but what?

Jonathan glanced past Jo toward the laundry room, craning his neck. "How about if we have a private chat out of earshot of Big Ole."

Calvin rolled his eyes and muttered, "Here it comes."

Jonathan caught Jo by her elbow and quickly ushered her back down the hallway, causing her to wonder if he actually would have been embarrassed had she decided to join the party or if he was out to have another good time at her expense. Calvin trailed along, but not without a hard-to-read smirk.

Before Jonathan could say another word, Frank, a new resident at the O.M. Harrington, hustled down the hallway and elbowed his way in. "Say, what's going on here?"

Oh, great. So much for not calling attention to myself.

Feeling an aversion and fearing a scene, Jo pulled back. Stout, tie askew, chewing on a fat cigar, Frank definitely had had too much Christmas cheer. "Hey, Jonathan, you didn't answer me," he grumbled.

"Follow us."

After all this time, the men were finally being friendly toward Jo. Still reeling from her breakthrough with Big Ole, she didn't want to take any chances. From where he stood, he could easily hear everything transpiring down at their end of the hall. Did these men have complaints about her work? Or were they merely playing games with her? No. They couldn't be. That would be cruel.

As they entered the laundry room, Calvin pulled on the light string and the men pressed in around her. Jonathan inhaled a large puff of cherry tobacco from his elegant pipe and said, "Mrs. Bremley, may we call you Jo?"

She felt closed in, outnumbered, and skeptical, to say the least. "Yes, Jo would be fine."

"Good. Jo, it is then."

"Hey, what is this?" Frank eyed the small gathering suspiciously. "Some sort of secret meeting?"

Jo looked past him, through the open door and out toward the hallway, wanting to slip through it and disappear. As if Jonathan could read her thoughts, he exhaled a sizable cloud of smoke, then stepped into the doorway, leaned his back against the doorjamb, and cradled his pipe close to his chest, looking quite pleased with himself.

The gleam in Jonathan's eyes held no cynical undertones. Jo was beginning to like the man. He wasn't playing with her, either. Or was he? No. He was too sincere. A smile cut across her face like a crack splitting across a thin patch of ice.

Jonathan turned to Frank. "Well, if you must know, we're about to put in our requests for ribbon color preferences for our laundry."

Completely caught off guard, Jo gasped. "You're what?"

"Hunter green ribbon was a clever idea," Jonathan said with a widening grin.

"Hunter green?"

"Yes, ma'am. Those suspenders. And that bow tie! We have a further request—"

Frank hadn't said anything, but Jo's insides shriveled as his narrowing eyes, which appeared to have little time for laundry ladies, found their way to her. She then glanced at Calvin, who stepped forward as though he felt he needed to come to her rescue.

"I don't believe you've met Mrs. Bremley, Frank. She handles our laundry now and does a great job of it."

"Help me understand this," Frank said, slowing his slurred speech. "You *gentle*men are crammed in this dark and cold little hole, huddled around a woman who does laundry for a living, and talking about the color of ribbon you want for your own personal laundry during a holiday party? The next thing you know, she'll be lining our collars with satin and our cuffs with lace."

Clean it up, Frank, or I'll sprinkle fresh rose petals on yours, compliments of the laundry lady. Jo suppressed a smile. Frank actually did have an excellent point.

Before any of the men could offer a quick comeback, Jonathan turned to her. "Seriously, we have given a lot of thought to the ribbon."

Unbelievable. "The ribbon?"

"Yes, ma'am. And we would greatly appreciate your color coding the rest of our laundry as well."

She had definitely misread him. He was playing with her. "You can't be serious."

"Oh, but I am. That way we won't have to worry about our clothes getting mixed up."

"But I try to be careful."

"There's no question about your work. Consider this a preventative measure. When the starch lady was here, she got the laundry mixed up all the time."

"The starch lady?"

Calvin stepped forward with a comforting grin. "That would be your predecessor."

"That's right," Jonathan agreed. "We weren't all that unhappy to see her go on maternity leave. Just one of those things, you understand. No harm done, really. Just the same, I'd prefer to have my laundry tied in a nice purple color of some sort. I like purple. It's rather rich looking, don't you think?" He clenched his pipe between his teeth and drew in another deep breath of the sweet-smelling tobacco then grinned playfully as he exhaled it in one long, thin cloud.

Jo was sure she had to be the object of some sort of joke. But when Doc requested charcoal gray, they had gone too far. She looked to Calvin for help. There could not be a man alive who gave a hoot about ribbon color preferences. That was beneath their dignity. If it wasn't, it should be.

Calvin smiled and nodded. "I told you so, remember?"

Just when Jo thought the charade was over and she could get out of there and back to Brue, Frank muscled his way past Jonathan. "This is way too nuts for me," he scoffed then cut a quick and swerving path back down the hallway.

Jonathan, Doc, and Calvin burst into laughter, but not Jo. Calvin appeared to notice her discomfort and looked at her, puzzled.

Jo remembered only too well the last time the men had had a good time at her expense and swore she would never let that happen again. She strutted out the door. Her feet carried her down the long hallway, shadowing Frank. Whatever she did, it needed to be appropriate with Big Ole in view.

"Frank," she said matter-of-factly, "I still have a deep royal blue left."

He turned on her. "Look, lady, I'm not interested."

Jo didn't flinch. She wasn't about to take no for an answer. "But it's rather regal looking."

When he took a step in her direction, the smoke from his cigar and the fumes from his Christmas cheer were enough to sear her nasal passages. She couldn't tell which was stronger. If someone lit a match within five feet of this guy, he would explode like a stick of dynamite.

"Very regal," she insisted. "I think binding your laundry with deep royal blue ribbon suspenders would be very appropriate for you."

The delivery of her words apparently caught him by surprise, and his surly countenance softened before her eyes. When he rubbed his stubby fingers along his bristly chin, Jo knew she had him.

"Regal, you say?"

"Yes, sir."

Calvin slipped past them, his cheeks bunching upward.

"Okay," Frank said and then strutted away like a preening peacock.

Calvin watched Frank saunter toward the punchbowl, and then he turned to Jo with a grin and a wink.

"I'll make certain the laundry is completely color coded the next time I drop it off," she said, giving him a purposeful nod, and then she glanced at Big Ole, who peered over Calvin's shoulder looking pleasantly amused.

Her cheeks growing warm, she dashed out the back door to find Brue waiting at the side of the boarding house.

"Mom, what's wrong?"

"I don't know. I'm not sure what just happened in there."

When they were halfway home, Jo burst into laughter.

"Honestly, those men."

CHAPTER FORTY-EIGHT

Sunlight glaring off the snow caught Jo's eye before she noticed the mailman trudging down the road, sinking into and climbing over high drifts. He struggled with the weight of his heavy bag, straining as he shifted it from shoulder to shoulder. He looked more like an Eskimo than a courier from the United States Post Office. Several minutes later, she heard the mail drop squeak, a thump hit the floor, and a final squeak as it closed.

"I'll get it, Mom," Brue announced as she dashed out to the porch. She shrieked and then darted back into the living room, wildly waving an envelope. "Hey, Mom, look! We got a Christmas card from Mr. Howland."

The iron nearly slipped from Jo's hand. "What? Are you sure?"

"Yup. Look." Brue raised the envelope. "In the top corner it says T.W. 'Tryg'—"

Jo seized the card from her daughter's hand and fanned her face. "Well, for heaven's sakes."

"Aren't you going to open it?" Brue asked impatiently. "Don't you want to see what he has to say?"

"Sure. Before I do, though, how about if we both go into the kitchen and have an oatmeal cookie?"

"But, Mom."

"Look, Brue, I need a little time first, okay?" Jo snapped. "I don't think I'm ready for this yet."

Brue flinched.

"I'm sorry, sweetie. I didn't mean to be short with you. I just need a few minutes."

Jo led the way to the kitchen. She pulled a few oatmeal raisin cookies out of the cookie jar, placed them on a plate, and set them on the table. As she did, her conflicting feelings betrayed her. Why did a card from Tryg have to hurt so good? Why did it have to make her feel closer to Case?

"Here, pumpkin. Have a cookie."

"When are you going to open the card?" Brue tilted her head and pressed her hands to her waist. The child was a textbook case for impatience.

"Okay, I'll open it." Jo sliced the envelope open and nudged out a tight-fitting card, the type of card a business would send.

"What does it say, Mom? What does it say?"

"It says, 'Merry Christmas and a happy 1945 to you and yours from the law offices of T.W. "Tryg" Howland, III, Attorney-at-Law.' And handwritten under the printed words it says, 'Meet me at The Copper Kettle at noon on Saturday, December twenty-third. Tryg.'"

Jo nearly dropped the card.

She thought for a moment. "That's not much notice. The twenty-third is the day after tomorrow."

"When did he send it?" Brue asked.

"I don't know. Let me take a look." Jo flipped the envelope over. "Hmm. It's postmarked December twelfth." She skimmed the address. "No wonder we didn't get it until today. He sent it to 537 Charles Place instead of 537 Charles Street."

"Are you gonna go, Mom?"

Jo looked at Brue thoughtfully before giving her a slow nod. She then turned and stared out the kitchen window, her gaze frozen on the snow-covered lake.

CHAPTER FORTY-NINE

Jo hadn't meant to eavesdrop, but the concerned voices of Calvin and the head elder of Village Church drifted down the hallway and into the laundry room as clearly as if she'd been in the great room with them.

"Really," she heard Calvin say. "I didn't realize it was that serious."

"I hope it doesn't develop into pneumonia," Mr. Johnson said. "Laryngitis set in a few days ago. He can whisper, but that's about it. I don't know who we're going to get to deliver tomorrow night's sermon on such short notice."

Jo stepped up the hallway. "I'm sorry, but I couldn't help overhearing. Is Reverend Collver all right?"

Mr. Johnson gave Jo a troubled glance. "No, I'm afraid he isn't, Mrs. Bremley. He's a very sick man, but we can't get him to go to the doctor. I think he belongs in the hospital, myself."

"What a shame. Is there anything I can do to help?"

Mr. Johnson folded his wool scarf loosely around his throat and slowly buttoned his overcoat. "I sure wish you could. I was just telling Mr. Doherty, here, that we're looking for someone to deliver the sermon tomorrow evening. I'm pretty lousy at that sort of thing, I'm afraid."

An immediate grin cut into Jo's cheeks. "Calvin, you'd be excellent. Absolutely excellent."

Mr. Johnson's face registered surprise. "Mr. Doherty?"

"He used to be a chaplain in the Army," Jo announced, her voice exuding pride.

Mr. Johnson's expression turned hopeful. "Why, I had no idea."

"No, Jo," Calvin snapped. "I'm not available. And even if I were, there's not enough time to prepare a sermon. Definitely not."

Disappointment revealed itself in Mr. Johnson's bewildered face. "If you change your mind, be sure to let me know. We could use your talent as a speaker, Mr. Doherty."

"Like I said, I'm not available," Calvin insisted, a razor-edged sharpness still evident in his tone.

Mr. Johnson drew back. "Well, then. If you'll excuse me, I guess I'd better be on my way." Before leaving, however, he hesitated, his look guarded. "Thank you again for all of your help with the Christmas barrel. That was amazing really. The presents have all been passed out, and I can assure you there are going to be lots of disadvantaged children with very happy faces this Christmas because of your hard work."

"It was my pleasure," Calvin said, his tone slightly softer.

The moment the door closed, Jo didn't hesitate to close in on Calvin. "I didn't mean to put you on the spot. That was accidental. But I have to tell you that I've never seen anyone as filled with life than you were when you coordinated the gift collecting for the Christmas barrel. I envied you. You have amazing talent. I hope you'll rethink giving the sermon."

"Jo, I know you meant well. But like I told the elder, even if I wanted to, I wouldn't have time to prepare. Nothing's changed. I still have no desire whatsoever to return to the ministry."

As she studied Calvin, he swiveled his chair away from her as if he were inviting her to leave. But then he swiveled back again and said earnestly, "I wish I had your faith, but I'm afraid I don't."

"My faith?"

"That's right." Although he leaned back in his chair and clasped his hands behind his head as though he didn't have a care in the world, his eyes looked troubled.

"But you're the one who talked me into giving thanks. You sounded like you believed what you were saying."

"That's not what I'm referring to. How is it that you could lose your husband at such a young age and still hold on to it?"

"What makes you so sure I did?" She took a step toward the laundry room. But then, reflecting on the awful thoughts that had plagued her mind with torment during the past year, she turned back and folded her hands lightly on the registration desk. "Case's death nearly destroyed me and my faith."

Calvin shook his head. "I'm sorry. I didn't mean to pry. That was pretty insensitive of me."

"Don't worry about it. I need to talk about Case. Maybe I should say I want to talk about him, thanks to your counsel."

Calvin gulped. He lowered his arms and rocked forward in his chair. "My counsel? You can't be serious."

"Oh, but I am. I'm talking about the in-everything-give-thanks counsel."

His jaw clenched. "Okay, I'm listening."

"Thanks. It turns out that when push came to shove, I thought I had let both Case and Brue down. During my worst days this past year, and let me tell you I had far more than I care to remember, I didn't think I had even an ounce of faith left. When Case was ripped from our lives the way he was, I felt like God turned His back on me. You have no idea how bitter I felt and how hard I fought it."

"But you still had Brue."

"That's true. I did." Jo looked past Calvin at nothing in particular. "I found out just how fragile life is. I could lose Brue, too, in a heartbeat. Just as easily as I lost Case."

"I'm sorry. I guess I hadn't thought about that."

"I hadn't either. How many of us do?" she asked, recalling how she had relied on Case so completely, as if relying on anyone or anything could possibly make her feel secure. "I learned the hard way just how vulnerable we are. Every last one of us."

Calvin nodded his agreement, but then his face turned hard, tension creasing his forehead. "How have you managed to keep your sanity after losing him?"

"Believe it or not, that's been the easy part."

He rested an elbow on his desk, smoothing his chin with his thumb and forefinger, his gaze probing. "You don't really believe yourself, do you?"

"Actually, I do. Regarding what you said about giving thanks, I hadn't realized it, but when it came to Case, that's what I've been doing all along. I've been keeping my focus on how fortunate I was to have him for eight incredible years, and I'll spend the rest of my life cherishing those days. If I don't, I'm going to grow into a bitter old woman, and I don't want to do that to God, to Case's memory, to Brue, or to myself."

Jo thought about Calvin and how he'd given bitterness a foothold in his life, remembering at the same time her struggle with Tryg these past months and how she'd batted it away at every turn. Where had it gotten either of them?

"I guess maybe knowing that I'll see Case again one day after this short life is over has also given me peace."

"I envy you," Calvin said, his tone drained of life.

"Why? You have faith, too. You've just turned your back on it."

A startled look flashed in Calvin's eyes, the sort of look that comes from having nurtured hurtful feelings for a mighty long time only to have them rooted up and challenged.

With Jo's friends-sharpening-friends-the-way-iron-sharpens-iron approach to life, she worried she might have been too blunt. Before she could voice a few words to soften the aftermath of their encounter, the front door swung open and a guest walked in. Maybe that was for the best. She retreated to the laundry room. At least there she wouldn't get in any deeper.

CHAPTER FIFTY

J o stepped around the corner of the O.M. Harrington to find Calvin sitting on the top step of the porch. With his shoulder resting against the balustrade, he lifted two mugs of tea high into the crisp winter air. Steam swirled above them.

"I've been waiting for you," he announced. "Thought you might like something hot to warm your insides before you head on home. This way we can also continue our little chat."

Jo instinctively glanced at her wrist, to the watch that wasn't there.

"I won't keep you long," Calvin insisted, taking note of her glance and smiling. "Just long enough for a quick afternoon break." Setting his cup on the porch behind him, he patted the top step with the flat of his hand. "Come, sit down."

"But I need to—"

"Come."

Jo dutifully pulled the wagon to the edge of the sidewalk and lowered its handle to the snow-covered ground. She climbed the steps and positioned her small form on the hard and cold top step. "It sure is nippy out here."

Calvin winked. "I know. Hence the tea."

Peeling off her gloves one finger at a time, she placed them on her lap and then folded her hands around the warm mug, holding it close, drawing in its heat. As she blew at it gently, the steam twining upward brought warmth to her cheeks as well.

"So, you want to have a chat?" she said with a wry smile. "I thought we had that a short while ago."

"We did. Seems you unwittingly nudged open a hornet's nest. Now, I wouldn't mind some help forcing those ornery little critters back in."

"Did I offend you, Calvin?"

"Your words smarted a little."

"I didn't mean for that to happen." She took a small sip of tea and said, "I'm curious, though. When did your hurting begin?"

Calvin looked as if he was about to choke. "When did my *hurting* begin?" he blurted. "My! You certainly don't waste any time asking the probing questions, do you?"

"I didn't mean—"

"It's okay. The answer is easy, actually. It's a long story, but cutting to the chase, I was rejected at the altar the week before I headed off to our First World War. In front of a packed church, I might add."

So that was it. Rejection.

"My lovely and kind bride-to-be refused to stop there," he chuckled guardedly. "Rainy—"

"Rainy?"

He nodded. "Lorraine."

"That's a name you don't hear often," Jo said thoughtfully.

"I know."

"You were saying?"

"I was about to say that she managed to marry my best friend while I was dodging bullets on the battlefield." Hurt and disillusionment were still evident in his eyes after all of those years. He looked away, his words spitting out soft, yet strong. "Here, I was crawling around in that god-forsaken hellhole trying to help the wounded."

Dumbfounded by the visual, Jo groaned.

"Some best friend," he continued. "That certainly sucked the life out of me. I gave it a lot of thought and decided I needed a faith that made sense and a God I felt I could trust. I'm not there yet. Don't know that I ever will be." He paused, staring down at a patch of ice on the sidewalk. "When your leg gets chopped off at the knee and the wound has had a chance to heal, I've found that the limp has a tendency to stay with you for the rest of your life."

Jo identified with his pain, but what was it with men? How could Calvin so effortlessly sort out and address the pain of others and yet bury his own, allowing it to eat away at him for years on end? Why would anyone tie their emotions to the very people they refused to forgive? Jo didn't believe in that kind of bondage and was disappointed to see that Calvin did—but then visions of Tryg came to mind and she grimaced.

Calvin held his mug loosely, cupping it with both hands. Leaning forward, he rested his forearms casually on his thighs. He appeared to be intrigued by the movements of a gray squirrel scampering in and out of a cavity in a large elm near the park's edge.

"What's captured your attention?" Jo asked. "That squirrel?"

Calvin nodded.

"It's so agile," she said thoughtfully.

"And free."

And free. What would it take for Calvin to break free? As Jo watched the nimble movements of the squirrel, she wondered how different Calvin's life might have been if his fiancée had been honest with him those many years ago. What if she told him that his best friend awakened passionate feelings in her even though she hadn't acted on them? Or what if his fiancée told him those passionate feelings confused and frightened her, making her feel as though she were cheating on him? What if she'd had the presence of mind to tell him she was walking away from his best friend, too, because it was the right thing to do? Would that have made a difference? Jo observed Calvin for a moment. It might have made all the difference in the world.

"By the way, you did a masterful job of handling Frank the other day," Calvin said, undoubtedly in a purposeful attempt to lighten their exchange. "He's not what I would call a particularly smooth or caring individual."

Jo grinned at the memory and the irksome feeling of having been toyed with. "Those men really did give me a hard time, didn't they? You have no idea how awkward I felt."

"I can only imagine. Crazy thing is they were sincere."

"I know, but I didn't figure that out until Brue and I were halfway home." Jo reached out and touched Calvin's arm lightly, just enough to draw his attention. "I didn't mean to offend you or to open up a hornet's nest."

"I know you didn't."

"The rejection wasn't God's fault, Calvin."

He cleared his throat and said with a heavy hint of sarcasm, "He could have stopped it, but He didn't."

Jo shook her head. "Maybe you just weren't paying attention."

"What are you getting at?"

"Can I ask you a question?"

"Of course. If I don't like it, I don't need to answer."

That was fair enough.

"Before the wedding, were there any signs at all that something wasn't right?"

"A few, sure, but nothing out of the ordinary." He raised a brow. "Everyone has misgivings."

"What did you do about your misgivings? Did you discuss any of them with your bride-to-be?"

Calvin's eyes widened. "Why on earth would I do that?"

Surprised by his response, Jo chuckled before turning serious. "That wasn't the right answer. Let me ask you a tougher question. I don't want you to answer me. It's none of my concern. But think about it, okay?"

"I'm listening."

"Did you feel in your heart that the marriage was right for both of you? Did you feel you were really *home* when you were with your bride-to-be?"

Surprise flickered in Calvin's vulnerable and transparent eyes, but he maintained his silence.

Suddenly, the gray squirrel bolted out of a hole in the trunk of the tree. It looked startled by the way its tail rode high in the air.

Not meaning to corner Calvin, Jo purposely deflected the conversation to give him a much-needed opportunity to regroup.

"You know, I had a cat once," she said, her eyes still fastened on the scampering little creature. "Made me wonder how much animals can feel."

"Why's that?"

"Cat's name was Rodie. That was short for rodent. When she was a kitten, she used to sit back on her haunches like that gray squirrel. When Rodie was sixteen, she got deathly sick. I took her to the vet. He said there was nothing he could do for her so I brought her back home. A few days later I was sitting in my mom's rocking chair with Rodie on my lap. I felt so bad for her the tears literally streamed down my face. When that cat peered up at me, I swear it looked like she was studying me. She had these innocent, caring eyes and with her little paw she patted my cheek. You would have thought she was trying to comfort me. Maybe she was."

"That actually happened?"

"Yes. It really did."

Jo drew the collar of her woolen coat tightly to her neck, and, while nudging her gloves back on, she said, "You know, Calvin, your fiancée and your best friend couldn't have handled things in a worse way, but it's just a shame you never stepped forward, either. Maybe things could have been different."

Calvin looked astonished, as though it hadn't dawned on him that he, himself, had the ability to participate in salvaging relationships he had with people he cared about.

Jo stood and gazed across the park. "The squirrel disappeared. You didn't happen to see where it went, did you?"

"No," Calvin said. "And I didn't see where the hornets went, either."

"Must have gone back to their nest." She looked at him with a coy smile. "Guess I'd better be getting back to my nest, too."

She made her way toward the wagon. Lifting its handle, she looked back. "I feel badly that you've suffered so much. I honestly didn't mean to be insensitive or glib, but it's not too late to move on with your life."

Calvin sat on the porch step, appearing to be reflecting on their conversation. And as she walked away with Brue's little red wagon in tow, Jo could have sworn she heard him mumble, "Ye shall know the truth, and the truth shall make you free."

But would he ever allow himself to be free?

Big Ole peered around the door of the coffee room. "You look a little ragged around the edges this morning. What's the matter, Calvin? Sleep escape you?"

Calvin reflected for a moment on yesterday afternoon's meaningful exchange with Jo. "Actually, I don't know when I've slept better."

"Good. Then come join me for a cup of coffee so I won't have to haul it all the way over to you."

Was it Calvin's imagination, or was Big Ole continuing to change right before his eyes?

CHAPTER FIFTY-ONE

I walked a mile with Pleasure,

She chattered all the way;

But left me none the wiser

For all she had to say.

I walked a mile with Sorrow,

And ne'er a word said she;

But oh, the things I learned from her

When Sorrow walked with me.

—*Robert Browning Hamilton*

After removing the letter from the Havana cigar box, Jo pushed the container to the side of the kitchen table, nudged the letter out of the envelope, and carefully smoothed out its creases. If she was going to face the past today with Trygve Howland, she might as well face all of her past, including the contents of the letter she had received over one year ago from Haskins & Sells.

She read the message slowly, savoring every word.

My dear Mrs. Bremley,

We couldn't have been more saddened when we received the shocking news in your telegram dated yesterday, 10 November 1943. Our initial interview with your husband had gone far better than we could have hoped. I can't tell you how excited we were when we learned Mr. Bremley would be joining Haskins & Sells. Our partners and I believed he would have represented our firm with a degree of professionalism that is rare in today's business world.

We would like to express our deepest condolences to you and your young daughter. Please know that your loss is our loss as well.

Should you be seeking employment in the not-too-distant future, do feel free to contact us. We have a clerical opening in our Chicago office that you may find to be of interest.

Again, our very sincerest condolences.

Yours truly,

Jo inhaled a room full of air then slowly let it out. She tucked the letter back into the envelope, slipped it into the cigar box, and snapped the lid closed.

To think Haskins & Sells had been as excited about Case as he was about them. Reading the letter, she was torn between gratitude and grief, but she knew Case would have been thrilled. How kind of them to offer her a job in Chicago, but a year ago she wouldn't have been ready. Her grief was too raw and consuming back then.

When the clock chimed half past eleven, she quickly approached the doorway of Brue's bedroom. "Have you finished changing your clothes yet?"

"I'm hurrying," Brue said.

"Do you need help? I don't want to be late for my dinner with Mr. Howland."

Jo gathered their coats, scarves, mittens, gloves, and overshoes from the living room closet. After shunning her for so long, why would Tryg invite her out for dinner now? Why would he want to meet in such a public place? And why of all of the days of the year would he want to get together on December twenty-third? Christmas weekend?

Jo walked Brue to the Tomlinsons' and then hurried on to town, arriving at The Copper Kettle a minute before noon. She stopped at the entrance and peered through the window and then up and down the deserted sidewalk. Tryg was nowhere to be seen.

Apprehensive and not in the mood to be the center of attention, she stepped inside and asked to be seated at a table at the far corner of the room. She draped her coat over the back of her chair and settled in. Contrary to the inactivity out on the street, the restaurant bustled for a lazy Saturday afternoon—the floor shaking with the stomp of heavy feet, knives scraping noisily against porcelain plates, cigarette smoke billowing toward the ceiling like a dense fog.

The oversized clock hanging high on the wall ticked away the minutes in slow motion—twelve o'clock, two minutes past twelve, five minutes past. When she looked again at precisely nine minutes after the hour, a sinking thought struck her. Tryg wouldn't stand her up, would he?

Ten minutes past twelve.

No Tryg.

"Sorry to make you wait so long. Would you care for a cup of hot chocolate?" a familiar voice asked.

Jo glanced up. "Oh, it's you, Alice."

"Yes, it is. And I promise to slow down and not spill it again," she said with a guilt-ridden smile.

"Actually, I think I might be more inclined to have coffee this time. Is it real or is it the toasted barley substitute?"

"It's real coffee, but we brew it on the weak side to make sure it stretches farther, if you know what I mean."

"We all do the same thing." Jo thought for a moment. "All right, I'll have some, then. Black, please."

After Alice poured the coffee and disappeared behind the counter, Jo took a slow sip. If Tryg didn't arrive by the time she finished drinking it, she would leave. Her apprehension lessened at the thought of getting out of there without having to see him.

At fifteen minutes past twelve, Jo jumped when the door swung open. A young woman with coal-black hair and lips the color of maraschino cherries stepped inside. She quickly scanned the restaurant as if looking for someone and then slipped out faster than she came in.

The minutes continued ticking by slowly and as they ticked, Jo's relief waned. Tryg was standing her up.

Nine years ago, with no small amount of effort, Jo had been successful in reducing his shocking outburst at her wedding into nothing more than an unpleasant memory, but now as she waited, the memory was taking on a life of its own. She could still hear his voice, as clearly as if it had been yesterday. The moment Reverend Collver said, "If anyone has just cause as to why this young man and woman should not be united in holy matrimony, speak now or forever hold your peace," Tryg didn't simply stand; he leaped up and blurted, "I do."

Jo could still feel a sickening crawling in her skin. Gasps rippled across the small chapel as she stood at the altar, unable to move. While Reverend Collver whisked Case and Tryg into the back room for what he called a quick little chat, she swallowed hard against a painful lump in her throat. Her mother had always told her that people who made people cry weren't worth crying over, so Jo used all the force she could muster to hold back her tears. She refused to let Trygve Howland ruin her wedding day.

But a bride can stand at an altar by herself for only so long. Just as Jo was about to lose her composure, her mother stepped forward and asked Jo to come sit with her. Her mother held Jo's veil as they inched backward.

Jo no more than lowered her thin frame onto the hard wooden pew when thoughtless whispering broke through the steely quiet. "Look at the poor little thing," someone said. "She doesn't know what to do with herself." Another barely audible voice murmured, "It must be awfully serious for that young man to object the way he did."

What had Tryg done? Why did he wait until their wedding day to take a stand? And why did he need to be so blasted public about it? *We're the ones who are supposed to be saying 'I do' today, not Tryg.* Shattered by betrayal, she couldn't help but wonder. *How could he do this to Case and me?*

Her mother seized Jo's hands. "It's going to be okay, sweetie. The way Case and you look at each other, everyone knows you're meant to be together." A moment later, the back door squeaked open and Reverend Collver, then Case, then Tryg stepped out from the shadows of the darkened room.

As suddenly as the memory of the wedding nightmare flooded her thoughts, Jo's thoughts were back in the restaurant. She took another slow sip of coffee. This wasn't the time to be reliving old memories. Tryg might walk through the door any moment now. She glanced at the clock. Twenty-five minutes after the hour. She needed to keep her emotions in check. But that hadn't been the end of the nightmare, and the long wait weakened her resolve.

While on their honeymoon, Case had mentioned that he understood why Jo found Tryg's outburst to be somewhat humiliating. *Somewhat humiliating?* Not only that, kindhearted Case insisted Tryg's public proclamation had nothing whatsoever to do with her. Tryg had merely feared that getting married too young might sabotage Case's chances for success. Case insisted he would have ended their friendship immediately had he sensed Tryg's motives were anything but honorable.

To this day, Tryg had never apologized and Reverend Collver had never attempted to make matters better, either. Jo could still hear the minister standing at the altar saying, "We've cleared up the confusion, folks, now let's proceed." What were folks supposed to think? And when Jo and Case stood in their receiving line, Jo could have counted on one hand the number of people who had the presence of mind to look her in the eye. Even then all she could see was pity. Months after the wedding, she could still feel their stares as though they needed assurance that something wasn't actually wrong with her.

Now Jo was back to square one, back to waiting for the door to open and Tryg to enter, just like she waited for the door to the back room of the chapel to swing open on her wedding day.

She glanced at the clock. Twenty-nine minutes before the hour of one. She hailed down Alice and apologized for leaving, explaining that the person she was going to meet hadn't shown up, and then she went to the cash register to pay for her coffee.

Jo stepped out into the cold, dry air, and headed back to the one place where she knew she could find relief—the place called home.

CHAPTER FIFTY-TWO

History repeats itself. Jo knew that. How could she have been so naïve? She pulled her coat snugly to her throat and butted headlong into the bitter wind.

Why hadn't she thought to send Tryg her regrets? He'd sent an invitation, for heaven's sakes, not a summons. If she'd declined, though, she wouldn't have known he would stand her up. Worse, she might have given him credit he didn't deserve. It was good to give people a second chance, she mused, holding her head high. That took courage, character, and generosity. Didn't it? But then, again, she hadn't been wise about knowing who deserved a second chance.

Rounding the corner onto Broadway, she heard something—a shout from behind.

She hesitated. It couldn't be.

The shout came again. "Jo!"

She looked back and saw Tryg rushing toward her with fast limping strides.

"I'm so sorry," he said as he approached her.

She took a half step back. Why did he have to look so disarmingly vulnerable and sincere? Whatever happened to the tough, velvet-gloved, steel-fisted Tryg?

"I just came from a meeting," he said, his voice breaking through breathless gasps for air. "A potential client approached me on my way out. I'm still building my practice so I needed to bide my time."

"I thought maybe you'd changed your mind."

He shook his head. "Oh, no, not at all. About an hour ago, when my stenographer walked past, I asked her if she'd mind stopping by to let you know I'd be a little late. She said she'd be happy to. Didn't she tell you?"

"No. I saw a young woman poke her head in the door and then leave, but no one else."

"Oh, no," Tryg said, appearing distressed over the confusion. "She must have assumed you'd be elderly. I'm sorry. I told her you were a widow."

Jo's insides crawled at the mention of the word *widow*, especially with it coming from him.

"I'm afraid I just neglected to tell her how young you are," he continued. "Look, if it's not too late, would you mind coming back to The Copper Kettle with me? I'm hungry and sure could use a bite to eat."

Alice seated them at the table Jo had just vacated. "I see you're back," she said with a hint of a smile.

Jo nodded.

Alice handed them menus and asked, "Coffee? Water?"

"I'm fine," Jo said.

Alice looked at Tryg.

"Uh, yes. Water, please."

Jo and Tryg held their menus high, their oversized bills of fare providing a convenient barrier during their first few awkward moments together.

Alice reappeared. After placing two glasses of water on the table, she plucked a pencil from behind her ear and held her order pad ready to write. "I assume the usual, Mr. Howland?"

"Yes. Soup and coleslaw will be fine."

The waitress turned to Jo. "And you, ma'am?"

"What kind of soup are you serving today?"

"Vegetable beef."

"Sounds wonderful. I'll have the same, please. Thank you."

As Alice walked away, Tryg rested his elbows lightly on the table and steepled his fingers. His gaze darted around the restaurant for another awkward moment. "Are you doing okay?"

"I'm fine."

"How about Brue?"

"She's fine, too."

Jo crossed her legs under the table. When her foot accidentally bumped Tryg's shin, she flinched. "I'm sorry. I can be a bit clumsy at times."

"Don't worry about it," he said, his tone sympathetic.

Her discomfort escalated with every slow second that ticked past. Dinner was just beginning and already she ached to scoot out the door. To be home. To be free from strife.

Tryg eyed the frost at the base of the windowpanes. "I assume you have your Christmas shopping done."

"Yes, and you?"

He laughed lightly. "I'm sorry. That wasn't a very bright thing to say. Of course you've finished shopping. It's Saturday. With the war raging on, the stores are all closed today and tomorrow is Christmas Eve."

Jo shook her head. This conversation was going nowhere. "That's all right."

Someone fed some change into the jukebox and in the background it blared, "Have Yourself a Merry Little Christmas." Jo welcomed the light distraction.

"That Judy Garland sure has a swell voice," Tryg said.

"Yes, she certainly does."

More uncomfortable quiet.

Alice plunked their coleslaw, forks, knives, and napkins on the table. "Your hot rolls and butter will be right up."

Jo played with her coleslaw, eating it with small bites. She tried to concentrate on the music flowing from the jukebox, but couldn't. Why hadn't she given this conversation advance thought? On second thought, this get-together was Tryg's idea. Let him take the lead.

After what seemed like forever, Tryg slid his coleslaw aside and placed his fork on his plate as if it were a fragile egg that might break. He leveled his attention on Jo. "Look, I had no intension of putting us both on edge," he said, leaning forward in his chair. "Let me get right to the point. I invited you to dinner for a reason."

Jo placed her fork delicately to the side of her plate. "Which is?"

"First, I want to apologize. I've been holding back, giving you a chilly shoulder every time I see you. Believe me, that hasn't been intentional or very gentlemanly of me."

Jo pivoted a quarter of a turn and swung her leg anxiously back and forth. "Don't worry about it. I'm a big girl. I can handle it."

"No," Tryg said, shaking his head. "That wasn't right. I just needed time. Time to think. Time to sort things out. Time to decide what to do."

Jo searched his face. His words sounded sincere, maybe too sincere. His expression was unreadable.

Tryg sat back and smoothed his napkin on his lap. "It's been over a year now since the accident. I live about half a mile from the office just north of Main." He indicated the direction with a nod of his head. "And I walk wherever I go. Haven't driven since."

Your point?

"Tryg, you don't have to do this."

The music stopped. Feeling suddenly exposed without the comforting sound in the background, Jo glanced around the room.

"Oh, but I do. I was the one behind the wheel."

Jo's eyes darted toward the floor, their movement swift and abrupt.

"What's the matter?" he asked.

Her jaw tightened involuntarily, her words spilling out cold and accusing. "Why were you driving? You were on crutches and you, of all people, knew that Case's car had a stiff clutch."

"Oh, that," he said nonchalantly.

Jo's eyebrows snapped together. She stared at him. His words had fallen off his lips as though they didn't matter. How could anyone be that cavalier? "Oh, that?" she repeated sharply.

Tryg reached into the inside pocket of his overcoat, pulled out a small box wrapped in satiny white paper with a thin silver ribbon, and handed it to her. "This is why I was driving. I'd forgotten all about it. When I went back to Case's car to collect my things, I found your gift in the backseat. Must have flown there on impact."

"But what does this have to do with your driving?"

"Case asked me to drive."

That couldn't be. Case knew better. Tryg's leg was still on the mend. "What? But why?"

"Because of that," Tryg said, looking at the small box. "I can't tell you how excited he was. He wanted me to see it. He thought if I drove, he might be able to carefully unwrap it so you wouldn't be able to tell he'd opened it."

Tryg stopped talking for a moment. Was he trying to collect his thoughts? "If you want, you can open your present now," he said finally.

She shook her head. Her insides fluttered from her stomach to her throat. Case's last gift for her. She slipped the small box inside her purse, keeping her hands below the table so Tryg wouldn't see her trembling fingers. "No. I think I'll put it under the tree and open it up tomorrow night. After all, it'll be Christmas Eve."

"Do whatever you want." He drew in a breath and slowly released it. "Back to my driving. To be honest, I was anxious to get behind the wheel again. My hip was still giving me a few problems. But my leg"— he picked up his glass and took a slow sip of water as if to buy time before going on—"my leg hadn't been bothering me as much, so I was sure it wouldn't be a problem. I was the one who wanted to drive faster. After all of those long hours on the train, I just needed to get home. I knew Case wanted to get home as bad as I did. The blizzard was getting worse and the drifts were getting higher the longer and farther south we drove."

Tryg stopped talking long enough for Alice to replace the coleslaw dishes with hot bowls of soup and walk away.

He looked down at the table. "Maybe we should finish eating before we go on. While we can still eat, that is."

From the quiet at the nearby tables, Jo sensed the locals were listening in on their conversation. Too many soft voices and stolen looks.

Jo and Tryg ate their soup and rolls halfheartedly, awkwardness hanging over them like a dam about to burst.

A short while later, Alice removed the half-emptied dishes from their table. "Would you care for coffee?"

"Yes," they said, too quickly and too in unison.

Again, the quiet voices and stares.

Alice reappeared with porcelain mugs and plunked them onto the table.

"Black? Cream? Sugar?" she asked while pouring.

"Black is fine, thank you," Jo said.

Tryg nodded his agreement, and again Alice walked away. Lightly stroking the stem of his mug, he hesitated as if waiting to regain Jo's undivided attention. "Case and I could barely see. We were afraid the roads would close if we didn't hurry."

We?

Tryg continued as if no time had elapsed since he began his oration. Jo was amazed at his honesty, the careful thought he'd given to his words. But that in no way hindered her resentment. She was not about to let her guard down.

"We'd been traveling for maybe an hour or so. I didn't see the deer until it was too late. I don't think Case saw it either."

Tryg appeared oblivious to the eavesdroppers, but Jo wasn't. She gave the surrounding tables a discreet glance. *Please keep your voice down, Tryg.*

She didn't know how to read him. She saw something in his eyes, but what?

He stopped speaking for a moment and squeezed his eyes closed. "When I slammed on the brakes, a horrific pain shot down my leg. My foot missed the clutch." He paused, his gaze finding the floor. "I lost control," he said more as a question.

He half-owned his recklessness at least, but what was behind his pained expression? Grief for Case? Or for the pain in his own leg? Overcome with guilt for challenging his motives, the questions dogged Jo just the same.

"The next thing I knew, we hit the ditch. Hard. I was in a daze when I looked up and saw how deep it was. Then I looked around. The deer was nowhere in sight. It couldn't have suffered a scratch. But Case—" Tryg's voice cracked. "No matter how you look at it, it was my fault. I was the one behind the wheel—and neither of us had automobile insurance."

Jo froze, horror-stricken by the words that slipped from his lips. Case had been killed and Tryg was worried about automobile insurance? *How could he?*

"I didn't need it while I was overseas," he said, oblivious to Jo's outrage. "I can't believe I didn't give the insurance a thought when Case asked me if I wanted to drive. For someone who passed the bar, what was I thinking?"

Tryg must have realized how loud his voice had become. He scanned the restaurant then looked again at Jo. Finally seeing the anger she had difficulty containing, he winced.

Jo sagged in her chair. "Case died and you're still worried about car insurance?"

"Look, I take total responsibility for Case's death, Jo, but I can't undo it. I'll never get over it. Never."

Jo's angry heart banged inside her chest. What about *her* inability to get over it?

"But just so you'll know," he continued, "I'm planning to take full responsibility for your future as well as Brue's. I know I can never make it up to you—"

He definitely had that right.

Jo rearranged her napkin on her lap. Had Tryg actually asked her to join him for dinner so he could absolve himself of guilt? Was that his motivation? How could he do that to her? This was no time for her to lose her composure. Not in a restaurant. Not anywhere.

"I've been completely focused on establishing my law practice," he said. "Earning a steady income. That's what this dinner invitation was all about. I took your future away from you. Now I need to give at least a part of it back."

Jo's breathing turned shallow. She looked away. Whatever happened to "I'm sorry for what I've done?" She wasn't about to let Tryg get to her. And she sure wasn't going to let him absolve himself of guilt. Not at her expense. She suffered the loss of her husband because of him. Catching herself, she stiffened and anchored her gaze directly on his. "You can't give it back. Not any of it. Not ever."

Tryg leaned forward. "You mean you won't let me."

How dare he!

"That's right," she said, her tone abrupt. She reached for her coat. "Thank you for dinner. Now, if you'll excuse me, I believe it's time for me to leave."

CHAPTER FIFTY-THREE

C alvin stepped around the corner. The moment Village Church came into view, he hesitated.

Jo Bremley, what have you done to me?

He walked on, approaching the small white wooden structure with slow, measured steps. The church sat alone on a low hill overlooking Amber Leaf Lake. Candlelight flickered through three tall and narrow stained-glass windows. Its bells tolled from the steeple atop its A-framed roof reminding the nearby community this was Christmas Eve.

Drawn to a lighted nativity scene nestled on a mound of hay near the front of the church, Calvin stepped up to the display and lingered. He wasn't quite ready to go in yet.

He tugged at his gloves then pulled open the front door. Its old hinges groaned. He entered the rear of the sanctuary smelling strongly of pine needles, old wood, and candle wax. "Hark! The Herald Angels Sing," resonated throughout the church as the organist pumped wildly at the foot pedals. Her shoulders swayed back and forth, her elbows and wrists lifting and dropping dramatically to the keyboard. She was staring out across the empty pews, but when she caught sight of Calvin, the organ fell silent.

"No need to stop on my account," he said, removing his fedora and fingering the edges of its rim.

"I need to stop anyway. Need to find more sheet music. I'm Mrs. Miller, by the way. And you are?"

"Calvin Doherty."

"Nice to meet you, Mr. Doherty. The church should be filling up pretty well in about another half hour or so."

He strode up the narrow center aisle, the hardwood floor creaking beneath his feet. Candlelit sconces illuminated its walls, a tall candelabra glowed beside the pulpit, and a Christmas tree glimmered in a gated square immediately opposite the organist. Charming as it was, he wished instead he could be settling in near the flickering fire at the O.M. Harrington.

Mrs. Miller glanced around the sanctuary. "Reverend Collver appears to be late, but—"

"He won't be with us tonight," Mr. Johnson said as he emerged from the back room. "I'm afraid he's under the weather with a horrific cold and an even worse case of laryngitis."

Calvin walked dutifully toward the elder with his hand extended. "Mr. Johnson."

"Nice to see you again, Mr. Doherty." Mr. Johnson's apprehension dampened his tone. Still smarting from their last meeting, no doubt. "And thank you, by the way, for agreeing to fill in on such short notice."

The church door swung open. Calvin glanced back. His stomach tightened when he saw a small number of parishioners shuffling toward the wooden pews.

"I'll introduce you immediately after the children say their pieces," Mr. Johnson continued. "Please, have a seat in the front row."

Calvin opened and closed and then reopened his Bible, pulled out his sermon notes, glanced at them, then fidgeted with the edges of the papers, unable to relax. The hard pew only added to his discomfort. His hardened heart had softened considerably after his conversation with

Jo, but hard feelings don't go away overnight. They beg for time to be worked through—time Calvin still needed.

Mrs. Miller resumed playing the organ and, as she predicted, within half an hour the church overflowed with quiet whispers, muffled coughing, and expectant worshipers. Would it ever be possible for Calvin to get past his conflicted feelings when he stepped inside a church? What irony that he would be the one delivering this evening's sermon.

Mr. Johnson stepped up to the lectern and said, "Ladies and gentlemen, we've listened to Mrs. Miller playing 'Oh, Come, All Ye Faithful' these past few minutes. Let's all join in by standing and singing the first, second, and last verses together. You'll find the words in your hymnals on page one hundred and forty-three."

As the congregation rose and burst into song, Mrs. Miller's fingers waltzed up and down the organ's keys as she vigorously pumped its foot pedals. She obviously enjoyed her own performance, which struck a chord in Calvin. An unexpected smile pierced his tightened cheeks.

After the first verse, Mr. Johnson held up a steady hand to quiet the congregation. "Let's go on and sing the second verse, but this time a cappella."

When the organ fell silent and the voices of the congregation rang out, a deep and distinct baritone boomed from the rear of the church. Calvin recognized Big Ole's voice immediately. He stole a glance at the big man standing in the back row. With the hymnal held high in his left hand, and leaning on his walking stick with his right, Big Ole bore a striking resemblance to Winston Churchill—a taller version, however. And Calvin's tension continued to abate.

After the congregation was seated, the Sunday school superintendent, Mrs. Hansen, asked the children to step up to the platform and share what Christmas meant to them. Most of the children said only a few words. When little Johnny Duncan stepped forward, he looked over the audience, but no words would come out. He rocked back and forth on the heels of his shoes, lifted his small shoulders, and mashed his little hands deep into his pockets. Mrs. Hansen whispered something in his ear, but he still had only wide eyes and no sound. After a long pause and with gut-wrenching innocence, he confessed, "I forgot the words." Heavy sighs rippled through the pews as the small boy's honesty melted more of the frost in Calvin's chilly heart.

A familiar sense of family took Calvin by surprise when Brue stepped forward. She recited her piece with a gentle and confident modesty. To her, Christmas meant loving those who didn't know how to love back and giving without expecting to get anything in return. Calvin reflected on the Christmas barrel and the joy that flooded his heart when it filled to overflowing. That was the best he'd felt in a very long time.

Calvin nodded his approval at Brue and she smiled.

After several more recitations, Mr. Johnson announced, "I regret to inform you that Reverend Collver is quite under the weather this evening. These past few days he's kept me apprised of his condition, but I'm sorry to say that it hasn't improved. If anything, I'm afraid it's gotten worse, and he didn't want to infect any of you. In Reverend Collver's absence, I am most pleased to introduce Mr. Calvin Doherty who has graciously agreed to step in for him. Mr. Doherty served as a chaplain both during World War I and in the European Theatre. He returned to the States earlier this year. Do help me welcome Mr. Calvin Doherty."

As Calvin approached the lectern and turned to face the congregation, a feeling of coming home, being home, overwhelmed him. But knowing what he wanted to say and having nothing to prove, he ignored it. Reverend Collver had made a point of letting him know he wanted to retire soon and would be looking for an ideal replacement. That wouldn't be Calvin. He was amenable to re-entering the faith, but he wasn't about to go that far. After he fulfilled his obligation this evening, Calvin would make sure to take proper measures so he would never again get trapped into speaking.

"When Reverend Collver phoned me this morning and asked if I'd deliver this evening's sermon," Calvin began, "I respectfully declined.

You see, I haven't prepared a sermon in quite some time. But I'm afraid Reverend Collver isn't one to accept no."

A few nervous snickers broke out, obviously from those who'd gotten a good dose of Reverend Collver's power of persuasion as well. Calvin confidently acknowledged them by pausing and waiting for them to subside.

"He told me that when he learned that I'd been a chaplain in the European Theatre, it reminded him of the story of the Four Chaplains, and he asked that I honor their heroism by recounting their story."

What Calvin didn't tell the congregation was that Reverend Collver had humbled—no, humiliated—him into speaking by asking that he set aside his personal struggles with faith and pay tribute to those brave men.

"You see," he continued, "they recognized and heeded their calling, even at the ultimate personal sacrifice, the way Jesus was born to do. And that, folks, is the reason I am honored to be here."

Calvin sensed the congregation was captivated. They grew quieter, increasingly attentive. He needed to stay focused.

"For those of you unfamiliar with the story of the Four Chaplains, it began in early November of 1942 when four young men met at the Chaplain School at Harvard University—a Catholic priest, a Dutch Reformed minister, a Jewish rabbi, and a Methodist minister were brought together by a desire to serve their country during this dreadful war. You might say they were brought together to help heal wounded souls. Although they were separated by faith, it's been said that they felt like brothers united by the same Father.

"One night, just under two years ago, the *U.S.A.T. Dorchester* was journeying across the frigid North Atlantic with nine hundred and two passengers on board when it approached the infamous area called Torpedo Junction. As many of you know, this is an area of the ocean where allied ships are vulnerable to German submarines. Most of the soldiers aboard the aging transport were frightened and many suffered from seasickness. They were packed below deck in close quarters, fretting about what lay in store for them on the fast-approaching foreign shores. The Four Chaplains put their own fears aside to minister to the needs of the many miserable and frightened soldiers.

"Suddenly, minutes past midnight, a German U-boat broke through the surface of the stormy seas. It fired at the *Dorchester* and hit it dead on. A second torpedo found the ship's hull, knocked out the power, and killed at least a hundred men. Men were tossed from their cots. With flaring, smoke-filled nostrils, they groped frantically as frigid water gushed through its blackened chambers. The ship started sinking rapidly, and in that 'living hell,' the Four Chaplains stepped forward to calm the chaos. They guided many of the soldiers to the ship's slippery deck. Some of the lifeboats floated away and others capsized when the panicked soldiers tried to board them. The chaplains' organized efforts reduced the panic and saved many lives that would have otherwise been lost."

For a moment, a deafening silence distracted Calvin. No one moved. No one coughed. Everyone remained completely quiet. All eyes were riveted on him. Even the candles stilled into steady plumes of flame.

This isn't supposed to be happening.

And then, rough with emotion, Calvin's voice cracked. He waited until he regained his composure.

"Before boarding the *Dorchester*, it had been said that Chaplain Clark Poling asked his father to pray for him, 'not for my safe return. That wouldn't be fair. Just pray that I shall do my duty, never be a coward. Just pray that I shall be adequate.'"

Calvin went on to tell how the chaplains worked against time, passing out life vests until none were left; and how during the chaos, they removed their own life vests and placed them on the frightened and distracted soldiers crowding around them. To enable others to live, the chaplains deliberately chose to sacrifice their own chances of survival.

"As the remaining lifeboats launched into the high seas to escape the yanking swells from the ship's plunge beneath the ocean's surface, the men turned back to see the courageous chaplains leaning on one another at the railing, arms linked. With strong voices they recited the Lord's Prayer in unison, and like those aboard the sinking *Titanic*, they burst into song as the ship disappeared into the vast and frigid sea. Reverend George L. Fox, Rabbi Alexander Goode, Reverend Clark V. Poling, and Father John P. Washington—vanished."

Calvin stopped and stared out over the congregation, the weight of the chaplains' message battering him.

"These men's lives were not taken from them." Calvin paused, holding back another eruption of emotion. "Not at all. They gave their lives so that others might live."

Calvin shifted from one foot to the other and leaned into the lectern, gripping its sides.

"The chaplains had the wisdom and courage to contemplate the cost of serving their Lord before they entered the ministry. And they willingly sacrificed their lives the way Jesus willingly sacrificed His life. His gift to us, like the chaplains' gift to the soldiers, was undeniable love. And that, my friends, is the true meaning of Christmas."

Calvin bowed his head, extended his hand over the congregation, and prayed the benediction. He then nodded at Mrs. Miller, who sat at the organ and softly played "Silent Night."

As the congregants filed out of the church, quietly and reverently, Calvin Doherty stepped forward and knelt at the altar on one knee, head bowed, resting his forehead against his hand in *The Thinker* pose.

My Lord, what have I done? How much time have I wasted?

CHAPTER FIFTY-FOUR

Jo lingered at the pew, her hand resting lightly on Brue's shoulder, amazed at Calvin's absorbing sermon, his spellbinding delivery, and the power of his words. The longer he had spoken, the more the emptiness in his eyes faded until it vanished completely. Church was his home. Judging by the reverent way he knelt at the altar, he knew it was his home, too.

Jo nudged Brue, guiding her by her shoulders. "Come, sweetie. Let's go home."

The late afternoon shadows settling over Harrington Park surrendered to the black of night. The moisture in the air from the sun's earlier warmth crystallized with the dropping temperature. Fine white flakes danced through the darkness, dusting the quiet earth with more white powder. Although the view was alluring, Jo couldn't stop thinking about Calvin. He had made peace with God. He couldn't have done that unless he forgave Rainy. How did he manage that? Then Jo thought about Tryg and her need to make things right with him. But how could she possibly forgive the man who stole her future, her very life from her and her young daughter? The hurt was far too fresh and deep.

Brue suddenly broke into a skip, intruding on Jo's musings.

"What's all the excitement about?"

Brue twirled around and yanked at her mother's hand. "I've got a surprise for you. It's under the tree."

"You do?" Jo pulled Brue close, pressing her fingers into the folds of Brue's coat. "Whatever it is, I'm sure I'll like it very much."

But then as they walked on, Jo glanced nervously at the snow. Wondering. What kind of gift could possibly make Brue that excited?

The aroma of scalloped potato soup and bread pudding greeted them as they entered their front door.

"It sure smells good in here," Brue said excitedly.

Jo lightly tousled Brue's hair. Scalloped potato soup was Brue's favorite—scalded milk, potatoes, salt, pepper, and, of all things, sliced wieners. Jo baked the soup rather than boiling it to keep the milk from burning at the bottom of the bowl. Baking it only scorched the upper crust of milk. Brue loved the scorched crust as much as she loved the soup. The aroma alone made the earlier preparation well worth the effort.

"You know, Brue, our home may be humble by a lot of people's standards," Jo said as they tugged off their boots, "but that doesn't mean it can't feel festive. It already smells like Christmas. How about if we make this place look and sound like Christmas, too? What do you say?"

"Yes!"

Jo headed toward the closet, coats in hand. "You go ahead and plug in the wreath. As soon as I finish hanging up our coats, I'll take care of the rest."

It took but a moment to accomplish the mood. The swirling scent of fresh pine needles. Christmas carols drifting lazily from the phonograph. The oil burner hissing and sputtering. The warm glow of the lights from the tree and the wreath on the window reflecting off the shiny linoleum. An appreciative smile worked its way up Jo's cheeks as she gazed at the small evergreen with its short needles and paltry branches. A glaze of tinsel, garland, colored bulbs, and lights made it look rich and full.

"Come." Jo guided Brue lightly by the nape of her neck to the supper table. "It's time to enjoy our Christmas Eve tradition. Just the two of us."

After a thoroughly satisfying supper, they were about to retreat into the living room when an unexpected knock hammered the back door.

Jo jumped. "Who could that be?" she asked, glancing at Brue. "You wait here. I'll get it."

A moment later, she changed her mind.

"Brue?"

Undoubtedly startled by the pitch of her mother's voice, Brue came running.

"Look who's here."

Brue tilted her head and peered around the door. "Santa!"

Poor Santa. His beard looked fake, his Santa Claus outfit had definitely seen better days, and his characteristic "Ho, ho, ho" fell a little flat. But his eyes sparkled. He winked at Brue as he handed Jo a plain white envelope then quickly turned and disappeared into the darkness with a parting, "Merry Christmas to all and to all a good night." Jo noticed a distinct familiarity in how Santa scurried down the steps. Thumbs tucked in his belt. Thickset chin jutted high into the air. He reminded her of the sight she'd seen uptown after bumping into that shiny new Packard and her conversation at The Copper Kettle over a second cup of hot chocolate. A deep stirring of warmth and peace enfolded her as she wondered how many more widows Santa would visit this Christmas Eve.

Jo returned to the bright light of the kitchen and ripped open the envelope, its contents accidentally spilling onto the floor. A twenty-dollar bill and a five-dollar bill. "Twenty-five dollars, Brue." Suddenly Jo's shoulders slumped. She scooped up the money and stuffed it back into the envelope. "Too bad we didn't have this sooner, sweetie. I'm so, so sorry."

Brue slipped her arm around Jo's waist, hugging her. "It's okay, Mom."

No, it wasn't okay. Jo had her heart set on buying the Cinderella watch and glass slipper.

"Come," Jo said, hugging Brue back. "Let's go into the living room. It's time to open our presents."

One by one, Jo presented her homemade Christmas gifts to Brue—a hand-knitted, red woolen scarf, mittens, socks, and a small box of homemade fudge.

Brue oohed and aahed, sincerely thanking her mother for each individual gift. She then announced, "Now it's time for your present."

Brue crouched down on the floor and reached far under the tree. She pulled out a small box wrapped in store paper and adorned with a delicate red ribbon. She twisted around and scooted to her knees. With a proud smile and her eyes radiating, she presented the gift to Jo. "Open it."

"What's this?"

"You'll see."

Jo carefully removed the ribbon, unwrapped the paper, and gasped. Words tumbled from her lips before she realized the impact of what she was saying. "Evening in Paris perfume. Oh, Brue. You shouldn't have. You could have bought the Cinderella watch with the money you spent on this."

Color drained from Brue's hurt-filled face. "Don't you like it, Mom?"

"Like it? Oh, sweetheart, I love it." Jo quickly pulled her daughter into a tight embrace while her heart shattered into a hundred small pieces. "It's wonderful. But I wanted you to have that Cinderella watch and glass slipper more than anything."

"I wanted you to have the perfume more," Brue said proudly. She hopped onto the sofa and pulled on her newly knitted socks and mittens with an earned amount of confidence. "Besides, Santa will bring me the Cinderella watch tonight. You'll see. I want to hurry to bed so I can get up early in the morning and open his presents."

"Brue," Jo warned, "I don't want you getting your hopes up only to have them crushed. We've discussed this before. Santa can't possibly bring you the Cinderella watch and glass slipper tonight. Like I said, the store was sold out; there weren't any left."

Brue sighed. "I know, Mom. I heard what you said, but sometimes a girl just needs to dream."

Jo quickly disappeared into the kitchen to keep Brue from seeing the moisture gathering in her eyes. She washed and dried the dishes, and after placing the last plate back into the cupboard, she and Brue cuddled by the tree. Jo read *'Twas the Night Before Christmas.* At eight o'clock they listened to *A Christmas Carol* on the radio, and then Jo finally announced, "It's time for bed."

She knelt beside Brue and listened as she said her nightly prayer. When Brue gave thanks for all of her blessings, listing her homemade presents one by one, Jo's heart broke all over again. How could she be so blessed to have a child that unselfish?

After Brue whispered, "Amen," Jo kissed her lightly on the forehead and tucked her under the covers. "Your gift meant the world to me. That's the best present I've ever gotten from anyone."

Brue wiggled under the covers and beamed.

"Sleep tight," Jo said then quietly closed the bedroom door behind her. Folding her arms over her red cotton apron, she went into the living room and plodded slowly toward the couch. Case's small box still peeked out from under the tree making her heart ache even more. She reached for the present, slid off the silver ribbon, and carefully unwrapped the paper. She nudged the lid open and gasped.

Case had bought her a brand new watch. A beautiful, gold watch. She could envision his face as she clasped it on her wrist.

Then came a deluge of streaming tears, tears she had to control with painful silence so she wouldn't upset Brue.

Exhausted after several minutes of raw grief, Jo took a deep breath and wiped her tears away. She recalled the self-assured look on Tryg's face as he pulled the gift out of his pocket and handed it to her. No wonder he was so confident. He knew what was in the box and how much it meant to Case. She thought about how she rushed out the door of The Copper Kettle, leaving him alone and defeated. She had misjudged him about one thing. He didn't ask to drive Case's car. *Case had asked him.* Was there anything else she'd been wrong about? What was he trying to say about helping her? About helping Brue? Didn't he realize there was nothing he could do to help them? Nothing—nothing, that is, other than to just say "I'm sorry," show some remorse, show that he'd been hurting, too. Hurting for Case. Hurting for Jo. Hurting for Brue. Not just hurting for himself.

She thought about Calvin and how his lack of forgiveness had ripped the life right out of him. She couldn't let that continue to happen to her, too. But the damage had been done. Case had lost his life at the hands of his best friend. There was no turning back. How could she forgive, sincerely forgive, the man who destroyed her life?

A light scratching noise intruded on her ruminating, catching her off guard. It was coming from somewhere near the front porch.

Not mice again.

Jo welcomed the distraction and shifted her attention toward the door. She remembered hearing mice on Christmas Eve before. It was when she was about Brue's age. That night, a mouse actually chewed the toe out of her Christmas stocking. Jo thought for a moment. If she could rig a cage of some sort to trap the mouse, she might be able to turn it loose in the wild. The thought of a trap that killed mice seemed cruel. She might be able to rig up a box of some sort first thing in the morning.

Easing onto the arm of the couch, she scooped up the small bottle of Evening in Paris perfume, gazed at it, and then at her wrist. Under the circumstances, how could she ever show her new watch to Brue? She couldn't do that to her. It wouldn't be right.

Jo squeezed the bottle of cologne tightly in the palm of her hand and then closed her eyes, reliving Brue's expectant look when she opened the gift. Brue had to have spent all of the money in her piggybank on

Jo. The cologne felt so small folded in her hand and yet so large at the same time.

Another light scratching captured her attention. Was it her imagination or did the scratching come from somewhere outside? She listened harder this time until another sound broke the quiet, a sound like whimpering.

Mice don't whimper.

Jo peered through the window, but didn't see anything. She pulled on her sweater, unlatched the living room door, and slipped out onto the front porch. Nothing there. But through the outside screen, she thought she might have seen something. She glanced up the road. It might have been an animal of some sort dashing around the corner onto River Lane. A dog, maybe? She wasn't sure. She then opened the outer door, astonished to find a basket sitting at the top of the porch steps. Nestled in the basket was a beautifully wrapped box with a small tag jutting out from beneath the bow. Jo reached for it, but before bringing it inside, she held it up toward the dim streetlight. She squinted to read the writing. All it said was *Merry Christmas to Brue.*

The doors slamming closed behind her, Jo dashed to Brue's bedroom. This would not wait until morning.

"Mind if I switch the light on?" Jo turned on the lamp without waiting for an answer. "I have something for you. I found it on the front steps."

"Huh?"

"Look, Brue, this is for you."

Still a little sleepy, but rapidly waking up, Brue grinned at the gift and carefully examined the note. She looked up at Jo questioningly.

"Brue, would you mind if I took the note?"

"Why, Mom?"

"I want to see if I can recognize the penmanship."

Brue happily handed the note to Jo then tore the paper off the gift. "Oh, Mom, look," she shrieked. "It's the Cinderella watch and glass slipper!"

CHAPTER FIFTY-FIVE

Jo situated the glass slipper on top of Brue's dresser, the same way it had been displayed in the display window, and tucked Brue back into bed with her new watch secured snugly to her wrist.

"Who do you think gave this to me, Mom?"

"I'm not sure, but I intend to find out."

Jo headed toward the door then turned around long enough to see Brue twisting and admiring her watch from every angle imaginable. "Will it be okay with you if I turn the light off? Or will you be needing more time to admire your new watch?"

Brue giggled. "You can turn it off. I'll admire it more in the morning."

Jo returned to the living room with the note in hand. The penmanship was neat, but totally unfamiliar. There was something about the card, though, that was familiar.

She laughed at the thought.

How ridiculous.

Big Ole?

Of course, he was the only one she knew who frayed the edges of things with his nervous fingers, but that made no sense whatsoever. Besides, he had no idea Brue wanted the Cinderella watch. But who could have possibly known? Other than Calvin and Evelyn, that is. Oh, yes. Miss Bickford. But when Miss Bickford learned the last two watches had been sold, Jo could tell by her surprised expression there was no way she would have bought it. Calvin wouldn't have bought it, either. None were left at the time Jo mentioned it to him. But what about Evelyn? Could it have come from her? No. Absolutely not. Evelyn offered her help, but Jo politely refused it. Evelyn wouldn't go against her wishes. Wait a minute. What about Tryg? No. He wouldn't have known Brue wanted that watch.

Jo thought further. She couldn't get past the note's frayed edges. Maybe she needed to reconsider that one. She recalled the beaten-up envelope at the car repair shop. Then there was the picture that had fallen on the floor at The Copper Kettle. How many times had Big Ole pulled it out of his pocket just to catch another glimpse of his late bride? And what about the nervous way he had fidgeted with the edges of his notepaper when she and Brue were in his office? Still it couldn't be him. Jo's cheeks burned at even entertaining the thought.

She slipped on her coat and boots, stepped out into the cold, and followed the paw prints down the porch steps. When she rounded the corner at the side of the house, a wave of goose bumps flowed through her like an electrical current. She found huge footprints in the snow made by very large boots. The tracks were accompanied by round marks pressed deeply in the snow. A walking stick? And next to those marks were more paw prints. Spitfire.

Jo followed the tracks trailing across the road. They meandered through the park and on toward the O.M. Harrington. She could hear Spitfire's bark before she saw him romping around on the porch of the boarding house and looking back at her, his tail wagging wildly for a tired old dog. She stopped in the middle of the park and watched as a light came on in the windows of a room on the second floor. That would be Big Ole's room. And a brighter light turned on in her heart.

Remembering only too well the words written in stunning calligraphy immediately above the gift barrel, Jo whispered into the night, "Nobility obligates, and you, Mr. Big Ole, are a very noble man."

> *In the depths of darkness with daylight long past*
> *And the glow from the lamppost on snow fallen fast,*
> *Tracks softened by snowflake dustings now came*
> *With markings most heavily poked in by a cane.*
> *With boot prints so giant*
> *Small paw prints reliant*
> *From where did they come and to where did they go?*
> *Frayed paper betrayed him and large tracks in the snow.*

CHAPTER FIFTY-SIX

At half past six the next morning, Jo hopped out of bed. On the first workday of each week, she routinely set off to the O.M. Harrington to pick up the soiled linens, but with Christmas Day falling on a Monday, the laundry would be given a day's grace—a day's grace she chose to forego. She wanted to express, at least in some small way, her appreciation for Big Ole's generosity by picking up his items ahead of time. With Calvin often out and about during the wee hours, it should be okay to arrive before sunup.

At five minutes before the hour of seven, she backed out onto the front porch locking the door behind her. Only being away for a few short minutes, she wanted to let Brue sleep.

Jo turned into the darkness to descend the steps, but suddenly stopped hard and reached for the side of the house.

What in the world?

At the foot of the stoop stood two large wicker baskets on wheels, linked together like the cars of a train with a full-sized handle at the front. A large red bow and a note card adorned the handle. Jo quickly padded down the remaining steps and knelt on the frozen ground, smoothing the sides of the baskets as if she needed assurance they were real, that she wasn't dreaming. The baskets were real. She gently nudged the note card loose, held it up toward the streetlight and read, *To Jo. From your friends at the O.M. Harrington House.*

The smile gliding across her face accompanied her all of the way across the park and into the boarding house.

Calvin sat near the hearth warming his hands. Looking up, surprise registered in his eyes as he slowly stood. "Good morning, Jo. What brings you out so early? Aren't you afraid of waking the roosters?"

Jo removed her gloves and slipped them into her coat pockets. "Good morning, Calvin. I've come to get Mr. Big Ole's soiled laundry."

"Mr. Big Ole, is it?" he asked with a contented smile.

"Yes, definitely. That man has certainly gained my respect."

"I guess I'm not at all surprised."

She took a few short steps toward Calvin. "By the way, there are two handsome baskets on wheels immediately outside the front door. They bear a striking resemblance to a small train. You wouldn't happen to know anything about them, would you?"

Calvin folded his arms and rocked on his heels. "Why, Mrs. Bremley!"

"I don't know how to thank you," she said, noting the complete absence of sadness in his eyes and his sheepish grin. "You have no idea how much they mean to me."

"It was our pleasure, I assure you."

Jo turned and took in the great room, the glow from the fireplace so early in the morning, the cozy sitting area, the small table in front of the far windows. Looking back at Calvin and realizing the days she'd enjoy seeing him at the O.M. Harrington were now numbered, she swallowed against a thick lump in her throat. "That was quite the sermon you delivered last night."

He lowered his head and looked at his shoes. "That wasn't a sermon. It was a retelling of a painfully true story. Those brave and honorable men deserve to be remembered."

"I know. That couldn't be more true." With an unhurried shake of her head, Jo added, "But your delivery, Calvin. You couldn't have possibly done a better job. You belong behind the pulpit. There's no question about it and you know it."

Calvin nodded a slow acknowledgement then said, "You've decided to do Big Ole's laundry on Christmas Day?"

Jo looked at Calvin for a long moment. "Absolutely." But then she hesitated. "This place is going to be painfully lonely without you here."

Calvin didn't respond. He didn't need to.

A short while later Jo crossed Harrington Park, listening to the whir of the basket wheels behind her. She looked up into the dark December sky, wishing there were a brighter moon. It would have been nice to have it reflect off the snowy path toward home so she could be more visible to any onlooking neighbors with her new gizmo in tow.

Immediately after sunrise, Jo poked her head into Brue's bedroom. "Wake up, sleepyhead. Your breakfast is ready—bacon, eggs, and orange juice this morning. How about that?"

It took a while for Brue to crawl up to the breakfast table. Half asleep, she pulled her chair up close. The watch was still on her wrist.

"I found out who gave your gift to you last night," Jo announced proudly.

Brue woke up fast. "Who?"

Jo poured the orange juice, taking her time placing the small glass next to Brue's plate.

"Who, Mom, who? Tell me."

"Big Ole."

Brue gasped. "Mr. Big Ole?"

Jo stood in front of the stove with Brue's plate in hand, ladling on a fair helping of scrambled eggs and plucking several strips of bacon from the iron skillet. "Yes, dear. Mr. Big Ole. He delivered the basket with the help of your good friend, Spitfire. Last night I found paw prints trailing down the front steps. The dog undoubtedly carried that basket between his teeth and dropped it on the top porch step. I also found Big Ole's boot prints and marks from his cane embedded in the snow at the side of the house."

"Wow! Wait 'til Poke hears this."

"Brue," Jo said, placing Brue's plate on the table, "do you have any idea how Big Ole could have known you wanted that watch?"

Brue thought for a moment. "Nope. When I told him I was sorry about almost bumping into him up by the dime store, I remember telling him I was looking at the Cinderella watch in the window, but I know I didn't tell him that I wanted it."

"He obviously figured it out. Who would have ever thought that man was capable of being so kind and generous." Pulling out a chair, Jo joined Brue at the table. "There's something you might want to think about."

Brue raised a forkful of scrambled eggs to her mouth. "What?"

"Mr. Big Ole. We choose our friends. Over time they become like family to us, just like Evelyn and Poke, Mr. Doherty, and the Wilders. I think Big Ole would make an excellent grandfather figure for you. He's an amazing man, and he's obviously learned to like you very much."

Brue lowered her fork, the look in her eyes hopeful. "Do you really think so, Mom?"

"Yes, I really do. Now, I'd better get back to the laundry."

Jo got up but hesitated before walking away. "By the way, wait 'til you see the baskets on wheels the men at the boarding house gave us for hauling laundry. They're terrific. Looks like a miniature train."

With the laundry finished by early afternoon, Jo stacked it in a basket, bound it, then topped it off with a neatly printed thank you note written and signed by Brue.

Jo rested her hand on the doorknob and turned back to see Brue peering out the window. "Are you going out to play with your friends in the park today?"

"Yup. I'm gonna get ready now."

"Okay. I'll be back in a few minutes."

As Jo descended the steps, she glanced across the park toward the O.M Harrington. Big Ole had just stepped outside, undoubtedly to make his daily trek to town. She remembered seeing a sign saying The Copper Kettle would be open on Christmas Day but only for coffee and pastries. That's probably where he was headed.

Suddenly, Brue shot out the door; slipped down the steps, sidestepping Jo; and tore off up the road at a fast clip, stuffing her arms through her coat sleeves as she ran.

"Brue," Jo called after her.

Brue ran far too fast to answer, to ask her mother's permission to go, or to bother saying good-bye. It didn't take much thought to know where she was headed.

Jo slipped back into the house and grabbed her purse and car keys. She then dashed out the back door and choked when she glanced at the bald white-walled tires that would be vulnerable to sliding on the slippery streets, but she jumped in anyway. In her excitement, she stomped on the gas pedal and nearly flooded the car. The car spat and sputtered before it kicked in. Backing out of the driveway, she floored it and swerved half the way up the road.

At the railroad crossing around the corner on Newton, Jo slowed to a crawl and looked up the tracks. Big Ole was walking down an adjacent path, rhythmically tapping his stick, his left arm swinging freely with Brue quickly closing in from behind. She trailed him like a hound on a fox then aimed and reached for his dangling hand. When she caught it, she raised her chin, looking very happy with herself.

Big Ole met Brue's gaze in an understated sort of way, but he didn't appear to say anything. From a distance, Jo sensed warmth in his eyes, and he walked taller with a sure-footed spring in his step.

Jo headed on up the hill, keeping an eye on them from the rearview mirror. They walked hand in hand, neither of them saying anything.

She sped ahead, parked across the street from The Copper Kettle, and waited for Big Ole and Brue to emerge into sight. When they stopped at the café's entrance shortly thereafter, Big Ole gave Brue a subtle smile, patted her head, and nodded. They parted paths, he into the restaurant and Brue back toward home and her friends at Harrington Park. As Brue headed off, she didn't walk—she strutted.

As for Jo, she opened the door of The Copper Kettle and asked if she might have the privilege of sitting in the empty seat across from Big Ole Harrington at his daily table for two, party of one.

CHAPTER FIFTY-SEVEN

Jo recognized the limp a block away.

Unsure of what to do or which way to turn, she paused at the corner of Broadway and East William to observe the man. This was an opportunity to turn things around, to make things right with Tryg.

But did she really want to?

Brue had certainly had enough encounters with Big Ole—the unintended mishaps and unpleasant feelings. What had Jo required of her reluctant daughter when it came to him? *You will handle it, and you will handle it well.* Had she been too parental? Not parental enough? *Aren't we all trying to find our way through life, mothers and daughters alike?* Jo calculated inwardly the high cost of her standoff with Tryg— the message it signaled to her daughter, the toll on Jo's emotions, saying nothing about her health. Although justified, she felt dogged by a cloud of shame. Hard feelings notwithstanding, she found her shoes carrying her swiftly down the sidewalk, sidestepping crusty patches of ice.

"Tryg?"

He froze in his tracks, appearing hesitant to take a backward look.

Jo took a wary step forward. "It's me ... Jo. I was wondering if we might be able to finish the conversation we started on Saturday." She hesitated then let out a ragged sigh. "I could understand if you choose not to."

The instant Tryg's gaze met then searched hers, Jo held a gasp in full restraint. His shoulders sagged badly. A pained expression painted his gaunt face and sooty-black circles framed his hollowed-out eyes. This could not be the same guy she left sitting alone in The Copper Kettle forty-eight short hours ago. Her getting up and leaving couldn't have bothered him that much. She didn't have that sort of power. Not over anyone. True, his driving was the cause of Case's death, but she didn't mean to punish him for it. She only pulled away to protect herself. No, that wasn't true. She pulled away because he was absolving himself of guilt and at Case's expense. She couldn't allow that.

"Could I possibly interest you in a cup of coffee?" she asked, disregarding a burgeoning fear that she might be getting in over her head. "It's on me."

He shook his head and with a voice weary and rough, he said, "No."

Feeling a well-deserved sting of disappointment, she said, "I understand."

"It will be on me."

Jo let out a low, strained laugh.

"What's so funny?"

The tight squeezing in Jo's stomach distracted her. Her response had been insensitive but accidental. "I'm sorry. It's nothing important. Um ... I just came from The Copper Kettle. Seems I've made more trips there this past week than I have in all the time we've lived in Amber Leaf."

"Would you rather come to my office? We'd have more privacy. It's a holiday so no one will be around."

Turning, they retraced their steps up the long deserted street. The tension between them during their silent trek cried for Jo's attention, but she refused to indulge it. She concentrated instead on the clap of their boots against the frozen sidewalk, the strangeness of their reflections on the darkened windows of the closed shops they passed along the way, and the T.W. "Tryg" Howland, III, Attorney-at-Law shingle just a few short yards away. How peculiar to enter the door beneath it.

With a light hand to the small of her back, Tryg guided Jo into his pristine three-room office suite and turned on the lights, revealing a cold and glossy white marble floor. The waiting area was simple. A brocade sofa. Lamps on dustless end tables. *Life* and *Newsweek* magazines stacked with unusual care.

"May I take your things?" he asked as he slipped out of his overcoat.

Jo peeled off her gloves and neck scarf and stuffed them into her pockets then handed him her coat. "It's warm in here."

"I was on my way home when you called out for me." He made his way to the coat tree. "Just came from here. I spent the morning working on a court case."

"On Christmas Day?"

"Yes, ma'am." He turned to Jo and, indicating his office through the door to the right, he said, "Go right on in. I'll be just a minute."

She stepped inside.

So this was Trygve Howland's office.

Drawn to the four double-paned windows outfitted with venetian blinds on the far wall, she crossed the room and looked out onto the deserted street. She needed to gather her thoughts and think of a way to accomplish the impossible—getting past her resistant feelings and finally making peace.

She turned and looked slowly around the room. Something nagged at her—Tryg's office and what it said about him. He was all business. No surprise there. A large philodendron stood like a sentry in the far corner. Two large cabinets filled with books in precise rows and a dark cherrywood credenza lined the far wall. Centered above the credenza, his framed law degree provided the only decoration on any of the walls, if a legal document could be called a decoration, that is. And he had a grand dark cherrywood desk with two leather chairs parked immediately across from it.

Vintage Trygve.

Meticulous.

All professional.

His office had the strange feeling of being inhabited without anyone having taken up residence, reinforcing an unwillingness to reveal who he really is. Jo shuddered at the sight. No warm pictures to remind him of family or friends. No personal artifacts. Cold. Impersonal. What happened to him? He always had exuded confidence with a hint of mystery. Except for Saturday. On Saturday, for the first time, Jo had been privy to something else—his vulnerability. Today his wall lay in ruins.

Tryg entered the room with his hand extended. "I believe you said you just had coffee, but I was hoping you might join me in another cup. I brought in a large thermos earlier this morning. Seems relatively hot yet."

Jo had her fill of coffee for the day. Didn't care for any more. "That would be great," she said, reaching for the cup. "Thanks."

Tryg remained standing, appearing unable to relax. Or was she projecting? "How was your Christmas?" he asked.

"Unbelievable, really."

He glanced at her with a quizzical look.

"People's warmth and generosity," she offered.

He nodded as though he understood.

"And yours?"

"Quiet," he said.

"Quiet?"

He nodded again. "I spent it alone."

His response didn't make sense. Why would he choose to spend Christmas alone when he had so many relatives close by? "But what about your family?"

"Let's just say that I needed some time to myself."

"What about Elizabeth? Is she still overseas?"

"I guess so."

That was unexpected. "You guess so?"

"She's married now."

"Really?" Jo blurted, unable to hide her shock.

Tryg looked down at his cup and swirled it slowly, looking at it as if a chunk of mold was floating around at the top. "Seems an Army doctor stole her heart away. Army doctors can be pretty hefty competition during wartime."

Jo took an ample amount of time to allow his words to sink in. "I'm really sorry to hear that."

He tried to laugh, but missed the mark. "Her loss, right?"

Jo nodded in resigned agreement.

"Where are my manners?" he asked, quickly pulling back a chair. "Please, have a seat."

Rather than sitting behind his desk, he pulled out the chair next to hers, a half smile curling his lips. "It's awkward again, isn't it?"

"I guess you might say that." Jo deliberately glanced at her watch and held up her wrist. "Would you like to see Case's gift?"

Was that reluctance she saw in Tryg's eyes? He barely looked at it.

"Case definitely had good taste," he muttered before nervously glancing toward the windows.

Jo heard a light tapping sound and looked down, surprised to see Tryg's shoe rapping against the front panel of his desk.

"I—" they both said in unison.

"You first. Please," he insisted.

"I'm sorry. Guess I'm a little too restless to sit at the moment." Jo got up and wandered toward the window. With her cup still in her hand, she looked back at him. "I want to apologize for leaving you so abruptly in the restaurant on Saturday. I'm usually not that rude. Suffice it to say, I wasn't particularly pleased with the way our conversation was going."

"I'm not sure I understand. Do you have any idea why I invited you to meet me?"

Jo needed a moment to think before responding. She had, in fact, given it a lot of thought.

"I figured maybe you wanted to absolve yourself of guilt," she said, more as a question, but then she added with a hint of sarcasm, "Can't say as I blame you."

"Is that really what you think?"

"Absolutely," she said shamelessly.

"But, then, what else could you think?" He stared across his desk and slowly shook his head. "I'm stuck in the middle of an unwinnable situation, I'm afraid."

"What are you talking about?"

He looked at Jo, his eyes hard. "It should have been me."

Jo glowered at his words too easily spoken. She cleared her throat, then returned to her chair, clenching her cup tightly with both hands. She hated the thoughts she was thinking, thoughts of how she agreed with him. What had become of her that her thinking could be so base?

"It was an accident," she said finally, but her words had no meaning, at least not to her.

"It was a dumb and foolish accident that didn't have to happen."

She lowered her cup lightly onto her lap, resenting her own indifference.

Tryg undoubtedly noticed, because he said, "I have the feeling you think I've been rejecting you all of these months."

"Haven't you been?"

He kept his silence.

"It sure felt like rejection from my end. Now, I suppose you're going to tell me you haven't been running away, either." She didn't particularly care for the way her words sounded, but it was a little late for that now.

"I didn't mean to reject you and I wasn't running away. Like I told you on Saturday, I just needed time."

"Time?" she asked, restraining a chuckle. "Time for what?"

"Time to think things through."

How disingenuous. His response didn't add up. Thinking things through didn't require an entire year.

The tapping of his shoe against his desk grew louder, the pain in his eyes deepening. Jo wanted to reach down and clutch that shiny, tormented shoe and still it—anything to stop his tortured countenance from penetrating her resistant skin.

"Every morning when I get up," he said, shifting heavily to the back of his chair and tightly gripping its arms, "I think of you and Brue getting up to face another day. Another day, that is, without Case. Every night when I go to bed, I think of you going to bed without him at your side. Every time I see you, I'm reminded that it was me who took him away from you. And I still don't know how to live with that. I only know that I have to. And I won't apologize—"

"What?" Jo said, suddenly unable to breathe out, unable to breathe in.

"I said I won't apologize," he repeated strongly, his defiant gaze penetrating hers. "There are no words in the English language or any other language, for that matter, that could possibly express my torment and regret or bring Case back to life. There are no words, Jo. I can only hope that my actions going forward can in some small way make up for them."

Tryg was right. There were no words, but the grief in his eyes was beginning to express what no words could ever say. The intensity of his pain was breaking her. Maybe it stemmed from guilt, but it actually hurt to see him crushed with remorse. If he didn't lighten up, the tension in his face was going to wrench his forehead into spasm. He'd always been stoic. Not anymore.

She studied him. Had she finally found what she was looking for? Having had no idea that satisfaction could possibly feel so empty, she looked away.

Suddenly, the screech of brakes intruded on their conversation. Tryg let out a muffled gasp, but Jo didn't give it much thought. She got up and peered out to see a boy in his late teens behind the wheel of a beat-up Model T. By the glee on his face, it was evident he was taking advantage of the deserted streets, braking hard and fast in the middle of intermittent and slippery patches of ice, making his car fishtail.

"Looks like that kid's having a great time," she said, but Tryg didn't respond.

When Jo turned, she was taken aback. His eyes were horror-filled. Was he reliving the accident with Case? Jo sidled back to her chair. Not only had Tryg assumed too much responsibility for Case's life when he was living, he now appeared to assume too much responsibility for Case's death.

"It wasn't your fault," she said, this time believing her own words. "It was an accident."

"What?" he asked, as though emerging from a dense fog.

"You didn't set out to take Case's life away from him or from us."

"You're wrong. It was my fault. I was the one behind the wheel."

Tryg's admission shook Jo to her core. To her dismay, as she attempted to polish him clean of guilt, it was as though she could see her own reflection in his eyes, and she wasn't all that happy with what she saw. Tryg had the decency to own his guilt. Now, maybe it was her turn.

She paused, needing a moment to gather a measure of strength. "Look, it's been easy for me to blame you. I actually believed myself. But if I'm honest, there's plenty of blame to go around here."

"What are you talking about?"

She placed her cup lightly on his desk and leveled her gaze at him. "I had a bad feeling when Case insisted on picking you up at the train station, but I ignored it. I let him go anyway without mentioning a thing about it. If I hadn't wound my watch too tight, you wouldn't have been driving. If I said yes to Case when he asked Brue and me to go along with him, again you wouldn't have been driving."

"But—"

"It was an accident," she repeated firmly. "If you don't accept it and let it go, you'll be in bondage for the rest of your life. Every time you hear the squeal of brakes, you'll relive the hell you're choosing to keep alive."

He struck his desk with the flat of his hand and shouted, "You don't understand!"

"I don't understand what?" she shouted back. "That deer run across roads? You swerved to miss a deer, for crying out loud. Should the deer feel guilty for running across the road? Should the automakers feel guilty about having built the car you were driving or the ditch diggers for having dug the ditch too deep? What about God? Should He feel guilty for having created the snowstorm? If Case had lived through the accident, should he have felt guilty for asking you to drive? It was an accident, Tryg. *It. Just. Happened!"*

The instant the last word escaped from her lips, a crazy, unexpected sense of relief flooded her heart. Was it possible that she'd forgiven Tryg completely? Deliberately released him? Had she forgiven herself? She noticed that the tension she'd been feeling had evaporated. He appeared less tense, too.

"If Case hadn't had hypertension," she said quietly, "he would have ended up overseas just like you did and worse could have happened. I'm grateful that at least he didn't have to suffer."

Tryg's eyes were still filled with pain. "But that's not the same. Case never went to war."

"That doesn't change anything. If it hadn't been for his health, he would have gone. Case and I were no different from you or anyone else. We're all vulnerable. Look what happened to you."

Jo noticed the incessant tapping of Tryg's shoe had ceased.

"You need to know you haven't been hurting alone," he said softly.

Jo squeezed her eyes closed and then looked back at him. "What?"

"You haven't been hurting alone," he repeated, this time firmly.

She inhaled a sizable breath, trying to hold back a sea of tears. If she allowed even one to fall, she wouldn't be able to stop the rest. Her throat ached. She listened to the utter quiet for a long while before she could breathe a word. "You have no idea how badly I've needed to hear those words."

The hard lines disappeared from his face. Although the wall between them crumbled before her eyes, Jo felt exhausted. Maybe sometime in the future they could learn to enjoy the memories of their common bond, but this was no time for that. Not yet.

"Brue and I are doing fine now," she said, maybe a bit too brightly. "I have a laundry business with the O.M. Harrington House. I work pretty hard, but at least I'm able to be home for her."

"That's what I wanted to tell you when I invited you to The Copper Kettle, but you refused to hear me."

"What's that?"

Tryg inhaled a deep breath and slowly let it out. "I'm building up my law practice. I want to share a significant portion of my earnings with you. I figure you could use some help raising Brue."

A half smile broke on Jo's lips.

"You find that amusing, do you?"

"No. I don't mean to be ungrateful. It's just that I have too much self-respect to accept your money or anyone else's, for that matter. I need to make my own way, Tryg. Besides, it's not necessary, but thank you just the same. That is incredibly kind and generous of you."

"Let me finish. Please."

"Tryg—"

His hand shot up, his voice coarse with emotion. "No, hear me out. There's something else you need to know."

"What's that?"

"I've given considerable thought to my practice. Eventually, I'll need more office help. Do you think you might be interested?"

Jo shook her head and sat back in her chair. "I'm afraid you've got the wrong person. I'm not any good at stenography."

"Who's talking about stenography? I'm talking about someone to handle the books, send out bills, handle collections, reconcile accounts.

That sort of thing. I've got a strong feeling you have the talent I'll be looking for. Give it some thought, okay? And you might want to prepare yourself."

"For what?"

"I have every intention of luring you with a generous income."

After finishing their coffee and a few light pleasantries, Jo and Tryg parted paths immediately outside his office. He mentioned something about having periodic get-togethers to keep current and she agreed.

As she strolled across the street toward her car, she felt tremendous relief. In the end, the war had taken its toll on Tryg, both physically and emotionally, but it appeared to have made him a much better person. How wrong she'd been to expect him to shoulder the blame alone for Case's death and for her to judge him for rejecting her. He hadn't been able to face her.

Jo had never thought in terms of office work before. She would have to give Tryg's offer further thought. With Brue in school, maybe Jo could work outside of home. At least that was another option. But she had put so much effort into building her workload at the O.M. Harrington she wasn't sure she wanted to give that up.

Looking up into the clear December sky, Jo inhaled a deep breath of fresh winter air. The blustery wind didn't feel quite as cold anymore. And then she thought about Case. He had been an unwitting casualty of the war. A number uncounted. Had Tryg not been injured, Case would not have driven to the Cities to pick him up and he would still be alive today. Case, the common bond that polarized Jo and Tryg, had now drawn them closer. She had made peace with Tryg, his oldest and dearest friend. Case would have been pleased. That thought alone lightened her spirits as she crawled into her car and drove home.

CPSIA information can be obtained at www.ICGtesting.com
Printed in the USA
BVOW071839180112

280846BV00001B/42/P